KW

13 116

F
Tho   Thompson, Anne Armstrong
              The Swiss legacy

7.95

DATE DUE			
Nov 9 82			
Jan 3 83			
Jul 9 '84			
Jul 26 84			
De 10 '90			
MAR 22 2001			

THE SWISS LEGACY

.

A SIMON AND SCHUSTER NOVEL OF SUSPENSE

BY

Anne Armstrong Thompson

SIMON AND SCHUSTER
.
NEW YORK

For my husband,
who encouraged me

13116

THE SWISS LEGACY

1

They were a handsome couple. The man listened absently to the woman holding his arm, but his eyes shifted to others in the street. She noticed but kept her smile. They crossed at Piccadilly and were caught in the swirling crowds. The woman became exhilarated and was laughing when he led her out of the throng, not toward the theater box office as they had intended but toward the sweeping curve of Regent Street.

"What about the tickets?"

"We won't be needing them." His color had changed. He was agitated.

"Why not? Are you ill?"

"I'm all right. Come on. We must go back."

"Back where?"

"To the hotel. If we hurry, we can catch that afternoon flight to New York."

"David! We just got here!"

"Shut up and come on."

He grasped her arm and pulled her roughly across Shaftesbury Avenue and up Regent Street. She continued to protest, but he ignored her. He jostled people out of the way in his impatience. She ran to keep up.

Then, just as abruptly, he stopped, his attention held by something ahead. Very clearly in the midst of the crowd he looked cornered.

The woman looked up into her husband's face and followed the direction of his gaze. Her expression became anxious, even fearful, but her fear was for him, while his was of something else. Once more she looked at his eyes. He was staring at the entrance to a department store. People were coming and going. One by one his wife looked at them, trying to find the object of his attention: an elegantly dressed woman entering her car, a housewife with parcels in a green string bag, two Americans with slightly blued hair and large maps protruding from black purses, a delivery boy in uniform, a slender man ducking into the store's vestibule. He must be the one. He wore a tan raincoat with epaulets, belted and buttoned down, and carried a black umbrella. His hat did not quite cover the gray hair straggling over his collar. Her eyes narrowed as she tried to see him more clearly. When she turned back to her husband, he was still watching the man intently, his face bloodless. Then the man disappeared into the store.

"Let's go," David said.

"Who is that?"

"No one important. Come on."

"But you know him. Who is he?"

"No one."

"What's the matter? What are you afraid of?"

"I am not afraid of anything. Something has come up. I can't stay here."

"David, what *is* this? Who *was* that man?"

"Damn you, stop pressing me!" His ugly tone made others turn and look as he propelled her toward the crosswalk. A crowd was gathering there.

"I want to know what is wrong. Why won't you ever confide in me?"

His fingers hardened on her arm and she winced away. His grip tightened. "Blast you. Don't start that again."

"Let go! You're hurting me."

"I meant to. Now, come on!"

He struggled to get through the people surging forward around them. She pulled away. "No. You go if you must. But leave me alone. I'll come on later."

"Carolyn, don't argue with me! Come on!"

But she jerked away from him. He lunged for her again, but then his gaze shifted from her. The hunted look returned to his eyes. "Have it your own way. I don't care what happens to you now."

Whirling, still looking behind her, he stepped off the curb.

Unexpectedly he was stumbling, his arms flung out awkwardly. His face contorted in some dreadful emotion. A taxi with an old-fashioned fender and front bumper was suddenly there, moving fast.

"David! Watch out!" She leaped forward, throwing out her hands to fend it off and bring him back beside her. But he was too far off balance. The fender caught his hip, scooping him up, tossing him over the hood, dumping him on the other side into the oncoming traffic. The taxi careened away, while cars and trucks behind it screamed and skidded to stop.

"David! Oh, please God, David—"

Her hands to her mouth, she stared at the man sprawled in the street, his head twisted, blood gushing from his ears and nose. Her first step was slow, tentative. Then she ran to him and fell on her knees beside him.

Recognition was in his eyes when he saw her. He raised his hand toward her throat, groping painfully, reaching out, searching. His fingers jerked convulsively. She caught his hand as it fell away and the life slipped from his face.

She stared at the fixed expression, looked in bewilderment to the people gathering tightly around them, then turned back to her husband. She still held his hand tightly. His blood was staining her skirt.

A policeman bent over her and felt for the pulse in her husband's neck. She looked hopefully up at him, but he touched her shoulder regretfully. "Come away, madam. There is nothing here for you to do." He lifted her easily to her feet, his hands under her elbows. He held her a moment until she was steady. "Is he your husband, madam?"

"Yes."

Still holding her arm, he waved the crowd back. "Step aside, there. Clear a space. Let the ambulance through."

Sirens shrieked and blue-coated men cleared the street, leaving David forlorn and shrunken on the pavement. She turned away from the constable, back to David. Flashbulbs exploded as the bearers unfolded the stretcher, lifted David onto it, and laid a blanket over him.

"Let me—"

"He's dead, ma'am. I am sorry. We will follow in the car."

She went with the constable then and climbed stiffly into the clut-

3

tered back seat of the nearest police cruiser. He followed her, fumbling in his pocket. He took out two notebooks, selected the yellow one, and put the other back.

"You are Americans?"

"Yes."

"So many Americans forget to look the other way when they cross the streets here. I am sorry. Your husband's name, please?"

Carolyn gave it and watched him print it carefully in block letters on a blank page. The letters blurred suddenly before her. David C. Bruce. She put her hand to her head to clear her eyes. She looked at her hands then, turning them over, staring at the blood on her palms. There were stains on her skirt and legs. "So much blood," she whispered. "So much. So much blood."

"Ma'am, are you dizzy? Are you going to faint?" the constable asked.

"No. I don't faint."

"Can you answer a few questions?"

"Yes."

The ambulance pulled away. The police car followed, easing carefully through the milling crowd. Sirens sounded for a moment, and then fell silent as the two vehicles reached a clear lane and accelerated. The driver reported their destination into the radio and a metallic voice replied.

To the city it was just another accident. But for her a life had ended. She could not yet comprehend how much of her own life it had taken with it.

She opened the window and turned her face into the wind. The air was cold but it carried the scent of coming spring. The street noises had resumed. Regent Street was as though it had not been disturbed.

2

Carolyn stood at the window of her hotel suite and stared into Hyde Park across the street. The trip to the hospital had not taken very long, she thought. The ambulance had pulled up to the emergency entrance and she had followed the stretcher into the hospital to a tiny curtained cubicle. She stood beside the examining table and looked at the long body and the drying blood. She touched him tentatively. His fingers were curiously cold. It wasn't David any longer, and touching the dead seemed a sacrilege. She withdrew her hand and folded it across her other wrist. Her hands were sticky with blood.

A man who had fallen from a scaffold was in the cubicle next door. His weak, querulous voice and the higher, more agitated one of a woman were interwoven with the peremptory tones of the medical staff. Unable to concentrate on David, Carolyn listened to the drama behind the rough hospital curtain. She didn't hear the doctor until he spoke to her. His examination was brief.

"I'm sorry, Mrs. Bruce. There's nothing we can do. Will you come with me?" She followed him wordlessly.

Outside the cubicle, the injured worker was being wheeled down the hall. The woman came out just as Carolyn emerged from behind the curtain. She stared at Carolyn a moment and then whispered shyly, "I'm sorry about your man. Mine's going to be all right."

The tears came to Carolyn's eyes. She reached for the woman's hand and gave it a hard squeeze. "I am glad for you. Take good care of him." Then she turned away from her. The doctor took her arm, gripping it hard above the elbow, and led her down the hall. She had to stop, her head down, to fumble for a handkerchief. He handed her a clean one, neatly folded. She turned away, her head bowed into the corridor wall, her shoulders hunched, hiding her emotion while she fought for control. Finally, blinking rapidly, she looked up. "A complete stranger," she said in disbelief. "For her to be concerned about me when her own husband is so hurt . . ." The doctor nodded and waited for her to follow him.

Sitting on the edge of a hard chair in the doctor's office, Carolyn waited while he completed filling in forms and handed the clipboard to a waiting constable. Then he came to sit beside her. Her hands were wadding his handkerchief. When she realized what she was doing, she smoothed it out and gave it to him.

"Do you have any family here?" he asked.

She shook her head.

"Friends? Anyone you can call?"

"No."

"You will have to arrange for the embalming of the deceased."

"I don't know anyone to call."

"I can give you a list of names."

"Please. Would you . . . would you call for me? The first name will be suitable, I suppose."

"Yes, I will contact them for you." He looked at her carefully, professionally; then he took a pad from his desk and scribbled on it. He tore off a single sheet and handed it to her. "Here is a prescription for a mild sedative. Have it filled and take two about an hour before you go to bed. You will need your sleep in the days ahead." He smiled briefly. "I'm very sorry, Mrs. Bruce. I wish there was something we could have done for him."

Carolyn nodded. Constable Harrod was standing quietly behind her. She hadn't heard him come in. "We can go now, Mrs. Bruce," he said. He helped her up and led her from the room, his hand strong under her arm. As he guided her down the hall, Carolyn wondered why people always assumed that grief created malfunction and collapse in the legs? It wasn't the legs. She was quite able to walk. Signals went from her brain and her feet responded obediently. But numbness made her feel as if she were in two parts. The head that hurt. And the feet that obeyed.

Once she was in the police car again, Carolyn's mind began functioning more efficiently. "Are there legal formalities here before we can return to New York?" she asked.

"Yes. Quite a few. The law requires the coroner to hold an inquest in the case of death by accident, which includes death in traffic accidents. The coroner must establish the identity of the deceased and order a postmortem. Once these two requirements are satisfied, he will issue a pink form. That is the burial order, which you must take to the registrar. He will issue the death certificate, and then burial can take place. In your case, you would then be able to remove the body from the country to the United States if you wish to bury him there."

Forms to be born. Forms to die. Forms to disguise the enormity of life. But she nodded politely, hiding her thoughts from Police Constable Harrod's earnest efforts to be kind. "How long will this take?" she asked.

"Several days. There is no question of the deceased's identity, and the postmortem can be accomplished promptly. This is Friday afternoon. You will probably receive the burial order Monday, Tuesday at the latest. However, the vehicle that caused the accident did not stop. If the search for it delays the investigation, the inquest may not be until later in the week, possibly Thursday or Friday."

"Do I have to attend the inquest?"

"You are the only relative of Mr. Bruce's here in England, are you not?"

"Yes."

"And you witnessed the accident?"

"Yes."

"Generally your presence would be required. If there is any possibility that your statement alone might suffice for the coroner, you will be advised."

"Is temporary burial required?"

"That depends. The embalmer can instruct you on that when you know more about the inquest schedule. Ordinarily these matters do not take very long and you could return home within five or six days at the most. But I cannot promise you that, of course."

"I understand. The embalmer. . . ? I forgot to ask . . ."

"He will call on you at your hotel for any special instructions you may wish to give him."

Carolyn nodded. They finished the ride in silence. In a very few minutes the car swung into the turnaround before the hotel on Park

Lane and stopped. Harrod helped her out. "Shall I come up with you?" he asked.

"That won't be necessary. I will be all right."

"Do you have any friends in London whom you can call?"

"No. But don't worry. I can take care of myself."

"There's one more thing. You should contact your embassy in Grosvenor Square. They will help you with the formalities. And please call the police station and arrange an appointment for sometime tomorrow. Here's the address. We will take your formal statement and settle any questions that you might have."

"You have been very kind, constable. Thank you."

"Not at all, ma'am. I am sorry indeed. Good day." He touched his hat and climbed into the front seat of the cruiser. Carolyn stood a moment and watched it ease into the flow of traffic. Then she turned wearily to the hotel. The liveried doorman had been watching their conversation with an impassive face, but his eyes were curious. Carolyn looked down at herself, at the dried blood, the run in her stocking, her dirty hands. She glanced at him. He made no sign that anything was amiss, but opened the heavy door for her. She nodded her thanks, but did not enlighten him.

Carolyn stood a while longer at the window, watching the dark close around the park and the mist begin to shroud the arc lights in softness. The minutes slipped by. Her mind wandered, not lighting on anything in particular, her thoughts not staying long enough for her to be really conscious of them. She felt a little disembodied, as though she had drunk too much. She moved her feet. They still followed orders.

Finally, with a long sigh, she turned from the window, drew the curtains and made the telephone calls that Harrod had advised. While she talked she looked about the bedroom. David's things were everywhere, assailing her, recalling his brisk movements. The sooner they were removed from her sight the better.

She selected David's new suit, a dark-gray flannel, which he had never worn, and put it to one side in the closet. Shirt, tie, shoes, all new, she laid in the drawer. He had modeled the suit for her when he had bought it. She had praised him then, thinking how handsome he looked. She hoped she approved her choice. His tongue would have been caustic had he not. Everything else she packed into David's custom-made luggage, checking the pockets first. Papers, keys, odds and ends, she put into an empty flight bag she had brought in

8

her own luggage. It was too much to look at these things now. She put the flight bag and the luggage at the rear of the closet, behind her dresses.

The work tired her. She was pouring herself a drink from David's silver flask when the phone rang.

"Mrs. David Bruce?"

"Yes, this is she."

"Mrs. Bruce, this is John Winfrey."

"Yes?" A familiarity in his tone ruled out the embalmer whose call she was expecting.

"We have not met and I *am* sorry that our first contact is under such tragic circumstances. My wife, Marjorie, and I heard the news about David on the radio just a few minutes ago and we came right over. David said this is your first trip to England, and we thought perhaps we could be helpful. We are—were—very fond of David, and we had been looking forward to meeting you on this trip. We are downstairs. May we come up and see you for a few minutes?"

John and Marjorie Winfrey. Carolyn searched her mind but could not recall that David had ever mentioned them. Did she want to see them? No, she thought, she didn't want to be bothered, but if they were David's friends, perhaps she had better talk to them. "If you wish, for a few minutes. It's such a shock . . ." She let her voice trail off.

Winfrey took the hint. "We won't stay long. But we do want to see you. We will be up in ten minutes."

Ten minutes. Carolyn checked the living room of the suite, then remembered that she hadn't changed when she came in. She put the ruined suit aside to give to the maid and was zipping herself into a gray dress when the knock came at the door.

Mrs. Winfrey preceded her husband into the room. A small woman who seemed much younger than her husband, she hugged Carolyn and kissed her on the cheek. "My dear, we are so sorry. David was a great favorite of ours. So gay. Such a good friend. We never considered him just a business associate, although he was that, too, of course. We had so hoped to meet you on this trip, but we never dreamed it would be under such terrible circumstances. Oh, Carolyn, how *awful* for you."

She put Carolyn away from her then and turned to her husband, holding out one hand to draw him into the conversation. "And this is my husband, John Winfrey."

9

He took Carolyn's hand, but she was grateful that he wasn't as effusive as Marjorie. He was the typical English businessman, dressed in the English businessman's uniform. He left his briefcase and black umbrella by the door and led the two women to the couch. He didn't hold Carolyn's arm, and she began to warm to him.

They urged her to describe what had happened. Not wanting to relive it just yet, Carolyn gave a guarded and very brief account while the Winfreys sat, one on each side of her on the sofa, and listened intently. Winfrey's head was cocked. His cool gray eyes watched her face closely, as if he were recording her words. Marjorie smoked, holding a heavy glass ashtray in one hand and dabbing the cigarette repeatedly on the edge, keeping the ash neat and rounded. Her heavy gold bracelets clanked with her gestures.

When she had finished, Winfrey shook his head. "It must have been a dreadful shock for you, seeing it happen and not being able to do anything to stop it. The traffic in this town is an invention of the devil. We are used to it, but visitors . . . I am sorry indeed about David. We shall miss him mightily." He shook his head in regret and Carolyn began forming a question to fill the silence that always follows such statements. But Marjorie covered the pause with a question of her own.

"We came to see if we could be of help to you in some way. Do you know anyone in London?"

Carolyn shook her head.

"Then you must consider us your good friends and let us do whatever we can. You should not be alone now. Won't you come and stay with us in the country for a few days?"

Carolyn looked at Marjorie, trying to determine if she was sincere or merely being polite. She saw that Marjorie was older than she seemed at first glance. She was cultivating the illusion of youth. "That is so kind of you. I do appreciate it. But I have obligations here and cannot leave London just now. I will be returning to New York as soon as the legal formalities are completed. Thank you anyway. I don't believe that I can accept."

"Then at least come and stay over the weekend. London is so dreary on Sunday. Absolutely nothing is going on. You will have trouble even finding a place to eat. It would be terribly depressing for you."

The implication that she might spend a day seeking London's social activities while David lay dead seemed crude, but a glance at the older woman's face assured Carolyn that she was unaware of her faux pas. "I know," Carolyn said, "but you need not be concerned about me. I will be quite all right."

John interrupted his wife's persuasions. "Marjorie is right. We will send a car for you on Sunday morning. Spend Sunday night with us and we will bring you back to town Monday in time for whatever you have to do. The authorities won't accomplish anything on Sunday and you won't be needed here. For David's sake, let us do that much. I would like to think he would want us to look out for you. He was such a good friend." Winfrey was leaning forward earnestly, his thin face concerned and anxious. Carolyn found that she liked him.

"Well, Mr. Winfrey," she said, smiling, "you put it so I cannot refuse. Thank you very much. I will come."

"Good. We must go now, Marjorie. The car will call for you at eleven o'clock on Sunday. We'll expect you for lunch. Here is our address and phone number in case you wish to come sooner or if we can help you with anything." He took a card from his wallet and handed it to Carolyn.

"Thank you for coming to see me."

"Is there anything about the authorities I can help you with?"

"No, thank you, Mr. Winfrey. I have been assured it will be routine."

"Good. Then we will see you Sunday."

As Carolyn ushered the Winfreys out, the embalmer was coming down the hall. She knew immediately who it was. He looked like an undertaker. She didn't want to see him just then, but he received her instructions attentively and refrained from any insincerity. Carolyn was impressed with him and with the reasonableness of his fees. She was grateful that it was over in ten minutes. She wanted to be alone to call her sister in New York.

Carolyn and Susie were very close. They were only a year apart in age and had shared everything from the time they were babies. First it had been dolls, then secrets, and finally boy friends. They had not shared Sam Mallory. Susie had met him when she was a senior in college and had ordered Carolyn to stay away from him. Carolyn had complied and had happily promoted the romance. Now she was almost as close to Sam as she was to Susie. The only thing that had ever marred her relationship with her brother-in-law was his disapproval of David Bruce. When she had announced their engagement, Susie had been wildly exuberant and excited for her sister. She was happily married herself and had never understood Carolyn's satisfaction in her single, career status. Sam had had very little to say, so little that Carolyn had made a point of asking him about it.

"It's not that I don't like him, Carolyn," Sam had replied thoughtfully. "I do like him, socially speaking. But there's something about him that makes me hesitate. He would be a fine drinking and poker buddy, but if I had several drinking buddies, he would not be the one I would choose to introduce to you."

"That doesn't make any sense, Sam," Carolyn had replied.

"I believe that he's insensitive. Even a little cold. That's insufficient reason not to marry him if you love him enough, but you are a warm and giving person. I see this incompatibility as a potential cause of unhappiness for you. But I am not in a position to lecture you on your choice of husband. And I won't grump about in disapproval. I just wish you were marrying someone else."

He had been as good as his word. Never again had he criticized David. He had given her away at the quiet wedding ceremony and kissed her as proudly as any true brother. He had welcomed David into his home and had been unfailingly cordial and friendly. But Carolyn had always sensed a restraint, almost a watchfulness, in Sam as far as David was concerned. It was so subtle as to be unnoticeable to the casual eye, and certainly David had never detected it. But Carolyn remembered Sam's words and long ago had forgiven him for being right.

The call to New York went through promptly and Susie's breathless voice answered. Carolyn clung tightly to the receiver, searching for the words to tell of David's death without provoking the emotional outburst that was Susie's response to any crisis. But after the first gasp, Susie sensed the precariousness of Carolyn's control and calmed herself. In tones flattened by grief they discussed funeral arrangements. Susie offered to fly over. Carolyn dissuaded her.

"But Carolyn . . ."

"I know, dear. But you can do more for me there. Please. I will be all right."

"Are you sure?"

"Truly. Now, don't worry."

The call ended quickly. If I say I'll be all right often enough, Carolyn thought, perhaps I can believe it.

But talking with Susie had been a mistake. It emphasized her solitariness, and Carolyn regretted not having gone to the country with the Winfreys. She poured out the drink that had become watery and made herself another. She took a bath and called down for supper to be sent up. When it arrived, she did not feel like eating. Finally she rose from the table, drew open the curtains and stared for a long time into the park. David had been afraid. And the man in the raincoat had had something to do with his fear. It was incongruous, really, to think that David could be afraid of a shabby little man who needed a haircut. David often boasted of profits of a million dollars on a single stock. He lunched with the Secretary of the Treasury and called White House aides by their initials and nicknames. He told her practically nothing of his financial operations, but he talked about the people, and he never failed to tell her when he had gotten the best of one of them. She had warned him once that he was going to make enemies if he wasn't careful. He had laughed and chucked her under the chin and told her not to worry about his business. Then he had walked away, leaving her infuriated at being patronized like a dull-witted child. But, then, he always sought to turn her mind from inquiring into his affairs. And she did inquire, because she was interested. He relished the constant struggle to make a good investment, and she enjoyed the sense of involvement. And since he had made her resign from her own job when they married, she hoped to find vicarious satisfaction in his successes. But he didn't let her. Her mind returned to the man in the raincoat. David was reckless and he hadn't paid attention to her warning, but she had never thought he was foolish enough to get into anything he couldn't handle. Had she been mistaken about his fear? Considering it carefully, she finally concluded that she might have exaggerated the extent of it, but she hadn't imagined the fear itself. It was real. And it posed a question that needed an answer.

It was strange, too, that he had never mentioned the Winfreys. They seemed nice enough, especially John. She wondered where David had met them and whether he and they had really been as close as the Winfreys said. Oh, but surely. She dismissed that thought. They certainly wouldn't want to be burdened with a newly made widow who was a complete stranger if they didn't feel they were obligated.

She turned from the window then, went to the closet and got David's leather address book from the flight bag. There was no John Winfrey under the W's. She turned carefully through the entire book. Each name and address and number was written neatly and completely in ink. Full name, full address, telephone number complete with the long-distance exchange number and area code. No Winfreys anywhere. But under the M's, written hastily and in pencil, there was the single initial W and a number. She got the London directory and looked up John Winfrey. The number could be a London number, but it was not for a Winfrey. Who was W? She remembered Winfrey's card, found it, and held it against the page, comparing each digit. The local exchange was the same, but there the similarity ended. Perhaps their country house had two numbers. She sighed and put the address book and the flight bag back in the closet.

She made herself prepare for bed. But she found herself standing with toothbrush poised or with slipper cocked, staring into space. She ran water for a bath, remembered that she had already taken one this evening and let it out again. She sat at the dressing table in the bedroom and brushed her hair, still unseeing, staring. Finally her eyes focused on the antique gold disk around her neck. It was set with tiny diamonds and emeralds forming a delicate flower. David had given it to her on their wedding night. He was not a sentimental man, and the gift had overwhelmed her, erasing the awkwardness she had felt.

On impulse she reached up and struggled to unhook the tiny clasp. She had worn it since that night more than four years ago. She held it in her hand, hefting the weight of the gold, savoring the soft yielding of the narrow chain, and looked, not at it, but at the bare place at her throat. Then, still not looking at it, she laid it carefully in her jewel case and closed the lid.

With that their marriage ended.

3
.

Carolyn took two sleeping pills and went to bed. But it was hours before they worked. She lay awake remembering David's ugly, cutting words, "I don't care what happens to you now." In the darkness, listening to the faint hotel sounds around her, she wrestled with that brief sentence, wondering whether David had really meant it. First dawn was coming into the room when she finally slept.

It was far later than she had intended when she awoke, headachy and sluggish. Her mouth tasted sour from the cigarettes she had smoked the night before and her eyes felt gritty. It was one o'clock. She had missed her appointment with the American Embassy. She made herself a cup of instant coffee from her travel kit and was sipping it when the phone rang.

"Mrs. Bruce? This is the desk calling. We rang you earlier but there was no answer. We have three messages for you, all of which seemed rather important. The American Embassy called about eleven forty-five. They changed your appointment with Mr. Richard Riley of the Consular Section to Monday morning at ten forty-five. If that is not suitable, you are to call them after eight o'clock on Monday. Then Police Constable Charles Harrod called to cancel your appointment at the police station this afternoon. He said to tell you that Detective Chief Superintendent Prescott of Scotland Yard will be contacting you instead. And finally, Superintendent Prescott's office called. He wishes to see you this afternoon at two thirty in his office at the New Scotland Yard building in Victoria Street. You are to confirm this time."

"Thank you very much. Can you place the call to Superintendent Prescott for me?"

"Certainly, Mrs. Bruce."

Scotland Yard's new office towers were impersonal, sterile and immaculate enough to be a laboratory. To Carolyn, who had expected the comfortable clutter and mahogany fireplaces of a thousand stories and movies, it was a little sad. She threaded her way through the maze of corridors, had to ask her way, and was late for her appointment.

Elsworth Prescott was a slight, wispy man with outsized ears and hands. His face was thin, chalky, and covered with fine wrinkles. A faint odor of age clung to his clothes, a relic perhaps of the ancient offices where he must have spent a lifetime. But the watery blue eyes behind sliding rimless spectacles were shrewd and the mottled hands were steady as he greeted Carolyn.

He settled her into a straight chair before his desk and sat down opposite her in a battered swivel chair complete with a red corduroy cushion. His old chair was the only personal object in the office, where efficient orderliness dominated, and the spreading view of London seemed the only element identifiable as human.

He had mugs of thick black tea brought to them, and while Carolyn was sugaring and stirring hers, he surveyed her quietly. He saw a slender young woman with light-brown hair, worn long and coiled about her head. She had enormous gray eyes with heavy lashes. Now, under the stresses of the last twenty-four hours, there were shadows under the lower lids. It was not unattractive. She was expensively dressed.

"Well, Mrs. Bruce," he began, "we have the statement you gave to Police Constable Harrod yesterday, but we require some additional information. We will get my secretary in to take down our conversation."

He punched the button on the intercom on his desk and a uniformed policewoman came in immediately with a pad and pencil in her hand. "Mrs. Bruce, this is Sergeant Hardwicke, my secretary." The two women nodded. Miss Hardwicke took a seat quietly to one side where she could see both Superintendent Prescott and Carolyn. "Now, Mrs. Bruce," Prescott said, "start at the beginning."

Carolyn nodded slowly and began to relate what had occurred. Early in her narrative Prescott decided that Carolyn Bruce was a very capable young woman. She spoke softly, in a husky voice, telling the events coherently and smoothly. Prescott listened critically. Occasionally he glanced at the typed pages clipped to a folder before him, nodding, as though she was confirming facts already known to him. Carolyn spoke deliberately, watching Sergeant Hardwicke's flying pencil. Carolyn knew shorthand herself and she saw right away that Miss Hardwicke was very, very good. But even the best court reporter needs pauses, and Sergeant Hardwicke's little nods showed she appreciated Carolyn's consideration.

"The sequence of events as you describe them checks with what you and other witnesses have already told us, Mrs. Bruce," Prescott said when she had concluded. "However, I have a few more questions I would like to ask to clarify the record. Can you describe to me exactly what you did?"

"What I did?"

"Your movements. Step by step."

"Well. My husband and I were arguing and I was holding back from him. He stopped and seemed to be looking at someone, a man. I asked who it was. He said it was no one important and pulled me on toward the crosswalk. We waited for the light to change so we could cross the street. He started forward and I pulled away. He turned back to get me to go with him. He seemed to change his mind then and went on across the street and . . . and was hit."

"And what did you do?"

"I went to him. Then he . . . he died right after that."

"How much did you see? Of the taxi, I mean?"

"Almost nothing. Just an impression, really, of something coming too fast."

"What did you do when you saw it coming?"

"I cried out."

"And then?"

"I ran forward. I was too late."

"How far were you from your husband?"

"About ten feet, I suppose. I don't judge distances very well. The distance from the curb to the second lane of traffic. Maybe not quite ten feet."

"Did you make any other gestures? Or movements?"

"No. I don't think so."

"Are you sure?"

"Yes. I think so."

"I want every detail, Mrs. Bruce. Every detail. Be sure on this point. It is quite important."

"I believe I've told you everything."

She seemed restive to Prescott, disturbed, and he changed the subject. "What were you and your husband doing in London?" he asked.

"We came on business. Afterward we were planning to travel in England and France for about a week. It was to be a vacation."

"What business did your husband have in London?"

"He was on assignment for the bank. At least, I assumed he was. He never discussed his work with me."

"Did you meet any of his business associates here?"

"No."

"Had he accomplished his assignment?"

"I believe he had. He went to a meeting yesterday morning. When he returned to the hotel, he said that everything was finished and now we were free."

"Where was the meeting held?"

"I don't know. Not in our hotel—I know that."

"Did he say anything about your meeting anyone on this trip?"

"No. He said since this was to be his vacation, he did not want to see any businessmen. He did not say anything about meeting anyone he knew. However . . ."

"Yes?"

"Just after the accident the John Winfreys called. I had not met them. They said they were friends of my husband's."

"But you knew of them from your husband?"

"No. No, I didn't. He had never mentioned them."

"Is that unusual?"

"What?"

"Your husband's not telling you of the people he met and knew through his work?"

"Sometimes he did. I doubt whether he did all the time, however. Probably not. I am sure he would see people every day in routine ways that he would not mention at home."

"Did your husband have any papers with him of a business nature?"

"Yes, I believe he did. A folder. He took it with him to the meeting yesterday morning and returned without it, so I assume he delivered it to someone he saw there."

"Anything else?"

"No. Just the usual things anyone would carry on a trip abroad."

"And you did not know what was in the folder he delivered?"

"No."

"Your husband was a banker?"

"Yes. He was a director of the New York Bank."

"Wasn't he a little young to be a director?"

"Yes." There was considerable pride in her quiet answer.

"What was his background?"

"His college degree was taken in economics at Harvard. Then he received an MBA from Harvard and went to work immediately after graduation for the bank. He was on loan to the United States Treasury off and on, but mainly two years ago for a six-month period."

"What facet of banking was his specialty?"

"Investments, trust and portfolio management, securities dealings, especially in the international area. He was also in charge of two mutual funds."

"Did he travel a great deal in his work?"

"Not a great deal. Once or twice a month he would take trips for three or four days. Occasionally for a week."

"Where did he go?"

"Wherever the bank had clients. Washington. Miami. San Francisco. Dallas."

"Did he ever come to London or go to the Continent?"

"No, not that I know of. I think he did travel to Europe for a summer when he was in college, but I don't believe he came to England."

"How many other passports has he had? Other than the one he was carrying, I mean?"

"I know only of the one he had when he was in Europe during college. It had expired and he had to apply for a new one to take this trip."

"How long were you married?"

"Four and a half years."

"Had you known your husband long before you married?"

"Yes. We met while we both were in graduate school in Boston and saw each other for several years, off and on."

"You said you were arguing. Did you argue often?"

"I don't believe that is pertinent to this, sir." Her voice was as soft as ever, but the tone was definitely steely, and the gray eyes were snapping.

"It may have a bearing on the case."

"I don't see how."

"One of the witnesses reported seeing you and your husband in violent argument just before it happened. I use the term 'violent argument' because that is the term the witness used."

"I see."

"Well? Was it a violent argument? For you and your husband, that is?"

"I suppose so. Yes."

"What were you arguing about?"

"He wanted to go home early. That day in fact."

"Is that all?"

"Yes."

"And you did not want to go?"

"No."

"Why did he want to go home? I take it you had planned this trip for some time?"

"Yes, we had. He did not give a reason."

"What did he say exactly?"

"He said he had to go back. That he could not stay here."

"What did you think was the reason?"

"That he needed to go back to work—to the bank, I mean. That was what usually interrupted our trip plans."

"Was his work one of the things you argued about?"

"I am not sure I can answer many more such questions."

"Forgive me. Tell me again what you did when you saw the accident happening."

"I cried out." She was speaking slowly, pointedly, a little aggravated with him and showing it. "I called his name. I jumped forward and threw out my hands."

"You didn't say that before. Are you changing your story?"

"What? No, I'm not changing my story."

"You omitted saying that before, that you threw out your hands."

"Yes. I forgot that. I tried to grab him."

"Of course. It confirms a detail reported by our witness. Are you sure you threw your hands out?"

"Yes."

"What did you touch?"

"Nothing."

"Nothing?"

"I was too late. He was beyond my reach. What are you getting at?"

"My dear Mrs. Bruce. It was a hit-and-run accident in which a man was killed. What's more, it is connected with a violent argument, which throws some question into the motives of the person or persons involved. Consequently I must investigate all possible theories. There will have to be a coroner's inquest next week, as soon as it can be scheduled."

"I don't care for your insinuations, sir. David Bruce is—was—my husband, and whatever our relations at the moment of his death, I loved him. I do not, I did not, wish him harm." She was sitting straight, eyes flashing angrily. Her voice was icy.

"I understand, Mrs. Bruce. You said something about your husband seeing a man just before the accident. Did you recognize him?"

"No."

"But he did?"

"That was my impression."

"Tell me again what he said about him."

"I asked who he was. He said he was no one important. When I pressed him, he just said he was no one."

"Could you identify him if you saw him again?"

"No, I don't think so. I didn't see his face. He was going into a store. His back was to us."

"Describe what you did see."

"He was thin and had gray hair, worn long. He was wearing a hat and one of the military-style tan raincoats, and was carrying a black umbrella. He was of medium height. My husband seemed afraid of him."

"Afraid? What did he say to make you think that?"

"He didn't say anything that I haven't told you. It was his attitude more than anything else that gave me the impression. After he saw the man he seemed to be even more eager to get somewhere else."

"I see. Could the man have been following you?"

Carolyn thought back. "I suppose it's possible," she replied after a moment. "We walked from our hotel to Piccadilly and were considering getting tickets at the Haymarket Theatre. We strolled slowly and it was very pleasant. David was a little tense, but not abnormally so. When we reached Piccadilly Circus my husband decided to get the tickets later. It was rather abrupt, now that I think back on it, his change of mood, I mean. Yes. I suppose it's possible."

"Hmmm," Prescott said. He took a blackened pipe from his pocket, his chair squeaking as he shifted his weight. He fiddled with the pipe a moment. "How long will you be in London?" he asked finally.

"As short a time as possible. How long do you think it will be?"

"Several days probably. You will be returning your husband's body to the United States?"

"Yes."

"Your situation is a bit unusual, and we will do everything we can to expedite the case so you can return home within the next week. However, you must attend the inquest, and your departure will have to be delayed until it is over. Now, if you will look through your husband's possessions and see if everything is there and then sign this receipt." He handed her a big manila folder.

Carolyn spilled the contents of the envelope into her lap. Black leather wallet with passport inside. Loose change. Keys. A vial of Dramamine pills. A checkbook for David's New York bank account. The blue folder of traveler's checks. She flipped through them. Three thousand dollars. He had not had time to cash any of them. She looked up at Prescott. He was watching her, but Sergeant Hardwicke had turned away and was looking out the window. "It seems to be all here," she said. Prescott handed her the pen from his desk holder and she signed the form he held out to her.

"Are you planning to continue at the same hotel?"

She nodded.

"Good. We have that address in case we need to call you again."

"I have been invited to the Winfreys' to spend tomorrow evening. I will be back in London Monday morning."

"Do you have their address?" Carolyn found the card that Winfrey had given her and handed it over. Prescott copied the address carefully into the folder before him and gave it back to her. "You said you had just met the Winfreys?"

"Yes. They came as soon as they heard about the accident on the radio yesterday evening."

"What time was that?"

"About six thirty. They stayed about half an hour."

"Well, then. Miss Hardwicke will transcribe this interview. Can you drop in Monday afternoon sometime after three o'clock—will that give you enough time, Miss Hardwicke?—and review the transcripts and sign them?"

"Yes, certainly."

"Good. Then I won't keep you any longer. Thank you for coming and for being candid with us. I am sorry your trip had to end like this. Your husband must have been quite a brilliant man."

"Yes, he was."

Prescott helped her into her coat, and then, at her request, pointed the way out of the building. She nodded her thanks and walked out, her back straight. To Prescott she somehow seemed very much alone.

"Well, Sergeant?" Prescott asked his secretary. "What's your assessment?"

"She's a very striking woman. Chic. I wish I had clothes like that."

"That wasn't what I meant."

"I know, sir. Well, as to that, I think she is smart enough and no doubt calculating enough. I wish you had asked about her background. I think she worked before her marriage. Did you notice how she let me keep up? I'd say she isn't the type."

"Hmmm," Prescott said. "I wonder." He took off his glasses, and holding them carefully by the wire earpieces, rubbed his eyes.

"Another cup of tea, sir?"

"Yes. Maybe I had better. I have a feeling this case won't let me sleep for a while."

4

●

It was late afternoon when Carolyn stood under Scotland Yard's revolving sign and pulled on her gloves. The sign was another incongruity. With a little shrug she walked toward St. James's Park, and reached it sooner than she had expected. Her boots made no sound on the damp sand walks as she wandered around the lake, seeking a place where there were no people. When she found it, she stopped and sat down. Wild ducks came tamely to the bank and pecked about for crumbs. Watching them calmed her and she could think more objectively about her interview with Prescott.

His questions about her relations with David had angered her. They meant he had shrewdly sensed that she and David had not been happy. Yes, they had argued. Or, rather, she had argued. David's response to anything he didn't want to hear was simply to walk away.

She had met David Bruce in Boston on a blind date and was instantly attracted to him. He was everything that she was not, and she felt the introvert's envy for the extrovert's ease with people. He was ebullient, flamboyant, laughingly outgoing, and she had been fascinated. Everyone who met him responded to his magnetism, and he appeared to like people in return. He collected anecdotes and could entertain a group for hours, telling stories with gusto, mimicry and a sense of drama. Even when expounding on the drier subjects of underwriting deals, the balance of payments, and the Senate Finance Committee, he interjected the comic and even ludicrous activities of the persons involved. Sometimes he became a little acerbic, discoloring a respectable personality by his innuendo and insinuating wit. At other times he was content with wit alone, and then, especially if the liquor was abundant, his listeners laughed until they were gasping. Carolyn sensed that the life-of-the-party image was something of an act, but she didn't mind. She enjoyed it. She was flattered that he singled her out and she liked being one of David Bruce's friends.

David was quieter with her. Sometimes he was a little remote when they were alone together and on occasion he was even abrupt. But these moods didn't alarm her. A person could not be a wit all the time, and she considered it a compliment that he could relax when he was with her. Sometime during that first year she realized that she loved him.

And he was attracted to her. She had no doubt about that. But at that time other things always came first with David—money, business, contacts—they were the most important things in his life. So the early years of their relationship were erratic. He would date her furiously for several weekends. Then he would disappear for several months, only to reappear as cheerful and familiar as if he had just seen her the day before.

She had been working in New York for some time when she realized that their relationship was not progressing and that David was hindering her friendships with other men. After that she went out with him if she was free when he called, but she never again broke an engagement for him and she didn't let him fill her calendar for days in advance. He had not liked her decision and had left her alone for several months. Then, suddenly, he began pursuing her with more intensity, with an ardor he had never shown before. He said he was in love with her, and his actions and words left her no reason to doubt it. The weekend after he had been promoted to vice-president he asked her to marry him. She did not hesitate long in giving her answer. David Bruce would not be very easy to live with, but she believed that he loved her and that they could be happy.

Once she had accepted, David wanted to marry immediately. She had been sorry to forgo all the trimmings of the big wedding that she had always dreamed of, but then, their parents were dead and there seemed to be no reason for a big ceremony. They were married quietly at her sister's apartment, with only a dozen good friends for the ceremony and breakfast afterward.

26

David's delight with his new life lasted about a week. Then he was off, day and night, working. After a month she felt that he wasn't head over heels in love with her, as he had told her. And after a year she wondered if he loved her at all. They lived reasonably well in the same apartment, sharing scrupulously half and half in closet space and catering to each other's desires in small ways, but the real sharing and the laughter and the little thoughtfulnesses eluded her. Then one night, bolstered by David's unusually mellow mood and an hour of lovemaking, she asked him why he had married her. "I like you," he said with more seriousness than she had expected. "I like seeing you at the foot of my table. I like you on my arm. I like you in bed. You are very good, you know."

"But you didn't know that before we were married."

"I believed that there was a hidden Carolyn. She looks out of those big eyes of yours when you are not thinking. And I was right. I am always right about people." And he caressed and made love to her and dispelled her doubts again. But they had come back, insidiously and against her will. She wished she hadn't asked him that question. He had omitted to say that he loved her. It was an important omission, and as the weeks passed, she came to expect no improvement in their relationship.

It was sometime later that he unwittingly revealed the reason he had married her. He had just been elevated to a directorship of the bank, which made him the youngest on the board. It opened new opportunities for him and he boasted to her of his success. "I knew I could do it," he said, his eyes shining with satisfaction. "I set my mind on the top, and here I am. This promotion relieves me of a lot of drudgery so I can concentrate on the next thing. The bank's usefulness to me is over. I've gone as high as I can there. Now I'm going to look around for a spot that will give me real power. God, wouldn't I love to have it, right here, right now." He closed his fist possessively and talked on. Carolyn didn't hear exactly what he said after that. It was grandiose and somewhat nebulous. The important thing was that he was bored with his accomplishment now that he had it. What excited him was not the job but the effort to get it. She remembered then that David's interest in her had quickened after she was no longer easily available to him. In her effort to reorder her life she had made herself a bastion to be stormed. He had reacted to the challenge. But as soon as he was assured of her he had turned to something else. If she had agreed to an engagement but had delayed the ceremony, would he have actually married her? Would his interest have lasted? She hadn't wanted the answer to that question, but hadn't he given it to her yesterday when he left her on the curb? "I don't care."

She stirred restlessly on her bench. Her sudden movement caught the attention of a mallard, which shied away and then cautiously waddled closer, clucking softly, importuning her. It was a welcome distraction. Carolyn shook her head at the duck and opened her empty hands. Then she remembered a packet of crackers in her purse. She opened them and crumbled them onto the ground. The bird found each morsel, ate it, and after checking around for more, returned to the lake. Carolyn sat on in the deepening twilight.

When Prescott asked about meeting people in London, she had answered in David's own words. She had been touched, made hopeful, by David's desire just to be with her, but wasn't it really inconsistent? David's love of his work and his diligence in pursuing a deal were such that, vacation or no vacation, he would not miss an opportunity to make some profit.

She had told Prescott that David had not traveled abroad on business, but did she know for certain that that was true? He went often to the places she had listed for Prescott. Yet for every time she knew where he went, there was a time she did not know. Once, when they were first married, he had gone hunting in the mountains of Vermont. She had called him, just to hear his voice and say she loved him. He had been so coldly furious, so cuttingly sharp with her, that her stunned surprise at his reaction turned to anger and she never tried again to call him. Later, when he was packing to go on another weekend trip, she had sat and watched and followed him forlornly from closet to bathroom and back to the bed, where the suitcase lay open. Finally she had asked where he was going. He said, "To spend a weekend with friends; you are not invited." The shuttered expression that crossed his face left her out. That time she had insisted that he leave her a number to call. He looked at her a long moment and then wrote a number on the desk calendar. "If it's a dire emergency, literally a case of life and death, you can call that number. The person who answers will always know how to get in touch with me. But you are not to use it just to chat." She said nothing. There was nothing she could say that would penetrate such insensitivity. She never again asked where he was going. She would go out or sit in the library and read while he packed. He could have had a separate passport for each continent and used them regularly for all she knew.

On one of the long days when he was away, she had begun to remember the little instances before their marriage when he had been abrupt with her. She wondered how she could have mistaken thoughtlessness for moodiness. The outgoing personality she had fallen in love with began to appear to be a façade. He was an actor. It was easy to believe in the friendly enthusiasm of his public appearances, but after they were married, she quickly discovered he could turn it on and off. Whenever they left a party in which he had been a main attraction, the smile would fall from his face and he would withdraw into his own thoughts as soon as the hostess shut the door behind them. Frequently he would make a harsh comment that showed a total lack of regard for the people he had just courted. Once, shortly after their marriage, she had remonstrated. He turned to her and ordered her coldly to keep her criticisms to herself. She clamped her jaw on her protest. That was the last time she tried to temper his opinions of people with any comments of her own.

She knew nothing of David's personal finances. She didn't believe in joint bank accounts, but she wanted to know, felt she should know, something of their financial status. She had been trained in business administration and had held a responsible job. She was fully capable of understanding anything he had to tell her. But he refused. He never asked her advice on any financial matters, either business or personal, and never told her of his personal investments. He gave her a generous sum with which to decorate the apartment, and when the bills threatened to run over the amount he had given her, he paid the difference without question. He gave her an allowance for the monthly household expenses, but he demanded an accounting of every single penny. Her books always balanced, but she never felt that he was completely satisfied with her stewardship.

He insisted that she resign from her job when they married. She had been willing to do so, but during the long days when David was at work, and the even longer evenings when he was entertaining clients, she was terribly lonely. She asked to join him in the entertainment part of his duties, but he brusquely refused. This she had not understood, because he was genuinely proud of her and her abilities as a hostess. She thought about it a great deal and came to the obvious conclusion that there was another woman.

Women adored him. Big, athletic, his summer tan maintained year round by a sunlamp, he attracted them without effort. For months Carolyn watched him at parties, while shopping, on any occasion in which they were thrown into the company of other women. Never once had she cause to be suspicious. Then one day she saw him having cocktails with six women at the Plaza's Peacock Room. She asked him about them.

He laughed heartily. "They are the Tuesday Night Investors Club of the Wilkes-Barre Western High School Teachers Association. They are in town for investment advice."

"Aren't they a little out of your league?"

He knew immediately what was worrying her. He laughed, enjoying her discomfiture. "You needn't worry about them. They compensate for their lack of looks and sex lives by playing in the stock market. They are worth roughly $265,000 at today's prices."

After that she hadn't worried about his female clients, although she still didn't understand why she wasn't asked to help entertain them.

But just recently she had begun to sense an answer to that question. When he invited her to accompany him to Europe, he gave her a ridiculously big check and ordered her to spend it all on clothes for the trip. It promised a new beginning for them, and she shopped carefully for things that would please him. She came home late one afternoon, her arms loaded with suit boxes. She dumped them on the floor of the hall, and as the rattle of cardboard and tissue paper died away, the sound of voices in the library became audible. She listened at the door. A man, whose voice was unfamiliar, seemed to be pleading. Her husband cut him off, refusing to listen. The stranger said, "You are unreasonable, Bruce." She was too near the door when it opened and the man came out. He was dripping with perspiration and there was a haunted look in his eyes. His shoulders sagged and his hands shook. He did not seem to see her, but she escorted him to the door and opened it for him. In the outer hall he turned and his eyes focused slowly on her.

"Are you all right?" she asked him. "You look ill."

"No, Mrs. Bruce," he said in a dejected tone, "I am not ill. But life will teach your husband a bitter lesson one day. I am just sorry I won't be around to see it. Good day." Then he walked quickly down the hall and out of her sight. She went immediately to the library.

"David, who was that man?"

"Ralph Stone."

"What did he want?"

"He can't meet his debt payment. He wanted more time."

"Did you give it to him?"

"No."

"But David—"

"That's enough. Won't you ever learn not to meddle?" He turned away from her, closing her out again.

The next week she read in *The New York Times* that Ralph Stone had died in a single-car collision on the Connecticut Freeway. He had crashed his car into a bridge abutment late the previous night and had died instantly. Carolyn circled the obituary, folded the paper and put it on David's desk. David did not mention the article. She found the paper the next day, still in its folds, dropped contemptuously into the trash basket. Slowly she bent down, took it out and reread the obituary. The tiny print blurred as the doubts rose. She sank into David's chair and stared out the window. The realization came that she was uneasy about David, even a little frightened of him. The paper slipped from her fingers. She didn't stoop to pick it up, but sat on until it was dark in the room.

And now? Prescott had identified the unhappiness in their marriage. He had not indicated that he believed she was in any way responsible for David's death. But she sensed that he was seeking a reason, a motive, sufficient to explain an accident that shouldn't have happened. She would always wonder whether it would have happened if she hadn't argued with David. But she hadn't wished his death. She loved him still. She felt grief for him, and sadness that their marriage had not been successful. But there was also a feeling of being freed, not from a union but from a bondage her love had created. That realization depressed her deeply.

It was dusk, almost dark. Her hands and feet were cold, and she rose and followed the edge of the lake. She was not yet ready to shut herself into her hotel suite and paused again to watch a pair of swans scavenge for the last crumbs. She wished she had some bread for them. She had fond memories of feeding swans when she was a child. Their aloofness had always appealed to her.

Suddenly she looked straight up into a clump of evergreens. They had tiny blue berries and were the only growth now alive in the park in February. A figure detached itself from the shadows on the other side of the bushes and walked swiftly away, umbrella swinging. He was wearing a tan raincoat in the military style. She watched him carefully. He was bareheaded and his long hair was gray, but was he the same man? He seemed a little broader through the shoulders, but could she be sure? How long had he been there while she sat by the lake? She knew he had been watching her. His stare had forced her to look right to the very spot where he was. She turned swiftly and hurried through the park, crossed the long open space of the Mall, and cut through Green Park. She looked from side to side as she walked, catching glimpses of people passing her. There were other men in tan military raincoats, but she didn't see the one she was seeking. He had vanished. Had he waited for her and taken up pace behind her? She walked quickly and purposefully, crossing the street and hurrying up Piccadilly. Just before she reached the brightly lighted entrance of the hotel, she turned sharply and looked behind her. Had a figure disappeared into a doorway? Her eyes narrowed, trying to penetrate the shadows. But she saw only the anonymity of the crowd coming and going, intent on its evening plans.

5
.

"Mrs. Bruce? Good morning. I am Haskins. Mr. Winfrey sent his car for you. It's just this way." The chauffeur took her overnight case and led the way to a gray Bentley parked before the hotel. He settled Carolyn into the rear seat and assured himself that she was comfortable. "It's a lovely day, madam. I hope you enjoy the drive."

"Thank you, Haskins. I am sure I shall." He shut the door and circled the car, paused a moment to wipe a microscopic speck from the fender, and then got behind the wheel. Carolyn was glad the glass partition between them was closed. She didn't want to have to make polite conversation.

Her interest in seeing the English countryside was disappointed. As soon as they left the main road out of London, long double rows of hedges on either side of the road blocked her view of the hills and fields. After a drive of almost an hour, a brick wall appeared on the right which extended for over a mile. Finally they turned through tall brick posts capped with lions. The car whispered down a long drive and turned to stop before an old Georgian house. It was an elegant house, a stately house, a rich man's home. Carolyn was even more amazed that David had never spoken of the Winfreys. David was impressed by wealth. He liked to talk of the people who had it. He would have known the Winfreys were well-to-do because he always had that kind of information about people. Then why hadn't he mentioned them? She shrugged. It must be simply another of the many things in his life that he hadn't shared with her.

Marjorie ran out as Haskins opened the door for Carolyn. "Carolyn, dear. Did you have a nice trip down? I am so glad the sun shone for you. Come in. We are just ready for lunch."

In the bright noon light Carolyn noticed that the older woman's hair was dyed. It was a masterful job, carefully reddish gold and beautifully coiffed. But her smile held no hint of her amusement as she pressed her cheek to Marjorie's and followed her into the house.

"Haskins, take Mrs. Bruce's luggage upstairs. And now, let me have your coat. We are eating in the breakfast room."

Carolyn had a swift impression of a wide paneled hall and a tantalizing array of antiques as Marjorie took her to a small dining room at the rear of the house. Tall windows poured sunlight over hothouse flowers and sparked the gold in the Crown Derby china on the table. Winfrey was waiting and held Carolyn's chair. "Welcome to Glenyck House, Carolyn. We are so pleased to have you with us." He turned to the butler standing quietly to one side of the room. "Neville, I believe we are ready now."

"Certainly, sir."

Neville looked more like an Italian longshoreman than an English butler, but he was skilled. He stepped without a sound on the Oriental carpet as he served Coquilles Saint-Jacques, broccoli and Pavlova, and kept their glasses full of a white wine. Conversation was light until the luncheon was cleared away and the coffee was served.

"Have the police located that hit-and-run vehicle yet?" Winfrey asked Carolyn.

"I don't believe they have."

"But they are making an investigation?"

"Certainly, I assume so."

"Have you talked to the police? Since the accident, I mean?"

Carolyn didn't want to go into Prescott's suspicions and her own suppositions. She decided to try to turn the conversation aside. "Yes. I saw Detective Chief Superintendent Prescott at Scotland Yard yesterday afternoon. He was most helpful and assured me that the legal formalities will not be allowed to delay my return to New York. My sister and brother-in-law are making funeral arrangements there."

"You went to the main Scotland Yard building?"

"Why, yes, the new one."

"Whom did you say you saw?"

"Detective Chief Superintendent Elsworth Prescott."

"I know very little about the Yard, but I believe that is one of the higher ranks. You must be getting very special treatment. How did you get onto him?"

"The policeman at the accident called Saturday morning and said I should see Superintendent Prescott instead of going to the police station, as he had instructed me. That's all I know about it. Marjorie, it was a lovely lunch."

"I am glad you enjoyed it. Are we all through now? Then, Carolyn, let me show you around the house. Coming, John?"

"No. You go on. I have a call to make. I will join you later."

"Very well, darling. Carolyn?" They left the dining room together. Carolyn had the feeling that something she had said had disturbed John Winfrey, but as she thought back over the conversation, she couldn't see what it was. She decided not to worry about it. She didn't know these people, and if something she said inadvertently upset them, that was unfortunate.

Marjorie gave Carolyn a brief tour of the house and then took her upstairs to a corner guest room. "I have to take a nap every afternoon, my dear. Perhaps you would like one, too. I will see you later. If you need anything, just ask me. But I think everything is here."

It was. The room was beautifully furnished with everything a guest could desire. There were comfortable wing chairs, good reading lamps, books. Behind the panels were large closets and a marble bathroom, complete to hot towel racks and outsized towels. Dried-flower arrangements brought the room to life. Carolyn liked everything she had seen of the Winfreys' house. Whoever had decorated it had perfect taste.

She unpacked, then slipped out of her suit and put on her robe. Everything was perfect, but the room seemed musty, and she went to the window. One side of the room overlooked a formal boxwood garden. Its focal point was a summer house, a miniature Palladian villa located at the end of the central path. She smiled with pleasure. It, too, was perfect. She tried the windows. Neither could be budged. The third window overlooking the entrance court yielded to her push and obligingly raised itself three inches. Content with her efforts, Carolyn stretched out on the bed under a comforter. She dropped off to sleep almost immediately.

She must have slept almost two hours, for there was no sun in the room when she woke. She lay quietly, her eyes resting on a portrait of a happy child over the mantelpiece. It was an engaging picture. It made one smile to look at it. Gradually she became aware of a murmur of voices. It seemed to come from below. Finally, fully awake and curious, she rose and went to the open window. Since she wasn't dressed, she concealed herself behind the curtain and looked down into the entrance court.

John Winfrey was talking to a man who was standing with his back to her. He was a full head taller than Winfrey, with wide shoulders and stout arms and legs. He wore no overcoat. They talked easily for a moment, their words indistinct to Carolyn. Then Winfrey clapped him on the shoulder. The man folded himself gracefully into an early Mercedes-Benz sports car, its powder-blue finish long since faded to chalky gray. Carolyn caught only a blur of his face as he lifted his hand to Winfrey and drove off. Winfrey watched him go, his hands jammed into his pockets, then turned and entered the house.

Carolyn dressed, carefully made up her face, and went downstairs. There was no one in sight. She wandered through the house, lingering to admire the things Marjorie had allowed her only a glimpse of. It was almost a museum and smelled faintly of wax and silver polish.

She ended up in the library, which the Winfreys obviously used as their main living room. A casual grouping of two wing chairs and a sofa around a coffee table stood before the fireplace, where a fire was burning. Mahogany bookcases filled with leather-bound books lined every wall from floor to ceiling. But the room was dominated by a massive fruitwood desk. Trimmed in brass, it sat squarely on a rectangular base at the right of the room. It looked as though it had grown through the floor. An elaborate baroque inkstand on its top contrasted oddly with the telephone and typewriter beside it. Remembering that she wanted to check the Winfreys' phone number, Carolyn crossed the room. The number on the telephone was the same as W's in David's address book. Then her eye fell on a folder on the desk. It was the folder that David had taken with him Friday morning. A letter, addressed to John Winfrey in David's handwriting, was clipped to it. Both had been opened. Carolyn remembered Prescott's questions. She had never in her life read anyone else's mail, but now she wanted to. She was opening the letter when Marjorie's footsteps clicked on the parquet floor of the hall outside the library. Quickly she clipped the letter back onto the folder and returned them to the desk. She was lighting a cigarette before the fireplace when Marjorie came in.

"Oh, there you are. Are you ready for something to drink?"

Was it her imagination, or did Marjorie glance at the desk?

Carolyn took an ashtray from the coffee table and sat down on the sofa. "Yes. Please."

"Good. So am I. John can't join us yet, so it's just the two of us." Marjorie tugged the bellpull, and almost immediately the butler came in, carrying a large silver tray with glasses and decanters. "What will you have, Carolyn?" Marjorie asked.

"Scotch and soda, please." Neville looked blank a moment and Carolyn shook her head ruefully. "Excuse me, I forgot. Whisky and soda."

"Certainly, madam." The butler's lips twitched. He placed the tray on a piecrust table near the fireplace and mixed their drinks. When they had approved them, he set the whisky decanter at Marjorie's elbow and bowed himself out.

Marjorie lit her cigarette with swift motions. "You must not mind poor Neville. He's not our regular butler. We hadn't planned to open the house this early in the season, but as soon as we heard about poor David, we wanted you to be with us here. It's so much more restful in the country, but it's a little difficult to get a staff together on short notice."

That answered one of Carolyn's questions. She had thought vaguely that there didn't seem to be enough servants around, and she couldn't visualize Marjorie polishing floors. "Then I am doubly grateful and appreciative that you went to so much trouble for me. It's most kind of you." In fact, she thought, it was extraordinary if what Marjorie said was true. "It's a beautiful house. David would have loved it."

"I know he would, and I am sorry he never got to see it. We usually met him in London. We have a flat there where we spend most of the winters, and he stayed at the Hilton, so the occasion never arose." So David had traveled abroad without telling her! Carolyn remained outwardly calm following this revelation, stifling the questions that rose to her lips. Her hostess took a hefty swallow of her drink, and with the hand that held the cigarette poured the glass full again from the decanter. Carolyn watched the ashes scattering on the table and chair. Marjorie ignored them. She tucked her feet under her in the chair. "A couple of our good friends are having dinner with us tonight," she said conversationally. "They are both bachelors and we dine often together."

Carolyn wasn't happy at the prospect of strangers, but she knew she was caught. She nodded and sipped her drink. "Were they friends of David's, too?" she asked.

Marjorie seemed a little relieved that Carolyn wasn't angry. "Yes, they were," she said. "Guillaume LeClere is a Frenchman. He's lived in London for years and has become quite an Anglophile. He has a gorgeous villa in Cannes. He says it's his only concession to his nationality, but I notice he's never changed his citizenship. We go down to Cannes every August to visit him. He keeps a yacht there. Last year we sailed with him through the Greek Isles. What a lovely cruise!"

"It must have been. Greece is a very special country, I think. It has a quality no other country that I have visited has."

"No other country has such gorgeous men," Marjorie said. "Such bodies." To this Carolyn made no reply.

"Then we spent a week in Athens," Marjorie continued. "Guillaume has an account there—one of the big shipping people, I think. While he was in town we had the ship all to ourselves. It was like owning it. He is a chartered accountant and has a fabulous practice all over the world. He earns enormous retainers as well as percentages of the taxes he saves his clients. He does John's tax work, too. He's quite good. You might consider using him now that you will have a big estate to settle."

Carolyn didn't want to comment on that. "Who's the other guest?" she asked.

"A Scotsman, James McAllister. Or rather, he's half Scottish and half English. He works for John, too, on a special-assignment sort of basis. He's one of my very favorite people. What a man! All the women adore him. You will see why. It's a shame that neither Guillaume nor James is married. We have introduced them to all the single girls we know, but nothing worked out. Now we have run out of girls. We have reached an age, I am afraid, where we don't know as many as we did. But maybe you will have more luck with them." She poured her glass full again. "Tell me, dear," she continued without noticing Carolyn's expression, "does David have other relatives or are you his sole heir—heiress, rather?"

38

Carolyn was finding Marjorie and her tactlessness increasingly difficult to take. Her instinct was to be rude, but Marjorie was her hostess and some semblance of civility was required if the visit was to be tolerable. "He has some cousins, I believe."

"Oh, cousins." Marjorie discarded cousins with a flick of her fingers. "Then you will be a real catch yourself now. And money always seems to marry money. But that leaves poor James out. He lives like a lord but he hasn't a sou that I know of. David was the one who was so brilliant with investments. Hasn't he made quite a windfall lately?" She paused, waiting for Carolyn to answer. Carolyn felt that her reply would have some significance for Marjorie. She wasn't just rattling heedlessly along. There was some purpose to this incredibly rude inquisition.

"You mean did he take his own advice? I hope he did. What time are your guests coming?"

Carolyn's tone was perfectly pleasant, but there was a hard glitter in her eyes. Marjorie knew she had gone too far. She accepted the rebuff and looked at the gold watch hanging around her neck. "Very soon now. And we aren't dressed. Something casual, dear. We don't dress up for these little dinners. Informality leads to better conversation, don't you think?"

Carolyn rose. Marjorie checked her glass, tilting it to see how much was still in it. She started to fill it again, but decided against it, and carrying the half-empty glass, she ushered Carolyn upstairs and left her at the door of her room.

Carolyn fumed inwardly. She thought it grossly inconsiderate of the Winfreys to have dinner guests when they had invited her for a quiet day and evening in the country. It hadn't occurred to her that there would be a dinner party, and neither of the two dresses she had brought was really suitable. She took the dress she had planned to wear back to London Monday morning out of the closet and looked at it critically. It was a gray designer dress with a trumpet-gored skirt that swung gracefully around her legs when she walked. The collar and cuffs of the hacking-style jacket were in soft white kid leather. It was severely tailored but elegant. It would have to do.

Carolyn was finding that she didn't like Marjorie Winfrey very much. To imply matchmaking with David not yet in his grave was crass to the point of boorishness. As a matter of fact, Carolyn thought, as she put on her lipstick and stepped into her shoes, Marjorie Winfrey was crude. Crude and tactless and prying. But, in honesty, she knew she was irritated mainly because Marjorie seemed to know more about David's financial successes than she did herself. Who were these people? What had they been to David that they had such intimate knowledge of him? She wished she had had time to read that letter.

She saw when she went downstairs to the library that the folder was no longer on the desk. The guests had already arrived and everyone rose as she entered the room. Marjorie's clinging black chiffon palazzo pajamas with sequins at neck and belt were not Carolyn's idea of informal wear, but a glance at the men's tweed jackets reassured her that they at least didn't dress for the "little dinners."

Marjorie performed the introductions while John Winfrey mixed a drink for Carolyn. "Carolyn dear, this is Guillaume LeClere, our good friend from France whom I told you about." LeClere was a small man in his late forties. His snapping black eyes and pointed face reminded Carolyn of a weasel.

"My dear Mrs. Bruce. How happy I am to meet you and how sad I am about your husband. He was such a fine man. A brilliant mind."

"Thank you, Mr. LeClere. You are very kind to say so."

"And this is James McAllister." Marjorie had taken McAllister's arm and led him forward. She clung to him as she made the introduction.

Carolyn recognized McAllister as the man she had seen talking to Winfrey in the drive earlier in the afternoon. In the muted light of the library she received an impression of decisive black brows and an imperiously hooked nose. He stepped forward, separating himself firmly from Marjorie, and took her hand. With a shock Carolyn realized that he looked intently and directly into her eyes, not vaguely somewhere to the left or right of her nose or mouth, as did most people she met. His directness riveted her attention on his face, on him. Eyes the color of cream sherry, deep set, hooded a little. A craggy face like a sculpture just begun, the features hacked with bold slanting strokes and then left rough and strong, like granite. Then McAllister smiled. And Carolyn felt a special warmth, a depth of feeling, a sensitivity in the man that promised much. She did not hear what he said and she murmured conventional words as she withdrew her hand and sat down in the wing chair. She accepted her drink from Winfrey. McAllister offered her a cigarette. As he held his lighter for her, she looked into his face, testing, to know if the directness was a thing of the moment or a characteristic of the man. The light eyes probed still, demanding honesty in response. He turned away and took a seat on the end of the sofa nearest her. As they all talked, Carolyn found that she turned often to listen to him. She was intensely aware of him. She sipped her drink and felt that she was waiting. There would be more from James McAllister.

6
.

LeClere possessed a droll wit and an amusing gift of mimicry. During dinner in the vast formal dining room, McAllister and Winfrey fed him lines and reminded him of stories. He talked well, pitching his monologue to Carolyn, sitting next to him, and explaining relationships and events so that she felt neither left out nor patronized. McAllister's easy laughter and the variety of wines encouraged him. Marjorie's voice drifted higher as the dinner progressed. Winfrey, Carolyn noticed, grew more silent as his wife's eyes brightened and LeClere's vocabulary became more salty. He seemed almost to be waiting for something to happen. Carolyn looked around the table. The others seemed unaware of his reserve.

As the dessert plates were cleared away, wheels crunched on the drive outside. Winfrey signaled Neville. "Show him into the library. I will be right there," he said quietly. Neville nodded and went to admit the caller. Winfrey waited for a pause in the conversation and then excused himself from the table. Marjorie and LeClere both jumped up and followed him from the room. Carolyn was startled by their abrupt exodus.

"Can I get you anything, madam? Sir?" Neville asked. He was looking at McAllister.

"Some coffee, please, Neville, and brandy," McAllister ordered.

"Will you have it here or in the drawing room?"

McAllister looked across the table at Carolyn. She shook her head slightly. "We'll have it here," he told the butler without taking his eyes from her. He was pleased that she sensed he didn't want to move and break the mood. She seemed mellower, softer, perhaps willing to talk. He felt she needed to talk. The table suddenly seemed too wide and the candelabrum between them too over-powering. He rose and took Winfrey's chair, turning it so that he could watch her face. He had watched her all night, quietly. Now he studied her openly, the intensity of his expression softened some-what by the dimness of the candlelit room.

She radiated glamour. The tailored suit encased her slender form austerely. He found it strangely provocative. Her hair was coiled in an elaborate braid on her head and swooped low on the sides to cover her ears. It seemed too heavy for her slender neck. And that, too, was provocative. Her sexuality was made of delicacy and courtesy, soft-spoken sweetness, and a stunning grace marvel-ous to see. He had watched her as they all walked to the dining room. She moved like a taut, sleek Siamese cat, proudly, softly, with a rippling rhythm that was totally unaffected, wholly hers. Now, as she sat quietly relaxed for the first time this evening, her body fell into graceful lines. His eyes lingered, then moved to her hands. What hands! Long, long fingers, with long almond-shaped nails, beautifully kept. Such hands as should grace a queen. She used them when she talked. When she was silent they absently stroked the velvet of the chair arm. They were rarely still.

Yet she was not beautiful in the face. The forehead was too broad, the nose too long, the mouth a little too wide, the eyes too keen and alert. The combination was altogether too decisive for beauty. But it worked. She had style. In a crowd she would be noticed. She was an interesting-looking woman. McAllister was intrigued, drawn as an artist is drawn to quality of line and purity of form. He was en-ticed by her drama, her grace and warmth. She challenged him. He wanted to see those gray eyes glowing with love, the lips softly parted, to see her expectant, a little breathless, turning to him to murmur deep in her throat. He wanted her.

The one flaw, slight though it was, was betrayed by the unquiet hands. She was not serene, not secure. She did not look, she did not act, she did not seem to be a deeply loved woman. There was the slightest sharpness, the smallest tautness, the faintest suggestion of tension. He felt it was habitual with her and emphasized now by her husband's death. She was under control. But the control was too total, and James, alert to her slightest reactions, felt she was too

44

tightly strung for her own good. She could explode, not into healing tears but into hysteria. He wanted to be with her when that moment came.

Neville saw that they were comfortable and bowed himself away. McAllister offered Carolyn a cigarette and lit it for her, then lit his own. The dining chairs were big armchairs, comfortable to sit and linger in. Carolyn took a sip of coffee and a satisfying breath of her cigarette. She lifted her head and blew the smoke in a long stream into the candlelight. To McAllister it was an alluring gesture.

He opened the conversation. "Have you known the Winfreys long?"

"Just since Friday. They came to see me after the accident. I hadn't realized David had so many good friends in London. I am glad to have had this chance to meet them."

"You mean David hadn't mentioned our little group?" There was a rueful smile at the corners of his mouth.

Carolyn realized immediately how her statement must have sounded to him. It was disloyal, a little accusatory of David. She sought to repair the damage. "Usually he told me of the people he met. But there were so many; I couldn't know them all." Again Carolyn saw very clearly that actually she knew almost nothing of David's life when he had not been with her. He had talked of people he met until she believed she had a nearly complete picture of his travels and acquaintances, but she saw now that he had actually revealed very little about them. She stopped as her thoughts turned inward.

"I would have been surprised if he had. We did a great deal of carousing about London, and wives are not supposed to be very understanding about that kind of thing. I believe that David was a loner, that he never told anyone anything unless it suited his purpose to do so. That is a valuable asset in international finance. I am sorry it had to end for him as it did. He would have gone far. What are your plans now?"

"To go home as soon as I can."

"When will that be?"

"I don't know. Scotland Yard has promised to do everything they can."

"What will you do after you get home?"

"I don't know," she replied. But his eyes commanded further honesty, and haltingly, she tried to continue. She gave up with a

45

little gesture of her hand. "I just don't know yet. I will have to see when the time comes."

"Is there anything there for you now?"

"My sister and her husband live in New York. She has three boys. I am their only aunt. We are close."

"Any other family?"

"No. My parents have been dead for some time. David was orphaned quite young, too."

"That's unfortunate. Three nephews may keep you busy, but they won't keep you from being lonely."

She looked up at him quickly, startled by the bluntness of his statement. She understood what he was saying. Susie and Sam were the souls of kindness and included her in all the important holiday celebrations, but she could not be totally involved in their lives. No matter how close they were, she would be a guest in their home.

"Yes, I suppose so." She hesitated, staring into her empty cup, knowing she would meet his eyes if she looked up. Somehow it seemed important to give this man an answer. "I may go back to work. My old job is still there."

"Why don't you come back to England?"

"What for? There's nothing for me here either," she said, even as she sensed the underlying tone of significance in his voice.

"Oh, I don't know. It would be a totally new life for you. London is a good city to live in. It's easy to make friends. If you want to count me, you have a friend here already."

He was smiling intently into her eyes, and again she was caught in his vitality. She was surprised at her enthusiasm for the idea but was afraid to show it. She was vulnerable, her emotions barely under control. The appeal of his suggestion lay entirely in the appeal of the man. Now was not the time to commit herself. "All right," she said, "I will consider it."

"Good," he replied, pleased.

As they had been talking, the voices in the library had risen until they could distinguish angry tones, though not any of the words. There was a thud, as if someone had slammed a fist into something. "Are they fighting?" Carolyn asked in alarm.

James listened, his head cocked. "No. Just arguing. Marjorie and Guillaume become contentious when they drink too much. It doesn't mean anything." But he knew he had lost her attention. The mood was broken. The shadows under her eyes seemed to be deepening, and suddenly she looked tired. "You look all in. Why don't you get some rest? It's late."

"Yes. I think I will." She was grateful for the suggestion. He walked with her to the foot of the stairway. The voices were more subdued now, but the argument was still in progress. At the foot of the stairs she turned to him, holding out her hand. He took it and held it, and she felt warmth and security and reassurance in him. "Thank you," she faltered, suddenly not wanting to leave. "I'll think about England."

"Good. I'll be in touch with you tomorrow."

"Good night." She climbed the stairs, feeling that he was watching her. At the landing she turned and met his eyes. She was touched by his thoughtfulness and involuntarily raised her hand in a little wave. He nodded and turned away toward the library.

Suddenly, chilled, she wondered if his kindness had been merely a ruse to get her out of the way gracefully so that he could join the argument. She listened. The voices momentarily were louder and then were extinguished as the library door opened and then closed again.

7
.

Carolyn took a book to bed with her. But reading was a worthless effort. McAllister's face, his quiet questions and suggestions intruded themselves into her thoughts, and she found herself reading and re-reading one paragraph without the least idea of what it contained. Finally she gave up and turned out the light. She lay a long time, comprehending her aloneness, wondering how to combat it, girding herself for the ordeal of building another life. At last she slept.

Suddenly she was frightened awake by a queer half nightmare. It took a moment to adjust herself to the strange bed, to recall the unfamiliar place, and to realize that the window was still open and the room was frigid. Shivering, she jumped up and rushed to close the window. It yielded easily, sliding downward firmly.

A small high moon was drifting in the sky, lovely and cold. Frost glistened on the ground. The entrance court shimmered in white-ness. Struck by the scene, Carolyn moved to the side window to see the garden. Evergreens and box hedges cast deep shadows over the paths. The summer house shone in the stillness. A sparrow fluttered sleepily, disturbed, off somewhere to the left, and was silent. Carolyn was turning reluctantly to go back to bed when something moved near the summer house. She paused, her eyes ranging over the garden, sifting through the shadows. A light glowed for a mo-ment and then was gone. A shadow moved again, toward the light, but then all was still and she couldn't see anything else.

Thoughtfully, she climbed into bed and pulled the comforter tight about her. She was alert, thinking of the events of the day and

49

of David's letter on Winfrey's desk. It might offer an explanation as to who these people really were. The letter assumed more and more importance as she considered it.

The house was quiet. Tempted, Carolyn pushed aside the covers and crept to the door, moving with more caution than necessary in her own room. The handle turned easily. The door opened silently. She listened. Not a sound. She drew on her robe, and carrying her shoes, eased out.

Moonlight flooded the hall through the windows. She went silently down the stairs. Not a step creaked to interrupt her progress to the darkness of the downstairs. At the bottom she paused, listening. One side of the library's double doors stood slightly open and a dim light burned inside. The room was empty.

She put on her shoes, moved swiftly to the desk, and tried each of the drawers—nine of them—but all were locked. The chest standing just behind the desk was not locked, but contained only games and playing cards. However, it had a key. Sometimes antique keys were interchangeable. She was reaching for it when a door slammed somewhere in the back of the house and footsteps came down the hall.

Trapped, she scanned the room for a way out. There was no other exit. Without thinking, she ducked under the kneehole of the desk and huddled against the wooden panel at the back, drawing her robe close in about her.

The footsteps came into the room, paused while another light was snapped on, then came directly to the desk. Immediately Carolyn regretted that a guilty conscience had prevented her from taking the easy way out. She could have said she was looking for a book, chatted a moment and exited gracefully. But it was too late. Caught in a cramped and bent-over position that made breathing difficult, she could only watch John Winfrey's highly polished black shoes as he stood on his side of the desk. What would she say if he discovered her? But he was too deeply involved in his conversation with two other people. They talked openly in normal tones. She could hear every word clearly.

"He's just finished that currency transfer," Winfrey said. "I think we should put him on permanent status. Give him a raise, perhaps promise an increase later if we continue to be pleased." Now Carolyn wished she had heard the first part of the discussion.

"How sure of him are you?" Carolyn didn't recognize the man's voice, but she would know it again. It was distinctive, light, rather high. The faintest of lisps reminded her of the Castilian *s* sound. Otherwise it was accentless and did not reveal the speaker's nationality. The man seemed to be standing in front of the desk opposite Winfrey. His voice came from above Carolyn's head.

"Reasonably so," Winfrey answered. "As sure as we ever can be at this stage."

"Your opinion, LeClere?"

"I agree with Winfrey," LeClere said from the other side of the room. "As it turned out, completing that transfer required a certain amount of judgment. But if you feel we should consider it a while longer before taking him into full confidence and partnership, then give him a raise and more important jobs until he's proven himself beyond doubt."

"Have you checked his record with the police?"

"He's clean. They have no reason to suspect him," Winfrey replied.

"Very well. Go ahead with the raise, but make it clear it's a probationary period still, as LeClere suggests. Now, what about this thing with Bruce? Do you have his original report?"

"It's here."

Carolyn shrank lower into the kneehole as Winfrey took a key from his pocket and unlocked the center desk drawer. He took out the folder and letter she had been looking for and dropped them on the desk. Carolyn heard the unknown man riffle the papers in the folder and then lock them into a briefcase. "You know," he said, his light voice seeming suddenly menacing, "I don't like this at all."

"You asked for an explanation and Bruce gave it. I don't think it's satisfactory, but then I have already expressed myself on that point."

"Yes, you have. Michaux still does not believe Bruce did it. He trusted him and he handpicked those two boards, which agreed to everything Bruce did at the Funds. But the money is gone. You know how Michaux is when someone crosses him. When I left him he was sitting in the dark in his office, driving his fist over and over into his left hand. He had been there for hours. He will get it back. You say Bruce had it. He said he was innocent. You changed your mind and backed him up, but couldn't name another suspect. And LeClere couldn't find out. We need to know."

"Who do you think has it?" LeClere asked thoughtfully.

"I don't know. If you consider forgery, there are several who might have done it, but Bruce would have been able to discover that. I think Winfrey's first suspicion was correct. Bruce was in the perfect position. If he took the money, we can't do anything to him. But what did he do with it? I do know that with Michaux in his present mood, whoever does have it will be very, very sorry. Does Mrs. Bruce know anything about his activities?"

"He wasn't supposed to tell anyone," LeClere murmured. "That was clear when we hired him."

"Marjorie thinks she knows," Winfrey said.

"He could have transferred the money to her," the man said. "He would think of something like that. From what the two of you have said tonight, she is as clever as he was." He paused. "Well, Winfrey. You are in the best position right now to find out. See what you can learn from her. Now, I don't want any bungling. If you fail, I will take over. I prefer to get it back quietly, without any fuss, if possible."

Winfrey must have nodded.

"Good," the voice went on. "That's understood. LeClere, we don't need you any longer. Keep your ears open and let me know if you can find any traces of the money and its whereabouts. Have you inquired in Switzerland? Don't we have a contact there?"

"Yes. I will check it out and report back to you."

LeClere left the library. Carolyn could hear him moving quietly down the hall. The two men waited until the front door closed before resuming their conversation.

"It's damned inconvenient that Bruce was killed. Do you have any idea who was driving that taxi?"

"No," Winfrey replied. "But we should find out promptly. Scotland Yard is giving Bruce's wife top-level treatment."

"What do you mean?"

"She talked to Detective Chief Superintendent Prescott. He's on the Murder Squad."

"Are you sure?"

"I'm sure. McAllister found out through his contact at the Yard."

"Why have they gotten into it? Roadway accidents are usually handled by the Yard's traffic department."

"He guessed because it was a hit-and-run of a foreigner. Apparently he couldn't learn anything else."

"Who is his contact?"

"I asked him that. All he would say was that his source has never been wrong in anything reported."

"Do they suspect foul play?"

"We don't know."

"The Murder Squad! It's hard to fool them." The man swore softly for a moment, more in thought than in anger. Then he made up his mind. "Well," he said decisively, "we can turn it into an advantage if we have to. But meanwhile we must know definitely whether the Yard suspects foul play and whom they suspect. That information is crucial to us. Can you find out?"

"McAllister can."

"I'd prefer to know who his contacts are. I don't like not knowing whom I'm dealing with."

"I don't know, but I suspect it's a female employee. It could be a snout, an informer, who squeals to detectives for gain of his own. They are a close-mouthed group of necessity, but so are the detectives. All in all, I believe it's a woman."

"And therefore unreliable, but it will have to do. It's all we have."

The man must have given Winfrey a thorough scrutiny, because Winfrey's feet shifted uneasily from side to side and he cleared his throat nervously. "Anything else you want me to do?" Winfrey asked.

"No. Not for now. But you listen to me. You are in real trouble. Michaux said to tell you that. He trusted Bruce and didn't appreciate having you undermine him and then weasel on your story."

"But he explained. We have no real reason to doubt him. Believe me, it's just as I said."

"For your sake, it had better be. Nevertheless, in my opinion, Bruce is the one. Now, you and Marge handle Bruce's wife with kid gloves. If you don't have any results, let me know immediately. I will do the pushing. If that money has gotten to Switzerland, our only hope is through her."

"I understand."

"Then good night. We will talk again later."

The two men walked to the front door. Carolyn waited. Winfrey returned alone and poured himself a stiff glass of liquor from the decanter. He drank it, letting his breath out after the first deep swallow. He poured himself more and drank that while he turned out the lights, leaving the desk lamp until last. He relocked the desk drawer and left the library, closing the doors after him.

Carolyn carefully shifted her cramped body and waited, counting the minutes until sufficient time had passed for Winfrey to get to bed. Finally she crawled stiffly out and rose to her feet. She crossed the room silently, eased the door open, slipped out and stood in the shadow of the doorjamb, listening. It was quiet. The house was dark. She crossed the hall and started to climb the stairs.

A sound caught her attention. She froze, her foot on the bottom step. It came from outside. Then, suddenly very much afraid, she gathered her robe around her and raced silently upstairs to her room. Carefully she closed the door and hurried to the window overlooking the garden.

At first she saw nothing. Then two forms approached the summer house from somewhere at the rear of the property. Moonlight gleamed on brass buttons and she recognized the chauffeur. The other was a heavy man of middle height, carrying a briefcase. Was he the third man in the library? If so, his bulk didn't fit his voice. The two men were speaking intently. They paused, then went on together, stepping carefully on the grass at the edge of the drive, staying under the trees, avoiding the rattle of gravel. Carolyn watched them out of sight. In a moment a car started up in the distance. Haskins didn't return. It was quiet. She was turning to go to bed when another form slipped around the summer house, moving away just as cautiously as had the first two. Her eyes strained to see who it was. The figure seemed to have disappeared. Suddenly a face gleamed in the moonlight and then vanished over the garden wall. It was James McAllister.

8

·

Deep shadows under Carolyn's eyes Monday morning told of her restless night. She made up carefully, trying to create a look of refreshed sleep. Whether they had heard anything or not, the assignment given to Winfrey by the stranger in the library meant that Marjorie and John would be watching her closely. She took a deep slow breath before entering the breakfast room.

They were already at the table. "There you are, Carolyn," John greeted her heartily. "Good morning. Help yourself to breakfast." Carolyn filled her plate at the buffet and John rose and held her chair. Neville poured her coffee. It was scalding hot and strong, as she liked it. Carolyn looked at John closely as he resumed his seat and folded his paper. His manner was natural and relaxed. He turned to her conversationally. "I think you and Marjorie will have a nice day for your trip to town. Do you have to be there at any particular time?"

"I have to be at the American Embassy at ten forty-five."

He checked his watch. "Then there's plenty of time for a leisurely breakfast. We know several of the people there. Whom are you meeting? Perhaps we know him, too."

"I believe his name is Richard Riley."

"Richard Riley?" Marjorie echoed thoughtfully. "No, we haven't met him."

"Well, no matter," John said. "It's always pleasant to be able to begin an interview with a comment about a mutual friend. But speaking of friends, what did you think of James and Guillaume?"

"They were both very pleasant and considerate, I thought. Mr. Le-Clere enjoys telling a good story, doesn't he?"

"He collects them," Marjorie confided, leaning across the table and lowering her voice so that the butler wouldn't hear. "He even eavesdrops in public places. He denies it. But I believe that's the reason he likes England so much. Conversation here is something of an art, and people can be surprisingly uninhibited in public where strangers can hear. He liked you very much. I can always tell. When he dislikes someone, he can be quite cruel, intentionally cruel. It is harder to tell about James, now. You seemed to be getting along famously, but when you disappeared so quickly after dinner, I thought you didn't want to be with him."

"He couldn't have been kinder," Carolyn replied. "It was just that I was tired, so I excused myself. I hope he understood."

"He did," John answered. "I hope you feel more rested now?"

"Yes, thank you. Much better."

Could he suspect? Carolyn wasn't sure. He was pouring himself more coffee with an air of complete normality. She glanced at Marjorie. She was buttering another piece of toast and seemed to have relinquished the conversation to John. Carolyn could not be sure whether she had been observed last night or not.

John sugared his coffee and stirred thoughtfully. He sipped it, nodded satisfaction, and sat back comfortably in his chair. "Carolyn, forgive me for asking, and please take it in the spirit intended. I think David would want me to satisfy myself on this point. Do you have sufficient funds to last you for several months?"

"Why, yes. Why?"

"I don't just mean expense money. I mean to live on, for everything you could possibly need, including emergencies, if necessary. I am assuming David left a will?"

"I assume so."

"Sometimes there are long periods before any of the estate can be distributed. In David's case it would be at least a year. Unless, of course, he transferred his assets to you as he acquired them?" He paused to wait for a reply before continuing.

"You needn't worry about my grocery money. I'll be all right."

"It could be quite a while. Didn't David make investments worldwide? The tax and inheritance laws of foreign countries can be even more archaic than the ones in your country. If you have a doubt at all, I would be glad to advance you any amount to tide you over.

I believe David would have done the same for me if our positions had been reversed and it was Marjorie who was alone."

"You are very considerate to be so concerned about me. I appreciate your offer. I have enough. And I can always go back to work. The company promised me my old position any time I wished to return."

"You must have been a valuable employee to have that kind of consideration. But let us hope that David avoided the problem for you by putting it all in your name in a neutral country, like Switzerland or Nassau. He may have done that." He was watching her closely, questioningly, behind a fog of cigarette smoke. Marjorie was licking marmalade from her fingers. She was avoiding Carolyn's eyes with studied normality. Carolyn sensed that they had planned this conversation carefully. She began to sympathize with the beetle wiggling on the pin.

"I am certain David did what was best for me," she chose to reply.

"David said you were shrewd and he could entrust you with his financial affairs whenever he had to be away. But please remember, if you ever need anything, anything at all—money, advice, a friend —let me know."

"Thank you. I will remember." She kept her face carefully appreciative but noncommittal. In view of his secretiveness, that was a very odd thing for David to have said. Had he actually told Winfrey that? If so, no wonder they thought she would have knowledge of David's financial activities.

Under normal circumstances a conversation such as the one she had just had with John Winfrey would have angered her. Her prior knowledge of his purpose made her tolerant. But if this was the conversation the strange man had instructed Winfrey to have with her, it was not what she had expected. She didn't feel that John had learned what he wanted to know. And she had learned nothing, except that the Winfreys had the very human characteristic of being curious about other people's wills.

Marjorie drove her own sports car. She was obviously proud of it and discussed its fine points with Carolyn as she exceeded the speed limit all the way into London. Once in town, however, she slowed to a more moderate rate, explaining ruefully, "I can't get another speeding ticket. They'll take my permit away."

"Awfully risky in this traffic," Carolyn murmured. She had been very quiet during the drive, merely nodding and saying little in response to Marjorie's steady chatter. She must have been too quiet.

"You know," Marjorie said after a pause, "you must not mind John and his questions. He is very concerned about you, especially since you are away from home at a time like this. There's a personal idiosyncrasy too. He has an absolute horror of being caught without money. Some people can carry not a pound in their pockets and be quite comfortable. Not John. He must have a wallet full of notes. Now, I never carry enough and always have to borrow from him. The nice thing is, I don't have to pay it back. When we married, John asked me whether I wanted a settlement or a monthly allowance. I told him I wanted neither, just for him to supply my spending money and pay my bills. And he does, dear man, even when I am terribly extravagant. Did David give you a lump sum or an allowance?"

"My dear, didn't David tell you? I inherited a sizable part of Kentucky."

"No, he didn't tell us you were from Kentucky. What part is it?"

"Fort Knox," Carolyn answered as Marjorie parked by the embassy.

Marjorie merely laughed. "You are annoyed. I am sorry. Do let me make amends and take you to lunch when you are through here. There's a quiet little restaurant nearby that John likes."

Carolyn wanted to refuse, but under the circumstances considered it best to go along with her. Neither Marjorie nor John had appeared suspicious of her, and she didn't want to raise any questions by seeming too anxious to avoid them. "Yes, of course," she said. "Won't you come in with me and wait? I shouldn't be long."

"Very well. I should like to see the inside of this building. It's not one of our favorites here, you know."

"I believe I did read that you considered the eagle too predatory." They smiled pleasantly at each other. Carolyn knew she could expect more questions over lunch.

Richard Riley saw that Marjorie was comfortable and led Carolyn into his office. Talking slowly and in oversimplified terms, he explained all the regulations for shipping a body from England to the United States. He sounded as if he had memorized his explanations. Carolyn suppressed a smile. He was very young and very earnest

58

and probably dealt with people far more confused than she. When her questions were answered, he asked if she could stay a few minutes longer to talk to another staff member.

"What is it about?" Carolyn asked.

"He will explain it himself," Riley answered, straightening the papers into a neat stack on his desk.

"Will it take long? I have a luncheon engagement."

"You will find Mr. Hood is very much to the point. He won't keep you any longer than necessary."

"Very well. Perhaps Mrs. Winfrey won't mind waiting for me."

Riley told his secretary where they were going and guided Carolyn and Marjorie upstairs to another suite of offices. He introduced them to the secretary there, Miss Simmons.

"Yes, Mrs. Bruce. Mr. Hood is expecting you. He's on the telephone just now. Let me have your coats. It won't be long."

Carolyn had a moment to thank Riley before a man came out of a private office and greeted them formally. "If you will just go in and have a seat, Mrs. Bruce, I will be with you immediately. Mrs. Winfrey, it's nice to see you again. I won't detain Mrs. Bruce long. Perhaps Miss Simmons could bring you a cup of tea or coffee while you wait." Carolyn noticed, as she went into Hood's office, that Marjorie didn't seem to remember him.

Jackson Forrest Hood III was the name engraved on the bronze plaque on the desk. A diploma conferring a bachelor's degree from the University of Tennessee hung on one wall, with a law degree and a master's degree in psychology from Georgetown University underneath. The other walls were filled with photographs. They showed Hood playing golf with President Eisenhower, shaking hands with President Kennedy, walking somberly just behind President Johnson. A fourth picture showed a surging crowd and a smashed automobile. She had to look to find Hood, clinging doggedly to the car, his raised arm warding off the assault of a Venezuelan mob on Vice-President Nixon. His face became sterner and stronger as the years passed and he matured. The pictures were all autographed. The one from Eisenhower read "To Jay, with thanks and warmest regards."

He has filled out and gotten heavier since then, Carolyn thought as Hood came in and closed the door behind him. He adjusted the window shade behind his desk so the light did not glare in her face and then settled himself in his chair. He regarded Carolyn gravely, his hands clasped one on top of the other on his desk. A bare quarter inch of cuff showed under his gray-flannel sleeves.

"I believe I met your husband once," he began, "when he worked in Washington with the United States Treasury."

"Yes. That was about two years ago."

"He was on loan, wasn't he?"

Her face warmed, her eyes softened. "Yes. That's correct," she answered, pleased that he remembered.

"Yes. I met him very briefly. He wouldn't have remembered me. He gave a briefing and I was introduced to him afterward. He was something of a maverick on monetary policy, wasn't he?"

Carolyn had never thought of her husband as a maverick. "How do you mean?"

"He was advocating drastic measures to salvage the dollar long before President Nixon made the idea respectable. He was preaching what the President finally practiced at least two years before it became policy." He picked up a manila folder on his desk, opened it and then closed it again with the briefest glance inside.

"I should explain, Mrs. Bruce, what it is I needed to see you about. I am a Revenue Service Representative for the Office of International Operations. We are under the aegis of the Assistant Commissioner for Compliance, Internal Revenue Service. The office has responsibilities for tax treaties, foreign trusts and estates, and foreign corporations with United States sources of income. American citizens resident abroad file their income tax claims with our offices. Our time is primarily devoted to American citizens and corporations resident abroad and to dealing with foreign governments and businessmen on customs and tax matters. Citizens resident in the United States, on the other hand, are under the jurisdiction of the Internal Revenue District in which they reside. The district office is responsible for making any necessary inquiries into individual and corporate tax matters, providing information and ensuring compliance with tax laws. As you probably already know, American citizens and corporations are subject to United States income taxes on income earned abroad. However, since district offices have no overseas representatives of their own, they ask us to obtain any information they need regarding income earned abroad by taxpayers at home." He paused to see if she understood him so far.

"What does this have to do with me?" she inquired.

"Your husband, Mrs. Bruce, had worldwide affairs." This was the second, or was it the third, such reference she had heard since the accident. But Hood was continuing. "He was building quite a reputation for his counseling and was in demand as an adviser to several Europeans and Americans in Europe with large trusts to invest. We believe he was paid for these services in foreign currencies and that he did not repatriate these funds to the United States."

"Is there some question concerning our income tax returns, Mr. Hood?"

"A question, yes. Several months ago audits of records of an American citizen resident in Switzerland showed that he had deducted expenses for counseling services rendered by David Bruce. A routine review of Mr. Bruce's claim for that year did not reveal that that particular sum had been reported. A letter of inquiry was addressed to Mr. Bruce at his place of business. To date there has been no reply."

"There must be a logical explanation for my husband's delay in answering. He would wish to clear up any misunderstandings."

"We sincerely hope so, Mrs. Bruce. The reason for my wishing to talk to you today is that you and Mr. Bruce filed your claims jointly. And since the sums in question were earned for services rendered in Europe, we wished to bring the matter to your attention promptly should you wish to make inquiries of your own while you are still here."

Jointly. The quietly spoken word leaped at Carolyn. She had reviewed their tax returns before she signed them. Her own income and deductions had always been reported accurately, and she had not questioned David's. "Mr. Hood, I am sorry, but you have caught me unprepared to answer your questions. I was not aware of a letter of inquiry from the Internal Revenue Service to my husband and I cannot explain why it has not been answered. How long ago did you write it?"

"About sixty days ago now." Hood checked a date in the folder. "Yes, in the middle of December." He closed the folder and leaned back, the chair creaking slightly with his weight. He was a big man, with a stark, almost nineteenth-century face. He steepled his fingers under his chin while he regarded her impersonally. She seemed sincere in what she said, but the situation was far more serious than he had explained and he was skeptical of her. Large amounts were involved, and if evasion had been intended, it was probable that she was implicated, too.

"All I can say to you is that I will look into the matter as soon as I get back to New York and will instruct our lawyer to answer the letter promptly. My husband handled all of our tax matters and I am unaware that anything was intentionally left unreported. I appreciate your wish to save me trouble here. Can you supply me with full details of your questions?"

"I am complying with the New York district office's request for certain information needed in their audit. I do not have the complete case."

"I will be here for several days. I would like to know something to tell my lawyer when I call him."

"Very well. I will cable for a report and let you know as soon as I get it. Now, another thing. Your husband was president and treasurer of the European Investors Mutual Fund and also of the Greater American Growth Fund. Are you familiar with those funds?"

"I know only that my husband was responsible for them. He didn't discuss his business with me, and I do not own stock in either one."

Hood's gray eyes were expressionless. He wasn't sure he believed that either. This woman had earned substantial salary in her own right before her marriage and it was inconceivable to him that she could be in such Victorian ignorance of their financial affairs. He changed the subject. She would be questioned thoroughly later in the investigative procedure.

"Were you in London on business or pleasure?" he asked.

"Both. My husband attended a meeting that morning, Friday morning. Then we were going to travel for a week before returning to New York."

"Was his meeting a personal matter or was he on assignment for his bank?"

Carolyn hesitated. She had assumed he was on assignment for the bank and had even told Prescott that, but now she wasn't quite so positive. "I believe he was on assignment for the bank."

"I see. I have a final question. Mr. Bruce participated in a conference at the Treasury Department last July. At that time, it is believed, he took with him three classified study papers. They should be returned to the Treasury Department now."

"Classified documents?" She was astonished, and her face showed it.

"The department contacted Mr. Bruce at his bank for their return. The bank reported it did not have them in its files. We would appreciate it if you would search for them when you return home and send them to this address." He wrote a name and address at the Treasury Department on a pad of scratch paper and handed it to her. "The man whose name I've written there will contact you in the next week or two if he has not heard from you in the interim."

Carolyn took the paper and folded it once. She had to ask. "Was there a date by which the documents were supposed to have been returned?"

"They were not designated for circulation."

The color began draining from her face as she considered the implications of what he was saying. "Are you quite sure," she asked, "that my husband has them and not someone else?"

"We are not positive. That's why no action other than inquiries has been taken."

"I do not believe that my husband had them, but if you wish, I will search. My husband's library is full of financial publications and pamphlets. What do these documents look like? May I read them?"

He smiled faintly. "You may have to read them to identify them. They will look like this"—he showed a page of Treasury stationery —"with the classification typed at top and bottom."

"Very well. Anything else?"

"It goes without saying that you should not repeat anything that you read."

"Of course not."

"Good. Thank you for coming. I am sorry indeed about Mr. Bruce. He was a brilliant man."

"Thank you. It seems I wasn't any help to you."

"You told me what I needed to know. I will be in touch with you when I get the information you requested." He held her coat for her and then shook her hand formally. She had calmly undergone quite a battery of questions. Hood wondered about it as he returned to his office and shut the door.

Marjorie was not waiting in the outer office. Her coat was gone, too. "What happened to Mrs. Winfrey?" Carolyn asked the secretary.

"Her husband came about fifteen minutes ago and they left together. She asked me to tell you that something rather urgent had come up and that she couldn't wait for you after all. Your suitcase will be at your hotel this afternoon."

Hood came out of his office in time to hear the last of his secretary's words. "Have lunch with me, Mrs. Bruce. I'm on my way now. There's a place near here that I like."

He was putting on his coat. Carolyn started to refuse. The long face, the sharp profile, the formal manner had been rather forbidding, and what he had told her disturbing. She wasn't in the mood to make polite conversation. Then she saw his eyes. Their expression profoundly wanted her to say yes. She found herself assenting.

A faint smile touched his lips and was gone. "Good," he said simply.

After they had ordered their lunch Carolyn asked if Hood knew Marjorie Winfrey well.

"Only slightly. The Winfreys gave a reception some time ago that I attended. I met her there for the first time, although I had worked with Mr. Winfrey on a customs problem. Are they good friends of yours?"

"They were friends of my husband's. I met them Friday and stayed with them last night in the country. I am afraid I don't really know anything about them."

"Winfrey is from somewhere in the Midlands and was educated there, I believe. He married the only daughter of a successful tradesman, but she died soon after he graduated. Using his inheritance from her, he and a partner set themselves up in real estate and became prosperous in a moderate sort of way. They were on the verge of concluding their first big deal when the partner was found dead. He was a diabetic. The autopsy revealed that a poison had been administered in the same syringe as his insulin. All of the man's friends and associates fell under suspicion at one time or another, including John Winfrey, but there was insufficient evidence to indict anyone. In fact, almost nothing was ever learned. The case simply came to a dead end. The man's will left his half of the business to John Winfrey. I am sure your husband knew of it. It was widely reported in the major European and American financial publications in addition to the usual speculation in the papers here. Well, Winfrey successfully concluded the transaction alone, and it was the foundation of his financial success. Since then he's been in land development, construction of apartments and tract housing, condominiums, and resort hotel development, both here and on the continent. He married the present Mrs. Winfrey several years ago. She was his secretary, I think. They bought that country place when they married. If I were you—" he said, and stopped.

"Yes?"

"If you wouldn't object to a word of advice, I would be a little careful of the Winfreys. There's some question concerning them still, stemming from the partner's death. There was a suggestion once that Winfrey might stand for Parliament, but the case and the questions were immediately resurrected and he dropped the idea. They moved in good circles, I know, but a few of their friends have doubtful reputations. Did your husband know them well?"

"They said so. I don't really know." She badly wanted more information, but with his position, she was uncertain how much she could ask. She decided to risk it. "Who is Michaux?"

"Lux Michaux, do you mean?"

"I suppose he's the one. I don't know the first name."

"Lux Michaux is rather a shadowy sort of a figure. He's a French Howard Hughes, jealous of his privacy, secretive about his affairs. He lives in one of the Loire's more spectacular châteaux and has a secret service to protect him that heads of state might envy. He's involved in everything—oil, minerals, land development, gold, even gambling, I believe."

"The Winfreys had two friends for dinner last night—Guillaume LeClere and James McAllister. Have you met them?"

"Yes. They were among the five hundred intimate friends at that reception I mentioned."

Carolyn laughed. "Tell me about it."

"The party was at Glenyck House, where you stayed. There were two orchestras and everything you could think of to eat and drink. Winfrey must have bought a champagne factory. And all the beautiful people were there, including some that one wonders about. McAllister is a likable fellow. He is in that group around the Winfreys and appears on the social circuit from time to time, but he's not the type. He's not dedicated to a party, like some of them. We talked for a few minutes that night. I had the impression he was almost forcing himself to be there. Professionally, he's a barrister, with an almost nonexistent practice. He has money, but no obvious means of earning it, unless you count the cards. He plays frequently and usually wins. But he never plays with his friends. Only with strangers. That night at the Winfreys' party he won about four hundred dollars by midnight and left. Rather an odd sort of fellow. Guil-

65

laume LeClere seemed to be sort of an official host that night, seeing that we had everything we could want. He's one of the ones I have some reservation about. I don't know anything definite against him. But there's a streak of cruelty there. He may even be sadistic. I'd be even more careful of him than of the Winfreys."

"Who else was at the famous party?" Carolyn encouraged him. "Anyone I've heard of?"

"Characters of one kind and another. It started out to be a pretty nice affair, but by midnight it was getting loud, and by one o'clock it had become raucous and rather ugly. I had stayed longer than I usually do."

"You don't like parties?"

"Yes, I like parties. Small ones, with good friends. I have been to so many big receptions in an official capacity that they are no longer any pleasure. I wouldn't want any of the so-called jet set on my side in a fight, but they amuse me." And Hood launched into a colorful account of the great and near great and their doings. He was an astute observer, with an unexpected eye for the comical. The gray eyes smiled at human nature and crinkled in pleasure when he coaxed a laugh from Carolyn. He made her forget and she was grateful to him for that. When lunch was finished and he said he had to return to the embassy, she was sorry.

On the pavement outside the little pub, he paused while she buttoned her coat. "Do you need a taxi?"

"Yes. I have to go to Scotland Yard."

He hailed a passing cab with a quick upward motion of his hand and it stopped neatly in front of them. "Where to, miss?" the driver asked.

"New Scotland Yard," Hood answered for Carolyn.

"Thank you for lunch, Mr. Hood."

A smile warmed his eyes and touched the wide thin-lipped mouth. "Good day," he said. She lifted her hand in farewell and he stepped back and waved the taxi forward.

Carolyn looked out the back window as the taxi moved ahead. Hood was standing on the pavement looking after her. The wind lifted the hem of his black coat and ruffled his dark hair. Slowly he turned in the direction of the embassy, head bowed, and soon was lost to her view.

At Scotland Yard Carolyn read the two original copies of the information she had given Saturday and signed them. Prescott was not there and there was no message from him. It took less than an hour, and she wandered out again and stood in the paved courtyard, debating whether to take a taxi. It was early, a beautiful clear day with no bite in the wind. She had nothing else to do. She told herself again that the experience Saturday afternoon had been only her imagination. It wouldn't occur again, and a groundless fear of it shouldn't govern her actions. She turned toward the park.

No one followed her today along the sand paths and no one lurked behind the clump of bushes that had hidden the man Saturday. Two nannies in blue uniforms sat on a bench, gently rocking old-fashioned prams. Two toddlers, a boy and a girl, played in the sun, their voices rising clearly in the air. Their very normality was reassuring, and Carolyn sat down on a bench nearby to watch them. After a few minutes the little boy darted up and gave her a curled brown leaf. He flashed a brilliant smile and ran away again to nanny's lap. Carolyn turned the leaf thoughtfully. David hadn't wanted children. On their way home from her sister's, soon after they married, he had said, "Those boys are a pain in the ass. I don't want any brats and you had better not have any." Children had never before particularly occupied her thoughts, but then, he had never expressed active dislike of them. His words stunned and hurt her. She felt denied. But as the years passed she came to feel that it was just as well they didn't have any children. David would have been an indifferent father. Yet sometimes, as now, she felt a pang of regret.

Her thoughts wandered. Hood, despite his quiet air, had been so pleasant and easy after the probing intensity of McAllister. Was McAllister the unnamed man the group had discussed putting on permanent employment status? Hood had given no warning about McAllister. Yet she felt she should be wary of him too. She tried to recall his face and couldn't. The features wouldn't go together. The essence of the man, his vitality, his direct gaze, were vivid, but not the face. He puzzled her. If the group trusted him, what did his stealthy presence in the garden signify?

Her first impression of LeClere, forgotten in his attention to her, returned to her mind. Marjorie's reference to his penchant for cruel jokes, and Hood's observation, honed by training in psychology, were too compelling to be overlooked. The warning about him was well made.

She wondered a little about Jackson Hood. Contained, disciplined, and in his official capacity intimidating, he must be a lonely

67

man. There had been no family pictures on his walls. He had been entertaining and courteous, even informative, but impersonal, a little more solicitous than his position as a federal official required, yet not friendly enough to permit any presumption. She wondered if it had been wise to ask him about Michaux. His face had remained perfectly controlled when he heard the name, but a wary stillness in his eyes betrayed a quickening interest. He had seen a reason behind her question and he wouldn't forget it.

Why was David neglecting a letter from the IRS? Then she realized that she had accepted everything Hood had said as the truth. He inspired credibility, while David, by his own actions, had created doubts which the conversation in Winfrey's library had done nothing to dispel. Four years of marriage and she knew of David only what he had wanted her to know. What had he really wanted in life? She had asked him once, and he had flippantly replied, "Money, bushels of it." She had begged for a better answer. What had he said then? Or had she done all the saying and he had agreed? That had been the way of it.

And he made money. His income each year ran into six figures. Carolyn had grown up in a family where money was used carefully for good purposes, and the lavish way in which she and David had lived was a new and enjoyable experience for her. Had she ever given him the impression that money was necessary for her happiness? She thought back. No. On that her conscience was clear. David enjoyed making it and spending it. He complained bitterly about paying taxes, but then, that was not so unusual. Even with tax-exempt investments, his IRS bills seemed enormous. He expended considerable energy in paring his tax obligations to a minimum, but would he fail to pay them altogether? The stranger thought he was guilty of stealing. Hood thought he had taken government documents. If they were correct, then omitting income from a tax statement was not inconsistent.

Stop it, she ordered herself. David was your husband. You loved him. You married him. If they don't know for sure, how can you doubt him so easily? It could be that none of this was true.

Putting down her thoughts, she rose quickly and walked purposefully toward the hotel. She saw no one and so didn't have to admit that she was afraid that she might. Yet when the doorman opened the glass door for her, she felt compelled to turn and look intently back the way she had come. A man in a tan raincoat, with gray hair

68

straggling over his collar, was climbing into a taxi. The taxi started and accelerated out of her sight. The face was averted. Again there was nothing to describe to Prescott. Suddenly depressed and chilled, she went quickly into the lobby and up to her suite. But as she inserted the key in the lock and struggled to open it, another thought came sneaking. If David was involved in something unethical and illegal, she was guilty, too. She had signed the tax returns. She had signed everything David had ever asked her to sign.

9
·

Her overnight case sat unopened on the luggage rack—delivered, as Marjorie had said it would be. Carolyn took off her coat, and running her hand over the fur, hung it carefully in the closet. She loved the coat, black mink, an extravagance from David on their first Christmas. That was one of the happy times. They had walked for hours in the snow, window-shopped along Fifth Avenue, talked nonsense. They had gathered up armloads of presents for the Christmas night party at her sister's. But then David had departed for a week. She spent New Year's Eve alone, forlornly watching television. Always disappointment had followed promise.

Wearily Carolyn unlocked the suitcase and began unpacking. As always, she took special care with her clothes, folding lingerie neatly into satin cases, hanging dresses on her own padded hangers, putting soiled clothes into a laundry bag. Immediately, she saw that her favorite amber nightgown was not in the laundry bag. Perturbed, she rummaged through it until she found the gown, halfway down, under a slip, some hose and a blouse. But it should have been on top, where she had put it Sunday morning before she left to go to the Winfreys'. It had been moved.

Immediately thinking of theft, Carolyn carefully went through the entire closet. Everything was there except the suit she had sent out to be cleaned. David's luggage was apparently untouched. His paraphernalia in the flight bag also seemed undisturbed. The traveler's checks and personalized bank checks were all there in sequence. The address book seemed intact. The W notation on the M page made sense to her now, she thought. Only the key ring seemed to have shifted. It was no longer in the right-hand corner of the bag, but the keys were all there on the ring in the order she remembered.

The locket in the jewel case! Carolyn fished the key from her purse, walked to the living room, and unlocked the desk. The jewel case was there, exactly as she had left it. Nothing had been disturbed. She took the locket out, remembering that when David gave it to her, he had said it was her security and she should wear it always. At the time she had been touched by his romanticism, but greater intimacy revealed that David was not a sentimental man. His words may have had another meaning.

Thoughtfully she turned the locket over and over, inspecting it closely for the first time, realizing that there was a minute catch at the circle where the chain went through. She carefully pried it open. Their initials, CB DB, and some numbers, perhaps a date, 12–12–70, were engraved inside. Carolyn turned the locket into the light. The engraving of numbers and letters matched. David had had the numbers engraved there, not some prior owner a century before. Puzzled, she closed the locket. It snapped tightly with a barely audible click. She held it in her hand a moment, then put it around her neck. She had always been particularly fond of it. More even than her wedding ring, it had symbolized their marriage. Was it significant that she had taken it off and let it lie virtually unprotected in a strange hotel room? Did it mean that she had not done enough to make their marriage work? That she had been too proud, too cold and angry and unforgiving when David disappointed her? There were so many questions and doubts, so little mutual trust and sharing. They had been married, but they had never been truly united. She continued to sit quietly, holding the locket in a closed fist, feeling the light drag of the chain around her neck, until her thoughts were interrupted by the telephone. She rose slowly and went to the bedroom to answer it.

"Carolyn, this is James McAllister." She sank to the edge of the bed, holding the telephone in one hand and feeling for the locket with the other. He had said that he would call, and she realized now that she had been waiting for it. The deep voice was a little guttural over the telephone. "I am downstairs. I have been thinking of you and wonder if you will have dinner with me tonight?"

Carolyn hesitated, remembering her resolve to be cautious. "Thank you. You are kind to suggest it, but I am tired. It's been a long day." But even as she said it, she knew she had not been final enough.

"Just for supper. You must. We won't be late."

Her watch said six o'clock. She looked around the empty suite. "All right," she said. "I will be down in a few minutes."

"I'll be waiting for you."

As she hung up and went to dress, she wondered again if she would be able to recognize him.

She need not have feared. The craggy face, the crisply curling hair, the giant frame, she picked out unerringly. She watched him a moment as he scanned the people leaving the elevator. Then, perhaps sensing her gaze, he turned and looked directly into her eyes. When he saw her his face leaped into life and she felt his smile. She found herself smiling back and was chagrined, a little shy with herself for her reaction. He strode forward and took her hand. "I'm glad you decided to come," he said. The tilt of his head, the light touch of his hand on her arm as he guided her to the dining room and seated her were solicitous, comforting, exactly right for Mrs. David Bruce, the grieving widow. But his expression as he savored her face and looked straight and searchingly into her eyes was deeper, more personal.

Carolyn was moved by McAllister's regard and yet a little wary. So far everyone she had met in London had grilled her on David's affairs, and there was every reason to think that McAllister would try to do the same. She studied him as he gave their orders to the waiter. He was big enough and broad enough and muscular enough to be Winfrey's thug, she thought. Yet he was not the type. He was handsomely dressed and freshly shaven. His boots shone with a high polish. His hands, she saw as he lit their cigarettes, were long and slender but powerful, with black hairs curling over the backs. They were immaculately kept, the square nails clipped precisely. He carefully modulated his voice to a soft burr, and it rumbled slightly, as though its natural inclination was to boom. She had never met a man quite like James McAllister, a man as attuned to her thoughts, as seemingly sensitive to her welfare, a man who made her feel surrounded by protection and masculinity. She felt guilty that he should attract her so powerfully, yet had she met him at another time, with David at her side, she would not have been impervious to his vitality. No one could be immune to the intense interest and

73

charm he projected. She wondered again what special assignments he carried out for John Winfrey.

It took a little prodding from her to get him to talk about himself. He explained that his mother was English and that she had met his father when she was visiting friends in Scotland. His father was an RAF pilot, and when the war came, his mother had taken him to live in London nearer his father. "Yet we hardly saw him. We had so few pilots, and he couldn't leave his base. He was killed in a dog fight with a Messerschmitt, the third he encountered that night. He got the first two. I think he knew his luck would run out. Mother thought about returning to the country, but she was a nurse in one of the hospitals and it didn't seem right for her to leave. I wouldn't let her send me back alone. A month later, almost exactly, an air raid came earlier in the evening than usual. We had practically no warning. I had gone on some errand down the street for Mother. When the sirens sounded I went immediately to the air raid shelter. I knew she would do the same. But she didn't come. I helped dig her out of the rubble. She had gotten as far as the front door when the bomb hit. She died in my arms. Her back was broken." He was white around the lips. Carolyn reached and touched his hand, her eyes full of her sympathy for him. "I haven't thought about it for a long time. It's a memory I try to push away." He was silent a moment, holding her fingers absently. He looked up at her, smiled briefly and released her hand. "I shouldn't have talked of it. You have sorrow of your own."

"But what did you do? You must have been—what, eight or nine years old?"

"Eight. I went to live with my Grandmother McAllister in Scotland." He talked on, painting a vivid picture for Carolyn of the long train ride to Scotland, and the stern life of growing up on a highland croft. There had been very little money. The land was rocky and unproductive. They grew their vegetables and raised what meat they had. He had longed for a dog, but they couldn't spare the food. He smiled in nostalgia as he described his pleasure when the farmer down the road gave him a motherless lamb to raise. Carolyn found herself smiling with him.

"After the war was over, things began to get a little easier. Our village was authentic and untouched. It had an old inn that became popular with the tourists. I started work there as a busboy, sort of a jack-of-all-chores. We needed the money. I couldn't spend any of it on frivolities. I didn't mind actually, but the thing I regretted most was not being able to go to the movies. I worked on Saturdays, and Grandmother didn't approve of going to the cinema on Sunday. There are hundreds of the old classics I have yet to see."

Carolyn smiled. "You can catch all of them now on television. I stay up past midnight myself for an old movie."

"The thing I never got used to was working for tips. Somehow, accepting a tip always made me feel degraded."

"Wasn't it part of your salary?"

"Of course it was. We weren't paid very much and were expected to keep the tips we earned. But that didn't make it any easier to accept them. It's so humbling to hold out your hand for a gratuity. I could never do it. And tips from women were the worst. One even propositioned me!"

"Only one?" Carolyn murmured, her eyes dancing with suppressed laughter at his remembered indignation.

He laughed ruefully. "I was fifteen. I grew too fast and was awkward and constantly falling over things. She was a Rubens nymph from Texas, fiftyish and trying to be kittenish. Marjorie Winfrey reminds me of her. I was so terrified I fled and didn't go near her again. When she left, the chap who worked with me got the tip that I had earned. It was a five-pound note, as I remember. And we could have used it. I was always proud to take my earnings home, and Grandmother made it a point to thank me very solemnly. But I never got over wishing that I had earned the money in a more professional way. I think that is what drove me to be a barrister."

"Don't you like the law?"

"I hate it. I knew it was a mistake almost as soon as I had started on the course of study. But Grandmother was ill by that time, and her dearest wish was to see me a barrister. She died just after I qualified as solicitor and before I became a barrister. But I finished the course. I owed her that much."

"What's the difference between a barrister and a solicitor?"

"A solicitor solicits legal work from people who wish to be defended. Since he can argue only before the lower court, he brings cases to barristers. Barristers aren't permitted to seek cases, but they are empowered to speak in the High Court and the county courts. Being a barrister is more interesting than being a solicitor, but not much."

"What did you want to do?"

"I didn't know. I owned the croft and my mother's farm here, but they didn't need my attention. So I entered the army. I didn't know what else to do. I spent most of my time in Aden, which is a place the Lord must have forgotten. For the rest of the stint I was stationed in a dreary camp here in England. I don't know which was worse. When I was mustered out, I had no money except my army pay, no career that I wanted, and no obligations. So I traveled. I worked my way across the oceans on tramp ships and traveled until my funds ran out. Then I waited tables, dug ditches, harvested rice, picked cotton, cut tobacco—you name it, I've harvested it. I've even been a steeplejack for a while. Next time I'll do it in more style. I think Switzerland was one of the places I enjoyed the most. Have you been there?"

"Yes. Just briefly. Did you ever discover what you liked to do?"

"I have thought perhaps I should have been a restoration architect. The old buildings fascinated me. In Reims I joined the crew that was doing some restoration on the cathedral. They couldn't let me do anything except the heavy labor of carrying materials, but it was the happiest work stint of the entire trip. Thereafter, in every town I visited, I investigated the possibility of maintenance and restoration work, whether I needed money or not. I worked all summer in Venice restoring the floor of a privately owned palace. But that was the last of that kind of job until I got to Washington and was employed to do hard labor on the National Cathedral. I enjoyed that, too, although I found that it is the challenge of restoring the old that interests me rather than building something new. It was a lucrative job. I earned enough to go through Central America."

"Would you want to study and become an architect?"

"It's probably too late for me. It would require two or three years of school, maybe more, since I don't have any engineering. At thirty-nine I would be a freak on a campus today."

"Wouldn't it be better than what you are doing?"

"What I am doing earns a living. And there's variety in it. I take a case or a commission occasionally, as long as it doesn't last too long. It's a carry-over from my days in school. I like the periodic holidays."

"And the different jobs include Winfrey?"

At this, he put her off. "Actually, I have joined the idle rich and do nothing of note. I just don't admit I am unemployed."

76

Irresponsibility sat oddly on him and conflicted with Carolyn's belief that wealth didn't excuse one from being productive. She changed the subject. "Who was in the little group you mentioned last night?"

"David, of course. The Winfreys, Guillaume and I. We were the nucleus, although others joined us from time to time."

"Others? Who were they?"

"Just acquaintances."

She had asked without thinking and the evasiveness in his tone told her what he meant. There *had* been other women in David's life. "How often did you meet?" she managed to ask quietly.

"About once a month, whenever David came. Didn't you know?"

"Of course I knew." She laughed, but it sounded a little false. Her face was averted, but he watched her closely, trying to catch each nuance of her emotion.

"Once we met in Paris," he said, trying to maintain the conversation.

"Paris?" Something clicked. Her mind turned inward. This final confirmation of Prescott's seemingly irrelevant question about her husband's travels brought a glimmer of a picture that hovered just out of sight around the corner of her mind. Finally she turned to face him and smiled a tight little smile.

"That's better. After all, I am the only friend you have right now."

"I have friends."

"Any like me?"

"No. None quite like you."

"Then you need me."

"What special assignment can I give you that doesn't last too long?"

But he wouldn't be drawn. "To make you smile again. Now let's finish supper. Besides, it is time to talk about you."

Carolyn studied him. Apparently he hadn't been instructed to tell her what was going on. That was Winfrey's job, she remembered. What she had learned so far she had learned through instinct. Instinct told her now that she couldn't afford to make McAllister suspicious. Still, his implied offer of aid put him in a different position. Would he turn against Winfrey to help her? Disloyalty wasn't an honorable trait. She couldn't depend on someone who swung with the wind. Or did he merely consider it another assignment? Like collecting a fee from both sides in the same case?

"I grew up in a small town in central Kentucky," she began. "Horses, blue grass, and fried chicken."

"Also bourbon—which you will have none of here—tobacco and politics."

"You left out the beautiful women."

"So you know about that corny old motto?"

"I cut tobacco, remember? All the way from Paducah to Ashland."

"Then you know what growing up on a farm in Kentucky is like."

"Can you milk a cow?"

"Of course."

"And ride a horse?"

"I trained and showed them."

"Do you hunt?"

"No. We had Tennessee walking horses."

"Did you win with them?"

"Yes. Two dozen blue ribbons, a purple or two, and four silver julep cups. I missed riding when I moved to the city, although I loved Boston and like New York. I rode once in Central Park. It wasn't the same."

"You must ride with me sometime. And the job you mentioned?"

"Montclair Oil Company. I was an analyst."

"That's not very descriptive."

"The job titles never are. I studied the economic advantages, or lack thereof, of the company's proposals for expansion. Also the nature of our competitors' activities and what threat, if any, they were to us. Production statistics, estimates of need, costs of development, projected returns from development. I traveled a good deal, mainly in the Middle East and the Far East. I was in Israel when the Six Day War broke out."

"Did you have to fight your way out? A female in khaki with a grenade hanging from her belt?"

She smiled. "I was well protected and hustled back to the States as soon as possible. I had finished my work there."

"And you gave it all up when you married? Wasn't that difficult?"

"No." Giving it up hadn't been difficult. Living without it when David wasn't home was what had been hard. Her brief response discouraged further questions on the subject of her marriage.

"And now?" he asked.

"And now I must go. I have stayed longer than I had intended."

"That wasn't what I meant."

"I know. I don't know about the future. I haven't ruled out your suggestion. There will be many things to settle before I make any decisions."

"Did you talk to Jackson Hood today?"

She was startled at his sudden change of topic and said yes without thinking. "How did you know?"

"Just accept that I know. Don't try to hide anything from him. He seems friendly, even easygoing when it suits him. It's part of his bag of tricks. But he's a tough one who always gets his man, or woman. One is always better off leveling with him from the start."

"Do you know him well?"

"By reputation mainly, although we have met."

"He said he knew you."

"And what did he say about me?"

"That you were a likable fellow who plays cards."

McAllister laughed. He seemed relieved. "Well, that wasn't too bad." He rose and helped her out of her chair.

They said their goodbyes rather formally in the lobby. "Someday," he murmured, "I want to hear you really laugh." He touched her elbow in farewell, then turned abruptly and walked away from her.

Carolyn stood a moment in the middle of the lobby, looking out through the glass doors of the hotel, watching McAllister standing on the pavement outside. He was joined by Guillaume LeClere and a man she did not know. So McAllister's rather sudden departure had its explanation. He had finished yet another job and was reporting to his employer.

As she rode the elevator up to her suite, she wondered if she had said anything that was significant enough to report? There had been an undercurrent in much of what he had said to her. What did this man want of her? He talked to her on an intensely personal level, yet she sensed he was acting on Winfrey's instructions. If the third man outside the hotel visited her in a little while, then she would know McAllister was merely carrying out orders. It depressed her. Carolyn liked McAllister. Instinctively she wanted to trust and confide in him, as her uninhibited admission that she had seen Hood proved. And certainly she had not meant to reveal her hurt over David's behavior. Not even her sister knew that she suspected

79

David had other women. Yet James had known, and his knowing was not as painful to her as she would have expected. McAllister would seek her out again, but it would be a difficult meeting. Because it was so natural to talk to him, she would have to be guarded. He couldn't be the man to trust.

10
•

Carolyn didn't get ready for bed right away. She was waiting, moving restlessly around the suite, staring out the window, picking up the evening papers, fiddling with a tourist bulletin. It was not long. The soft rap on the door introduced her caller. She went to open it.

"Mrs. David Bruce?" She knew immediately he was the third man in Winfrey's library, the one voice she hadn't recognized. "I am Alfred Ingram. May I speak with you for a few minutes?"

"What about? It's very late."

"It's a financial matter concerning one of your husband's clients." The stubby fingers of one pudgy hand held the door frame. She wouldn't be able to slam the door in his face.

"Very well. Just for a moment."

Ingram stepped inside and stood by the door, waiting for her to lead the way into the room. She did not ask him to take off his coat, but he took it off anyway and dropped it on the end of the sofa. He hitched up his trouser legs as he sat down, revealing shiny nylon socks with a pattern on them. Carolyn didn't know they still made such socks. She took a seat in the armchair beside the sofa.

"My card." Ingram handed her a heavy mat card engraved with his name and, in small discreet letters in the lower left-hand corner, his address and occupation. Barrister. Carolyn held the card between thumb and forefinger and tapped it on the chair arm as she studied him. He was stocky, almost square in build, beginning to go to fat. The light voice came strangely from the big chest as he expressed his shock and dismay over David's death. The lisp was unpleasant, repugnant to her, making his words sound false. Carolyn lit a cigarette with her own lighter and waited.

"I am sorry to disturb you at such a time over a matter as mundane as money, but it is a question that can be so easily cleared up that I thought I would speak to you before you leave London. Settling these affairs at long distance can be difficult."

He sounded patronizing. Carolyn nodded noncommittally.

"I represent a client whom your husband served as investment adviser for some years. Mr. Bruce was a brilliant manager, canny with finances. My client was pleased with him and with his recommendations. An incredible success record, I might add."

Carolyn waited again, carefully rolling an ash into the big crystal ashtray, listening to the little crackle of burning cigarette paper.

"It is indeed awkward now that he is dead. Such a tragedy. He was destined for great things. My client feels his loss personally. He was quite fond of David, had planned a fine future for him. But now that hope is gone. He wishes only that this important matter be cleared up. I have been told that you are intelligent and sagacious and shared your husband's confidence. We should be able to resolve the matter tonight."

Carolyn hated clumsy compliments from people who wanted something from her. "What matter?" she asked.

"Mr. Bruce had in his care some money, quite a substantial sum, which he was investing for my client. There was an error on your husband's part concerning this money. I assure you it was the only error he ever made. My client wants to make new investments and wants the money returned as soon as possible. Mr. Bruce had promised to deliver a check for the amount due today. If you could return the money for your husband, the matter will be closed."

Carolyn stubbed out her cigarette and reached for another. "You are mistaken. I know nothing about this. My husband conducted his business at the bank and respected his clients' desire for discretion. He never discussed their affairs with me. But if, as you claim, Mr. Ingram, my husband had some money belonging to your client, it will undoubtedly come to light when his affairs at the bank are settled."

"Mrs. Bruce, this was not a bank matter. It was a personal matter between your husband and my client. His New York bank is not involved."

"Is it something concerning either one of the mutual funds with which my husband was engaged?"

"I see that you are informed. No, not directly. It was a personal arrangement."

Carolyn measured him. He was sitting forward on the edge of the sofa, watching her intently. He licked his lips. The pale eyes were dead. She didn't like him. She didn't like him at all. "Then, if it was a personal matter, you should contact his lawyer in New York. He will be handling the estate and will naturally wish to satisfy all legitimate claims. He is Allen Blackman, at the RCA Building, fiftieth floor, New York City. Undoubtedly records do exist regarding my husband's dealings with your client, and you can get your estate check promptly from Mr. Blackman. I'm sure you understand that under United States law, all my husband's assets are frozen until they are turned over to the estate?"

"I'm afraid you don't understand. This is a *personal* matter between my client and your husband. It will not be a part of the estate. At least, that was the understanding, that it should be separate."

"Who is your client?"

"I'm sorry. He wishes to remain anonymous. If you will write a check for him, you can make it out to Corbett et Compagnie and I will deliver it for you. Corbett et Compagnie is a French banking and investment firm which also serves my client."

Lux Michaux. It was on the tip of her tongue to ask, then she decided ignorance was the best policy for the moment. She had not liked his response to her innocent question about the mutual funds. "If he wishes to remain anonymous, it will make the matter very difficult to trace. You are not giving me sufficient information. You also have not given me identification to prove that you are indeed the authorized representative of your client. I will have to discuss the matter with Mr. Blackman when I return home."

Ingram shot his cuffs and fiddled with the black onyx cuff links. A diamond winked on his little finger. "I'm a barrister. I can advise you, if you wish," he said with assumed modesty.

"Mr. Ingram, I was not aware that a barrister was permitted to solicit business. I would not dream of involving you in a conflict of interest or of ethics. You file your claim with Mr. Blackman. I'll inform him of our conversation. The matter will be settled as expeditiously as New York law permits. How much shall I tell him to expect the claim to be?"

"My dear Mrs. Bruce." Ingram rose. His pleasant words belied the acid in his tone. He paced the floor while Carolyn watched him carefully. He was the man she had seen in Winfrey's garden walking with Haskins, she decided. "Your charade is touching. But I am not fooled. I know from reliable sources that you are fully cognizant of your husband's relationships with my client and that it is within your power to deliver the sum that your husband had promised. It is to your advantage to do so without delay. Tonight."

"I must protest, sir. You are badly misinformed. I have no idea what you are talking about. What is more, I have no authority to act for my husband in any financial capacity whatsoever, and have never had such authority. You must contact Mr. Blackman, as I suggested." She rose to dismiss him.

"Not so fast, lady." Ingram was unmoved. "A mutual friend of ours, James McAllister, informed me that you would take this tack. I see you are going to be difficult. I should warn you that my client is a very powerful man, with varied means at his disposal. It should not be too hard to bring you to see reason. Shall we have to use force? Or would more subtle means be convincing?" He stared at her, then picked up his coat and walked slowly to the door and turned. Carolyn stood by her chair, watching him. She still held his card and was stroking it gently between her fingers. She didn't seem frightened. He nodded slightly. "Think about it," he said as he closed the door softly behind him.

Carolyn stared at the door for a long moment before she went to take her bath. She lay in the hot water trying to relax, to pretend that all was well, that David was undressing in the next room, pottering, putting away the gold cuff links she had given him on his last birthday, buffing the polished Gucci shoes. There was the irony. She knew his little personal habits so well she could predict his every move, but she knew him not at all. And while she had been careful to show an unruffled expression to Ingram, he had shaken her badly.

When the water was tepid, she climbed out and wrapped herself in a towel. The locket swung from her neck with her movements. There were so many problems and so little to go on. It would be a relief to call the lawyer tomorrow and leave it for him to settle.

She went to bed, but not to sleep. It had been a painful day, and all the problems went relentlessly through her mind. Was David involved in questionable financial operations? She had felt that David shared her belief in honesty and integrity. Had she been mistaken? Was yet another illusion to be mercilessly stripped away? Then so be it. She was wiser now and would keep her own counsel, from the Winfreys, from Ingram, from McAllister. Especially from McAllister. Like David, he was handsome and astute, but he was the one to watch. His misplaced principles, his predilection for making money wherever and however he could, without regard to honesty or ethics, made him untrustworthy. Her last conscious thought as she finally went to sleep was of McAllister. His hand, as he greeted her, had been hard and calloused, not the hand of an idler.

11
•

The telephone rang three times before Carolyn realized what it was and sleepily reached for it.

"Mrs. Bruce? Long distance calling. One moment, please."

"Carolyn? Carolyn, can you hear me? It's Susie." Her sister's voice, as warm and comforting as Susie herself, came clearly over the line. Susie was shouting, compensating unnecessarily for the distance.

"Susie. Yes, I can hear you just fine. What time is it?"

"It's the crack of dawn here, but I wanted to catch you at the hotel. Something terrible has happened."

"The boys? Sam? Are they all right?"

"Yes, yes. They're fine. It's not that terrible." Susie's affection spilled over the transatlantic lines. "It's your apartment. It was broken into and absolutely wrecked! The manager found it. The plumbing was destroyed and water was leaking downstairs." Carolyn held the phone tightly, remembering David's precautions against burglary. "Carolyn? Are you still there?"

Carolyn was very alert now. "Yes. I'm here, Susie. I was just thinking. What time did it happen?"

"The manager found it about six this morning and called me right away. It could have happened any time within the past twenty-four hours. The police are at the apartment now, checking things and questioning the staff on duty. All I know is that they think it was someone who had legitimate access to the building. They used a key to get in. Sam is there now, so we should know more later. Carolyn, when can you come home? The burglars must have read about David in the paper and known your apartment would be empty. It won't be safe for you to be alone and unprotected. You must stay with us. You can have the bed in the den. Carolyn, I am so sorry. It seems that troubles go in bunches. Carolyn—" Her sister's voice was rising and Carolyn hurried to reassure her.

"Susie. It's all right, dear. Don't worry about the apartment. Call Allen Blackman for me. He has the insurance inventories and can tell if it was theft or vandalism. David probably had everything well insured, so there will be no financial loss. Another apartment might be good for me anyway. Tell Allen I will call him, but you call him now in case I don't get a line right away."

"You are so brave, Carolyn. David, and now this. You will hurry home so we can look out for you?"

"Of course, dear heart. You know I couldn't stay any place else."

"All right. Let us know. Sam and the police are coping, so don't you worry."

"I won't. My love to you all. I will let you know when I'm coming. It shouldn't be too long now."

"Okay. Bye now."

"Goodbye."

Carolyn hung up thoughtfully. The burglars had had a key. Her suite had been searched. Ingram had threatened. She worked out the time difference on her fingers. It was possible, just possible, that he could have arranged it. She went immediately to get David's keys. They were all still there on his key ring. She felt each one. Was it her imagination or did they feel waxy? Ingram was not omnipotent. There was the possibility, but it was a remote one. She put the keys away and ordered breakfast and the morning papers to be sent to her. While she waited she made coffee from her travel kit. She was just finishing it when Prescott's secretary called. Carolyn agreed to see Superintendent Prescott in his office at three that afternoon.

At two o'clock she called Allen Blackman. The connection was made promptly and Allen's broad-A Boston accent, a weak travesty of the rich London speech, was on the line. Carolyn came to the point right away.

"Has my sister telephoned you yet?" she asked.

"Yes. She caught me just as I was leaving home. I had to come into the office to get the lists from the safe. I'm on my way to your apartment now. I have talked to the police officer in charge of the case by phone. The upholstery was ripped apart. Rugs pulled up. Drawers torn open. Even the heating and cooling ducts were wrecked. He said they had plenty of manpower and plenty of time, but he didn't think that anything had been stolen. It was his opinion that they were looking for something and didn't find it. Everything was totally destroyed. He said it was one of the worst such cases he had ever seen. And the police can't find anyone who saw or heard anything out of the ordinary."

Carolyn absorbed that. "Everything was insured?"

"Oh, yes. No problem there."

"Allen? Did David leave a will?"

"Yes. He dashed in here just before you left and we wrote one, using a standard form that we use on such occasions. Everything goes to you. The amount will depend on the market value of securities, of course, but you should clear $150,000 to $170,000 after all expenses, debts and everything are settled. I don't know if he had any margin accounts at his broker's. They could be anything."

"That brings up a question I wanted to ask you. Was David involved in market speculations for other people—Americans or Europeans resident abroad, for example—on a private account basis?"

"Not that I know of. He had a world of accounts at the bank and did the investing for the mutual funds, but he never mentioned any private customers at all. Why?"

Carolyn related her conversation with Ingram. "Does that make any sense to you?"

"No, it doesn't. And it isn't likely to without names and amounts. Do you have anything to go on at all?"

"I have the names of people who have turned up as David's friends or acquaintances here. They are quite interested in his estate. I had never heard of any of them until after the accident. Have you a pencil there? Good. John and Marjorie Winfrey. They called immediately after the accident and I spent Sunday with them. Guillaume LeClere, a friend of theirs and David's. Albert Ingram, of course. And they seem to have some sort of relationship with a man called Lux Michaux. I suspect he's Ingram's client."

"That could be significant. He's a pretty unsavory character, I hear. Anyone else?"

"One more. James McAllister."

"You're not sure about him?"

"What?"

"You hesitated. Do you have a doubt about him?"

"No doubt at all. He's in the group and does some sort of work for Winfrey. I have no idea what. He's a lawyer, the nonpracticing kind. They all knew David quite well, apparently."

"Okay. I will see what I can find out."

"Do you know anything about David's affairs with the Internal Revenue Service?"

"No. What about them?"

"I talked with an IRS agent at the embassy here, a man named Jackson Hood. He told me that the IRS is concerned about under-payment of taxes and nonrepatriation of funds to the United States from overseas. David had omitted reporting a counseling fee he earned from a client in Europe."

"That could be anything or nothing. I can find out about it."

"I took it that the IRS hadn't finished its investigation."

"Then, now is the time to start talking with them. Had they contacted David at all?"

"Yes. An initial inquiry was made about two months ago. David had not answered it. Mr. Hood did promise to get the details of the case for me. He also said there were some missing Treasury documents that David may have had."

"Good Lord! Anything else?"

"Did David ever tell you of any trips he took abroad?"

"No. I didn't think he liked to travel. What are you implying?"

"Would David have had a bank account in Switzerland?"

"He never mentioned it to me. Is there one?"

"I don't know. I think it's possible."

"You didn't say anything to the IRS man about such an account, did you?"

"Heavens, no. It's pure speculation on my part."

"Well, don't mention it until we know for sure. Once money reaches Switzerland, it is beyond the reach of the IRS. You'll pay enough taxes without their jumping into something that might not concern them. Now, listen. You handled Ingram and Hood properly, so don't worry about it. Keep me posted on anything else you turn up there in London. I will handle it from this end." He was ready to hang up.

"Allen. Allen, wait a minute."

"Yes?" The line crackled and cleared. "Yes?"

"Let me know, won't you? The minute you find out anything? Anything at all?"

"Of course. I will keep you informed."

His hearty confidence didn't reassure Carolyn. As the outlines of David's tangled affairs emerged, she felt increasingly uneasy. Honest and naïvely trusting, Allen Blackman faced the world with bright hope and the expectation that it would return his faith in full measure. He and David were lifelong friends. Could he be objective about such a good friend? As Carolyn finished dressing, she wondered why dumping the problem into Allen's lap didn't reassure her. Perhaps it was because Allen had not connected the apartment search with Ingram's threat. Then she realized that she herself had accepted the incident as a search and not a burglary. If Michaux was as organized and powerful as everyone said, he would have a crew already in New York equipped for such jobs. The promptness and the thoroughness of it alarmed her. She wanted very much to discuss it with someone who was not involved with David. Superintendent Prescott was the only one who could help her there.

It was raining when she left the hotel and directed the taxi driver to Scotland Yard. The cold depressing drizzle matched her mood exactly as the heavy traffic delayed them for long periods. When Carolyn finally realized she would be late, she looked anxiously around at the crowding cars. Just then the taxi found a clearing in the traffic, darted through it, and turned down a side street. A green sedan behind them followed. Suspiciously, Carolyn twisted sideways, sitting well back from the rear window so she could watch it without being observed. When the taxi drew up in front of the Scotland Yard building, the sedan went on and turned off at the next corner. She still had no faces to describe to Prescott, but this time at least she had jotted down a license number. It could be coincidence, of course, but Carolyn no longer believed in coincidences.

12

•

Superintendent Prescott seated Carolyn in the same straight chair she had occupied on Saturday. He pulled out his smelly pipe and rummaged in his clothes for matches. Carolyn finally handed him her book of souvenir matches from the restaurant where she and David had had dinner Thursday night. When Prescott got his pipe going, he leaned back. "Well, Mrs. Bruce. I don't quite know how to begin. I have a confession to make. I don't usually have to admit a mistake."

Carolyn was intrigued.

"When I gave you your husband's effects Saturday, I thought I had them all. This item wasn't in the envelope I gave you, nor was it included on the list of articles taken from your husband's body. I wish to return it to you now. I *am* sorry and hope it has not caused you any inconvenience. If you will just sign for it." Carolyn signed the form he put before her and Prescott slid a black bankbook from an envelope and handed it to her.

"A checkbook? You gave me his checkbook the other day."

"I know. No doubt that is how this one was overlooked."

Carolyn opened the book. There were a few checks, inscribed with the name of a bank in Geneva, Switzerland. The checks were slightly larger than American checks. "A Swiss account?" she asked.

"It seems so."

"Are you sure this is my husband's?"

"Quite sure. It was in his inside breast pocket. I assume it's a personal account. There's no name on the checks, as you will notice. It may be a numbered account."

Carolyn thoughtfully tapped the book in her fingers, hefting it a little, then put it in her purse. "Well, I'll turn it over to my lawyer. Perhaps he will know what to do about it. Was there anything else you wanted?" She looked up and noticed that Prescott and his secretary were watching her closely. They recovered themselves quickly.

"Yes. Several things. You told me that the Winfreys came to call on you after the accident occurred. What time was that?"

"They were with me about half an hour. From six thirty to seven o'clock, roughly. I didn't notice the exact time."

"And how did they learn of the accident?"

"They heard it on the radio."

"Ah. I thought that was what you said." He knew quite well that was what she had said, Carolyn thought. It was in the transcript of their interview. "I checked with the news station broadcasters. It was not on the news until later that evening. It was mentioned at nine o'clock without giving a name. Complete coverage of the accident was not given until eleven o'clock."

"That's strange. I know they said they heard it on the radio. In fact, now that I think about it, I was a little surprised that they came as quickly as they did. Mr. Winfrey must have come directly from his office. He had his briefcase with him, I remember. How could he have known about it?"

"That's what I would like to know. Do you know where the Winfreys are now?"

"Aren't they at home?"

"No. There's no one at the country house or at their flat here. We checked. Mr. Winfrey has not been at his office since Friday evening. What time did you leave them after your visit?"

"Mrs. Winfrey drove me into London Monday morning to the American Embassy. We left Glenyck House about nine thirty. We left Mr. Winfrey there."

"And you didn't see him again?"

"No."

"When did you leave Mrs. Winfrey?"

"I didn't. We had planned to have lunch together, so she came into the embassy with me. I was longer than I had expected, and when I was through, she was gone. Mr. Hood's secretary gave me a message from her that something urgent had come up and she could not have lunch after all. The secretary said that Mr. Winfrey had come for her."

"But you did not see either one of them leave?"

"No. They told the secretary that they would leave my suitcase at the hotel, and it was there when I returned that afternoon. But I have not heard from either of them since."

Prescott was leafing through a paper-bound booklet. "Whose secretary gave you the message?"

"Mr. Jackson Hood's."

"Yes, here he is. Office of International Operations, Internal Revenue Service."

"That's right."

"And what was the secretary's name?"

"Simmons, I believe."

"Very well." Prescott was making notes on a pad of paper before him. "What time did you arrive back at your hotel?"

"About four thirty or five o'clock."

"I can check all this out. Perhaps someone in the hotel can remember seeing them. Why were you talking to your Internal Revenue Service?"

"They wished to ask a question concerning my husband's tax reports."

"I see." Prescott's tone indicated that he suspected considerably more than Carolyn had told him. He gnawed the end of his pipe thoughtfully. "You know, there's no sign of that taxi yet. A taxi has been reported stolen and its license number jibes with what one of the witnesses remembered. Do you recall anything about its appearance that would help locate it?"

"No. It was only a blur to me."

"Well. We will find it in time." He paused to doodle on his pad. "Another thing. One of the witnesses to the accident reported seeing you push your husband."

"No!" It was a cry of astonishment. "Why didn't you tell me?"

"Didn't I?"

"No, you did not! If you are being clever, sir, it doesn't suit you. David was my husband. I wouldn't hurt him. It's . . . monstrous!" Her voice rose in indignation and anger.

"Don't agitate yourself, Mrs. Bruce. I remember I didn't tell you. Rather, I verified your account of the accident and your actions.

You should not be overly concerned about this woman. She is an eccentric, a crackpot actually. She was somewhat inebriated when we questioned her and her story was not too coherent. She thrives on publicity and is forever reporting imaginary burglaries, calling the firemen to rescue her cat, that sort of thing. It's unfortunate that she happened to be at the scene of the accident. She is a nuisance and could even be troublesome, but I believe she's no real threat to you. She will have something to say at the inquest. However, two more witnesses called in just a while ago. We will take their statements later this afternoon. Have you told me everything that happened that afternoon?"

"Yes. Yes, I did."

"You've left nothing out?"

"No."

"Good. I had to be sure. The other witnesses have confirmed your story. I don't know what these two new people will say, of course."

"Superintendent," Carolyn said chillingly, "whatever you may think, I did not kill my husband."

"I didn't say that you did. I just have to be certain that all the facts are coming out."

Carolyn controlled herself. He was only doing his job, after all. She considered her original intention of asking him about Ingram, and decided that she couldn't afford not to. "Superintendent, add this to your picture and see what it does." He listened intently to her account of Ingram's visit and of the search of her apartment in New York. "I told Ingram plainly that I didn't know what he was talking about and that he should contact my lawyer in New York," she concluded.

"I think Ingram's visit and the destruction of your apartment are unrelated, Mrs. Bruce. Ingram is a specialist in international corporate law. He has a few questionable clients, but he himself is quite legitimate. His calling on you in behalf of a client could not be said in itself to be sinister. Was there an announcement of your husband's death in the New York newspapers?"

"Yes."

"The thieves doubtless saw that and thought it was a good chance to pillage."

"What if Ingram's client was Lux Michaux?"

"Ah." Prescott leaned forward and carefully tapped the blackened ashes from his pipe into a vile tin Dubonnet ashtray. "Michaux is an interesting character indeed. What makes you think he's the client?"

Carolyn hesitated a moment, her eyes thoughtfully looking out Prescott's big window to a city obscured by mist. She turned back to him with a little smile. "I overheard a conversation at the Winfreys' Sunday night." And she recounted the entire scene in the library as well as the one in the garden. When she had finished, Prescott and Sergeant Hardwicke both sat back in their chairs.

"That's most interesting, most interesting," Prescott said. "Did they know you overheard?"

"I don't think so."

"How did you happen to hear it?"

"I was under the desk. I got caught in the library and hid rather than have to confess that I was snooping."

"Under the desk!" Prescott chuckled until he had to remove his glasses and wipe his eyes. "My dear young lady. Well." He wiped his eyes again and put away his handkerchief. Miss Hardwicke was grinning broadly. "I trust I don't have to tell you that you took a very foolish risk. But a useful one. Very useful indeed. So you were not too surprised to see the Swiss bankbook?"

"I suppose not, although I do not in fact know such an account exists. I talked to my lawyer this morning. He, too, was unaware of it."

"Let me have those names again, the ones you saw and heard."

Carolyn repeated them and he wrote them down. "Miss Hardwicke, call down to CRO and have them search the files and send up everything they have on these people immediately. Also, initiate an inquiry to Interpol. I know we have information on Winfrey," Prescott said as Miss Hardwicke left the room. "I don't know the others."

"Superintendent, as I've told you, I believe I am being followed."

"Can you describe in greater detail the person or persons following you?"

"No. I still haven't seen his face. I believe it is the same man my husband saw just before he died. Today a green sedan followed us for several blocks as I came here. This is the license number."

"Quite frankly, Mrs. Bruce, the description you gave me Saturday is pretty tenuous. Every London male must have a tan raincoat, and many have gray hair. We can check this license number, but it will probably turn out to be innocent."

"But suppose it's not? I must admit that I am uneasy."

"That's only natural. You have been under a strain and the things you have learned since Friday have not done anything to lessen the tension. But I believe it will turn out to be nothing."

"But if Ingram threatens me again? What do I do? I don't like that man, Mr. Prescott. He's dangerous!"

"Now, don't exaggerate the situation. He may well come to see you again. He may even make threatening statements. But as long as they think you have or know something that they want, you are in no physical danger. If Ingram does contact you, use the opportunity to learn as much from him as possible. Give an appearance of cooperating insofar as you can. And let me know immediately what transpires."

She had to accept what he said. "Very well. But that doesn't lessen my apprehension." Her words were interrupted by Miss Hardwicke's return. She was carrying several folders.

"Excellent. Excellent. Faster than I expected. Now, let me see." He scanned through them quickly. "There's nothing here that concerns your husband, Mrs. Bruce," he said when he had finished. "James McAllister has only a traffic citation, and it is old enough to be dropped from the record. There's sufficient on the others to warrant investigation into their involvement in this case. We shall do that straightaway." He closed the folders and handed them back to the secretary. "I have one final thing to tell you. The inquest is at two o'clock tomorrow afternoon. The witness I mentioned could impugn your reputation. You should consider retaining the services of a solicitor to speak for you. If you are unable to find one in the time remaining, you can always speak in your own behalf. Our inquests are informal hearings, although a thorough record is made and can be used in evidence should the case come before court." At that point the phone on the desk rang. Miss Hardwicke answered it.

"Yes. Yes? Just a moment, please."

She handed the telephone to Prescott, who listened for a moment. "Good. Excellent. It's about time. I will be right there. Start dusting for prints."

He put the phone down and turned with satisfaction to Carolyn. "They've just found the taxi at the docks across the river. The license plate is missing, but it is the one. Now maybe we'll learn something. Miss Hardwicke will show you out."

"Thank you, Superintendent."

98

Prescott was already shrugging into his coat and reaching for his hat. He passed Carolyn going out the door. He tipped his hat, polite always, and hurried ahead of her, moving at an astonishingly rapid pace down the hall, a small shapeless man in an overcoat too long for him.

13

Carolyn quickly caught a taxi outside Scotland Yard. The weather was bad, and in spite of Prescott's assurances, she didn't feel safe walking alone. As the taxi headed toward her hotel, the green sedan appeared again several lengths behind. After a block she managed to see its license plate. It was the same car. Her hands turned icy inside her kid gloves. She admitted to herself that she was afraid.

The car followed them to the hotel. As Carolyn got out and the taxi pulled away, the sedan stopped just ahead. The gray-haired man in a trench coat climbed out and crossed Park Lane toward Hyde Park. The green car lurched off and was immediately lost in the traffic. The man was still in sight, walking fast. Carolyn could see the scraggly hair dribbling over his collar. He half turned his head as he walked, showing a sharp nose. She ran, taking terrible chances in the heavy traffic, to follow him. It was deep twilight, wet and misty. She could barely see him ahead of her. Once he looked back and Carolyn had a brief glimpse of a thin face. He seemed to know that she was following him, for he quickened his pace. Then, maddeningly, he disappeared down a long path.

Thick bushes lined each side. Bare branches met overhead. Carolyn ran after him. It was darker here. Intent on the chase, she did not hear the drumming noise until it was upon her. She whirled, comprehended the danger, and instinctively leaped to the side of the path.

She wasn't fast enough. A rider, leaning low, swerved his mount and lunged against her. A heavy fist against her shoulder sent her hurtling, off balance, into the wet scrub and leaves. She fell heavily, scratching her face and hands viciously on the clinging branches. She fought them away and scrambled up to glare after horse and rider. A dark horse with four white feet. The rider's face had been hidden. "You could kill somebody riding like that!" she shouted after them. But they had vanished around a bend in the path.

They hadn't meant to kill her, she thought. She had been set up! And she had fallen for it! Angrily, she retrieved all the things that had spilled from her purse and ran back to the hotel. The doorman inquired solicitously about her cuts as he held the door for her.

"An accident. I will be all right, thank you. Tell me, did you see a green sedan pull up over there just a few minutes ago? A man got out. Did you see his face?"

"Why, no, madam, I am afraid I didn't. What kind of car was it?"

"I don't know. A small one."

"I am sorry, madam. I didn't see either the car or the man."

At least, Carolyn thought bitterly as she went upstairs, I should have some bruises to show Prescott.

Ingram must have been waiting for her. She had no sooner taken off her coat than he was knocking at the door.

"Well, Mrs. Bruce," he began. Without waiting for response from her, he advanced into the room and looked her over deliberately. "In a more tractable frame of mind?"

She returned his stare coldly, without answering.

"Are you prepared to give me the check for the amount due?"

"The estate will give you a check when it receives a legitimate claim."

"I want it from you."

"I told you I know nothing of it."

"I believe you do."

"Then you are wrong."

His square face hardened. "You are not being wise, Mrs. Bruce. Other accidents may happen."

"I cannot give you anything I don't have. Now get out. We have nothing more to say to each other."

"We are not fools. We know you have the money. We know you have the authority to disburse it. The moneys were stolen from my client. Now give them back."

"So that's why you can't contact the estate. The claim is not legitimate."

"Are you calling me a liar?"

"I know nothing of your alleged affairs with my husband. You have told me neither the name of your client nor the amount of money you claim was stolen. I can only conclude that you are trying to take unfair advantage of me for your own monetary gain. Now, get out before I call the police."

He did not move. She went to the bedroom and picked up the telephone. "Get me the police," she ordered when the desk clerk answered.

Ingram was beside her in four silent steps. He shut off the connection and wrenched the receiver from her hand. She pushed him away. The phone fell to the floor with a jangle as she stumbled against the table. He picked up the phone and held it tauntingly in one hand, the receiver in the other, before her, waving it a little.

"No police. We handle this our own way." Mockingly, he dropped the receiver back on the cradle and put the telephone on the table. He reached for her purse on the bed behind him. Carolyn darted around him, heading for the door of the suite. But he was too fast. He grabbed her arm, whirled her around to face him. He held her with one hand and dumped out the contents of her purse with the other. He saw the checkbook immediately. "So you know nothing about it. You little bitch."

"No."

He wrenched her wrist sideways until she cried out. "Get *out* of here."

His reply was interrupted by a firm knock on the outer door. Carolyn jerked away from him and ran toward it. He blocked her way. "Are you expecting someone?"

"Yes." The knock was heard again, louder.

"Very well. I will be back. You've had your warning."

Before he opened the door he paused again. "I see that you are not used to pain, Mrs. Bruce. Interesting." He left then, politely nodding to Jackson Hood, who stared after him.

"Who was that? Was he annoying you?" Hood asked.

"Yes. Am I glad to see you. Is he gone?"

"Yes. What happened? You're a mess. Did he do that?" He indicated her scratches.

She touched her face with shaking fingers and sank slowly into a chair. The color was draining from her face. "Not directly." Her voice caught. "Not directly," she repeated.

She fumbled for a cigarette. Hood took the case from her, lit one and handed it to her. "Have you contacted the police?"

"Yes. They said I was in no physical danger." She laughed wryly. "Imagine! I don't know what would have happened if you had not come when you did."

"Who is he? What does he want of you?"

"His name is Alfred Ingram. He says I have some money that belongs to a client of his, a client he refuses to name. I don't know anything about it. Look in the cabinet over there and make us a drink. Straight bourbon for me, please."

"Of course." The phone rang just then. "Do you want me to get it?"

"No. I'm all right." She rose slowly, and moving carefully, left the room. Her hand hesitated over the receiver, then she picked it up. "Hello?"

"Carolyn? I tried to get you earlier, but you were out. This is James."

"Yes?"

McAllister sensed the coldness in her tone. "Is anything the matter?"

She heard the quick anxiety in his voice and steeled herself against it. "There is. A horse ran me down in the park."

"Are you hurt? Who was it?"

"Don't you know?"

"I? Why would I know anything about it?"

"Your friend Ingram seemed to. Don't you work for him?"

"What are you implying?"

"It wasn't an accident, Mr. McAllister. It was a deliberate attempt to harm me. It almost succeeded. Ingram has threatened me and virtually admitted he arranged it. I am tired of this harassment and I want it stopped."

"You don't think I had anything to do with it?"

"Did you?"

"No, I did not. But you have only my word for that. Well, I called to ask you to have supper with me again tonight, but I suppose you don't want to now."

"No."

"As you like. But be careful. Don't go wandering about alone."

He rang off. She sat a moment, remembering that he had also

104

warned her that he was her only friend. So many warnings since David had died. Clearly there was danger.

Before returning to the living room, she inspected her face and hands carefully. The scratches were minor. Her generally disheveled appearance was what made them seem so bad. She rearranged her hair and changed her dress.

Hood was quietly reading Carolyn's evening paper when she entered. The drink at his elbow was untouched. He rose immediately, and the stern face eased into a little smile when he saw her. "Here's your drink," he said.

"Thank you." She accepted it from him and sat down in the armchair.

"It's none of my business, Mrs. Bruce, but are you in some kind of trouble here?"

"You overheard?"

"I couldn't miss it. What is it about?"

"I don't know. Something concerning my husband. I am being followed."

"By whom?"

"I don't know."

"It's easy enough to find that out."

"How?"

"You could take a walk."

"I was just warned not to go about alone."

"You wouldn't be alone. I will follow you and see if anyone is interested in your whereabouts."

"Well," she considered. "Yes. I would like to know."

"All right. We'll go when you finish your drink."

"I don't want to inconvenience you with my problems."

"No trouble at all. One purpose of an embassy is aiding travelers in distress. Usually the difficulty is not as acute or as colorful as yours seems to be. But we will see. Do you want to tell me about it?"

"There isn't anything definite to tell."

"Does it concern Lux Michaux?"

She smiled. He had remembered. "Possibly."

"And your husband?"

"Definitely. And I'm being dragged into it."

"What does McAllister have to do with it?"

"I don't know that either."

"What makes you think your accident was staged?"

She described what had happened in detail. He listened intently, weighing her words carefully. "How does it sound to you?" she concluded.

"In conjunction with what you said earlier, I think you have analyzed your danger accurately. Why does Ingram think you have his client's money?"

"Apparently he has been told so."

"Do you have it?"

"Not that I'm aware of."

She was clearly troubled and Hood didn't think she was feigning it. "Do you know how much is at issue?"

"No. Ingram won't say. I wonder if he knows himself."

"Maybe he doesn't."

She was startled. "Oh, come now, Mr. Hood. I was being facetious."

"I'm not. Why not tell you? It might be appropriate to protect a client's name. Under certain unsavory circumstances, one could see intimidation being employed to gain financial restitution. But to withhold the amount due makes no sense at all. Unless he doesn't know."

She thought back. No figure had been mentioned in the conversation she had overheard at the Winfreys'. There it was said that LeClere hadn't been able to find out. She had thought Ingram meant LeClere hadn't learned who had the money, but he could also have meant he hadn't figured out how much was missing. "Perhaps you are right," she admitted at last. "But it doesn't help me."

"Did they contact Mr. Bruce about it?"

"Yes. He made a report to them. Then he was killed."

"I see."

"Did you learn anything about my husband's tax case?"

"Yes. That is why I called to see you. I received a cable today from the New York district office. Comprehensive computer analysis indicates that Mr. Bruce failed to report $643,000 of counseling fees received during the years 1965–1970. The taxes on that alone would be upwards of $300,000, plus interest. This is only the beginning of the audit. A letter was addressed last Thursday to Mr. Bruce requesting his complete financial records. Of course, he would not have received that inquiry. One of the unreported counseling fees was paid in cash by the European Investors Mutual Fund, of which he was president and treasurer. When inquiry was made to the fund, your husband happened to be absent. The matter was handled by another officer. Such consternation was caused by our investigation that a thorough audit of the fund was begun. There is indication of malfeasance in both the European Investors Mutual Fund and the Greater American Growth Fund. Substantial sums have disappeared."

She looked as if he had struck her. "Do you know how much?" she whispered.

"No. Not yet. I know what you are thinking. Don't reach your conclusions too fast. There is another suspect, although I will admit that your husband is the primary one because of his position. It looks serious for you."

"Why would it be serious for me? I have no connection with either fund."

"If your husband is responsible, and if the funds are in your possession, you are guilty of receiving stolen goods. Moreover, if he failed to report it as income to him, then you are involved again through the joint tax statement."

She made no reply. She was suddenly haggard. The long red scratch across her temple stood out cruelly.

"I have perhaps gained unfair advantage of you, Mrs. Bruce. I can delay further questions until you have legal counsel with you."

She made a deprecatory gesture. "Mr. Hood, I may have signed the tax returns, but it was not *my* intention to evade financial responsibilities. I don't have $300,000, but if that is what is owing the government, I will see that it is paid. I instructed my lawyer this morning to respond to the IRS inquiry of mid-December. As for the other, I just don't know." She caught his look of doubtful inquiry. "You don't believe me?"

"Not entirely, Mrs. Bruce. You were married to the man for four years or more. It's inconceivable that you could be so totally ignorant of what he was doing."

"Ours was not a happy marriage, Mr. Hood. He didn't confide in me."

Her answer carried the conviction of truth, and Hood suddenly felt she was innocent of wrong in this case. Yet he realized that, guilty or not, she would act exactly as she was acting and say precisely what she was saying. She had not been happy with Bruce. She was telling the truth there. The grief in her eyes was understandable. But there was something else that had been there a longer time, a sadness, a resignation, a brave front shown to the world for so long it had become a habit. Perhaps it was the lack of spontaneity. Bruce was callous and arrogantly insensitive. Another four years with him would have hardened her. Hood had expressed sympathy for her loss, but he had said only what minimum politeness required. He had not liked Bruce. He had felt that he was too glib, too quick with his radical suggestions. True, he was a brilliant man—a "bright young man" was the term in vogue—but he was too prone to play at government when he didn't know the effect of the policies he advocated. Bruce was too handsome, too ambitious, too quickly successful as a financier to be much of a success as a husband. He wouldn't have had the time.

Hood found Carolyn Bruce immensely attractive. She was self-sufficient and could probably take care of herself without his assistance. But even so, he felt protective toward her. The ugly red marks across the wide brow were a sacrilege. His eyes lingered on her. Most men would not call her a beauty, but there was something beneath the cool exterior, the aristocratic poise, that drew him. There was something sexually potent about her. He couldn't define it exactly. She didn't flaunt herself. She was too ladylike for there to be any thought of that. But it had something to do with the sinuous grace of her walk and the delicate gestures of those incredible hands. Her dress was cut with a deep collar at the neck and the long line of her throat tempted him so strongly his hand raised involuntarily. She turned to look at him. "Are you ready for an evening stroll?" he asked quietly.

"Yes. Where do I go?"

"When you leave the hotel, turn right up Park Lane to Curzon Street, then turn right down Curzon to Half Moon Street. Partway down Half Moon are some antique shops. I'll join you there. I will leave first. Follow me in ten minutes exactly. That will be my signal that you haven't been waylaid on the way downstairs. Try to look natural."

"Where will you be?"

"I'll be there. But if you see me, I have lost my touch."

It was raining when Carolyn left the hotel. She walked briskly. There were few people and they passed her quickly. There was no sign of Hood. Even knowing he was near her, she was apprehensive. By the time she turned onto Half Moon Street and saw the shops Hood had described, she wanted to run. She stopped before the bay window of one shop and studied the silver and small decorative objects inside for what seemed an endless time. Finally, uneasy that Hood had not come, she turned. He was standing behind her, his hands in his pockets, watching her with a pleased little smile. He greeted her as though he had just chanced to meet her there. She smiled.

"How long have you been there?"

"I just got here."

"I didn't hear you."

"Good." He turned down the street and she fell into step with him.

"Am I being followed?"

"Yes." There was a little surprise in his tone.

"Then you didn't believe me?"

"I was surprised to have it confirmed. It makes your problem a little more serious, I think."

"Is it a gray-haired man in a trench coat?"

"No. It's James McAllister."

"Where is he now?"

"Behind us. On the other side of the street. Don't look back."

"Did he see you?"

"He has now."

"Well! I didn't expect it to be him."

"You told him about the accident. His shadowing you doesn't necessarily have a sinister purpose. Perhaps he is just concerned."

"Maybe."

They had reached Piccadilly. "Do you want to go back or would you like to walk a little?"

"Do you have time?"

He looked down at her with concern. She seemed emotionless, so complete was her self-control, but he wasn't entirely fooled. What he had just told her had somehow increased her worry. She was suffering deeply and alone. He wondered if anyone would ever be allowed to see her pain. "All the time you want," he said.

"Then let's walk."

They strolled slowly down Piccadilly and over to Trafalgar Square. The rain had stopped momentarily, but the wind blew the water from the fountains in misty spray across their faces. Carolyn was preoccupied, walking apart and a little ahead of Hood. He would think she had forgotten his presence until she would turn and wait for him with a little comment. They wandered down to Buckingham Palace and stood with a knot of people for a while, but the crowd made her nervous and he led her out and toward the parks.

At Constitution Hill she lagged behind him suddenly. "You don't want to go through the parks?" he asked.

"Every time I do I see faces in the bushes."

"There are no faces tonight. McAllister left us when we turned off Piccadilly." He reached for her hand and drew it through his right arm to guide her across the street. His manner was cool and formal and Carolyn did not pull away from him. His left hand rested on his right arm, near but not touching her fingers, in a courtly little tribute to her.

"You were in the Secret Service?" she asked at last.

"For thirteen years."

"And you protected three Presidents?"

"How did you know that?"

"I saw the pictures at your office."

"I should have remembered."

"Why did you leave it?"

"I had been on the White House detail for nine years. It was long enough. I had proved to myself everything I wanted to prove."

"And what was that?"

"We have elaborate defense tactics and the most efficient weapons and gadgetry to use, but if they fail, the last defense of the President is the agent's own body. Every Secret Service man wonders if he can actually put himself between his President and an assailant. He doesn't get the opportunity to find out very often, fortunately."

"And you can?"

"Yes."

She waited for him to tell the story. When he didn't, she was afraid she had pried too much into an intensely personal experience. They walked in silence a moment before he continued.

"A man came out of the crowd at President Kennedy in 1963. He had a knife. Surprisingly, no one else saw it. I stepped before the President and stopped him. The knife turned out to be a rubber one and the man an escaped patient from the state's mental hospital.

I didn't know that at the time. All I thought was, My God, he's got a clear path to the President. We knew about him. He was one of the poor souls who have a hate complex against the presidency and write threatening letters to the President describing the ugly things they are going to do to him if they get the chance. They don't understand that it is not the man but the office they are trying to destroy. This particular incident was one of the freak occurrences that are our constant worry. No one knew that the patient had escaped until he lunged out of the crowd. But I had satisfied myself that I could do the job. It was not too long after that that the President was assassinated."

"Were you in Dallas then?"

"No. It happened that I was in Washington. I watched the morale of the Service sink to nothing. It seemed to have lost its sense of cohesion, and there wasn't anything we could do about it. I stayed through the transition to President Johnson, and when an opportunity came to transfer to the Counterfeiters Squad, I took it."

"And was that a letdown after associating with Presidents?"

"On the contrary, it was challenging and exciting and I enjoyed it immensely. I was totally immersed in it. Am I boring you, Mrs. Bruce, with all this? Details of other people's lives can be pretty tedious."

"Your life is so far from my range of experience that it is like a story. What happened then?"

"I was working on a case, and the whole thing came to a conclusion in a gun battle. I was wounded. Not seriously, but enough to put me in the hospital for several days. While I was there, a man who had retired the year before from the Service came to see me. For forty-five years it had been his entire life, to the exclusion of everything else. Now he has no wife, no children, no family of any kind, no friends. When he was finally unable to avoid retirement any longer, he was literally brokenhearted. All he had left to live for was coming back to visit around the building. It was pitiful. And lying there with nothing to do but think, I saw myself at his age. So I called a friend in IRS and asked if he had a job. He did, and I resigned from the Service. I took six months off to learn to live again. I discovered I hadn't bought a new suit in three years. Washington is a transient city and it is hard to make lasting friends there at any time. But I had not realized how isolated I had become. I spent the next four years in the IRS in Washington, learning my tax law and enjoying all the things I had been too busy for before. When an opportunity came to join OIO, I grabbed it and came to London. Now I am getting acquainted with a kid sister I hardly knew."

"How old is she?"

"Nineteen. My brother and I were in college when she was born. She was reared very much like a grandchild. She was naturally spirited, and was indulged and spoiled in addition. She got in with a bad crowd her first year away at college, had an affair with a real hippie type, and left school without telling anyone. The police found her in a commune in Arizona and brought her back. Her boyfriend ended up in jail for possession of marijuana. She was mad and rebellious and everything anyone said to her brought a blank stare or an ugly remark. My family is ultraconservative, and her troubles were completely outside their abilities to cope. Finally they packed her off to me in desperation."

"And have you tamed her?"

"I wouldn't if I could. I insisted she get a job and stick with it and that I always know where to get her. Other than that, she's free. She had learned her lesson, although it took quite a while for her to admit it. But she's a good kid, and her judgment of people is considerably improved. The move to London was a good idea."

"I'd say she's lucky that you were willing to help her out. Not many brothers would be bothered. Do you like living in London?"

"Very much. It's a city on a human scale, and that appeals to me."

"It's been suggested that I move here."

"It's not a bad idea." They had reached her hotel and he held the door for her.

"I suppose my decision depends on whether you find me guilty or not."

"I hope that won't happen."

"But it doesn't look very hopeful, does it?"

"I suppose not."

She swallowed hard, but was fully composed when she looked up at him. "Then thank you for bringing me back."

"You are most welcome. It was a pleasure for me. Good night."

He touched her hand briefly and saw her into the elevator. He gazed at her until the doors closed. There was a bemused little smile on his face.

14

Carolyn let herself into the silent suite and flipped the wall switch, flooding the living room with light. She went to the window and stood a moment, watching the traffic below moving steadily, constantly, silently, its noise muffled by the thermal panes. It was drizzling again, and the lights of the automobiles were casting their reflections against the wet streets. It would be gray again tomorrow. She was reaching for the cord to close the curtains when she saw James McAllister running across the street. He leaped into his car and wrenched it sharply into the flow of traffic. The car jerked as he rammed it into higher gear, darted around a slower car, picked up speed and disappeared. Thoughtfully she closed the curtains and went slowly into the bedroom.

The light from the living room illuminated the room only slightly, but it was enough to undress by. Carolyn was reaching to unzip her dress when she saw something in the mirror over the chest. She froze, staring into the mirror, trying to penetrate the dark behind her. Slowly she reached for the lamp on the chest, groped for the chain and turned it on. There was someone in her bed.

Cautiously she turned, eyes fastened on the bed. The person, stomach apparently grossly distended in pregnancy, did not move. "Who are you?" she rasped. She cleared her throat. "Who are you?"

There was no reply.

"Now, listen. This is my room. Get out of here!"

The figure did not move. And Carolyn saw that something was

very badly wrong. The body was stiff, rigid, inhuman, bloated-looking.

Staring at the form, Carolyn crossed the room. Her steps caused no response. Still nothing could be seen of the figure under the covers except the crown of shiny hair. She put out her hand and shook the shoulder. It was hard. Unyielding. Slick under the layers of clothes and blankets. As she drew her hand away, the cover slipped down, revealing an egg-shaped head, perfectly oval, with a collection of smiling features distorted into unearthly flatness. It took a tremendous force of will to strip the covers back.

"Oh, my God!"

She edged back, gasping, staring, her hands clenched at her mouth, her body shuddering hard. Suddenly nauseated, she fled to the bathroom and was violently sick. She knelt for a long time on the tiles, her head on the cold porcelain of the toilet, swallowing hard. The dank coldness felt good, and gradually she stopped gulping and got her breath. Finally she rose heavily and washed her face.

Taking a deep breath, she went back into the bedroom and inspected the thing in the bed. It was a mannequin, almost completely covered by a pall of black carnations, with a wide satin bow just under the creature's chin. The pall was heavy, awkward to lift. Underneath it the mannequin's ankles and wrists were shackled together in a complicated arrangement of black chains. Carolyn recognized the suit she had worn Friday and had sent out to be cleaned. The truth came to her and she looked closely at the face. A photograph of her own face had been carelessly pasted at an awkward angle on the oval head, and the gaudy wig was in Carolyn's own hair style. The whole was a grotesque travesty of herself. Sickened, she lowered the pall back into place. A florist's small envelope fell to the floor. It was addressed in heavy black pen strokes, "Mrs. David Bruce." She bent and picked it up and slipped the card out. "I find I can't let you go. James McAllister." Slowly she slid the card back into the envelope, and holding it between thumb and forefinger as if it had been reptilian, dropped it onto the pall as a firm rap on the outer door sounded.

She thought immediately of Ingram. Fearfully she tiptoed to the door. There was no peephole to see out. She waited, hardly breathing, listening to the impatient knocking. "Mrs. Bruce?"

It was Hood.

She unbolted the door and swung it wide.

"Mrs. Bruce—Carolyn—" He reached for her hands, then stopped. "What's the matter? You look ill!"

"I—" She could not finish. Hood's gaze followed her pointing finger questioningly, and at her nod, he strode into the bedroom. There was silence. Slowly she followed him.

There was an expression of intense revulsion on his face. "Did you just come in and find this?" he asked grimly.

She nodded.

"Something told me I should have come up with you. Whoever did this is a maniac. He—or she—should be in a maximum security hospital." He took his handkerchief and carefully lifted the card. "May I read this?"

"Go ahead. It takes care of any theory of McAllister's concern for my safety."

"It would certainly seem to. Have you called the police?"

"Not yet. I was going to when you knocked. I'm sorry I didn't let you right in. I didn't know—"

"That was wise. Go ahead and make your call. I'll wait for you in the other room."

Prescott came promptly. Carolyn introduced him to Hood and led the way to the bedroom.

"Ah," Prescott said when he saw the mannequin. "That would give one quite a turn." He opened and read the card and then stood thoughtfully tapping it on the envelope. "I've found out something of this chap, McAllister, since you told me about him. This doesn't seem his style. Have you touched anything?"

"No. I lifted the flowers and put them right back where they were."

Prescott studied the picture glued to the mannequin's face. "When was this taken?"

"I have been thinking about it. I finally remembered that Friday afternoon before the accident we were walking along Piccadilly. A photographer was there taking pictures of tourists. He snapped a picture, but we didn't buy any copies. I hate that sort of thing. It could have been then, although without any clothes or background to use for identification, it is hard to tell."

"Could you identify the person taking the picture?"

"I doubt it. A young, rather woolly-haired fellow. He was wearing a blue jeans outfit—pants and jacket, I think. But features—no. I didn't look at him very closely. I didn't want to encourage him."

"Of course." Prescott looked at the card and the envelope again. "This is from the hotel flower shop. We can check that out. Have you seen James McAllister or talked to him recently?"

"Tonight. He called and asked me for supper, but I refused. I told him about an incident in the park this evening, which happened after I left you. A horse tried to run me down. I was angry, because I thought he had had something to do with it. Mr. Hood was with me when Mr. McAllister called. We talked here for a while and then went out. When I came back upstairs, I saw McAllister running across the street as I closed the curtains. He got into his car and drove off rather fast. That's all."

"And then you discovered the dummy?"

"Yes."

"What time was that?"

Carolyn looked at her watch. "About forty-five minutes ago."

"You didn't call until eleven o'clock. What were you doing in the meantime?"

"Being sick." Carolyn wished he hadn't asked.

"I shouldn't wonder. May I use your telephone?"

"Of course."

From the living room, Carolyn and Jackson could hear Prescott's conversation clearly, ordering men from the Yard to come and check for fingerprints and take pictures. Prescott joined them as soon as he had finished his call.

"We will want to examine the suite carefully and question the hotel staff. Are the dummy's clothes familiar to you?"

"It's wearing my suit. I had sent it out to be cleaned."

"Where did you send it?"

"I gave it to the maid who cleans in here every morning. I don't know her name. She said the hotel had a reliable cleaner it used regularly. She didn't say its name, only that it wasn't too far away. The shoes are mine, too. They were in the closet."

Prescott was making brief notes in his tattered little notebook. "Anything else? Anything missing?"

"I haven't looked."

"Would you check now, before my men get here?"

Carolyn made a quick search. When she returned to the living room Prescott was hunched in a chair studying McAllister's card. Hood was moodily pacing the floor. "Nothing has been taken," Carolyn reported.

"Good," Prescott said. "Mrs. Bruce, did I understand you to say that McAllister had something to do with the accident in the park?"

"Yes, I thought so. He denied it."

"Why did you think he would have?"

"He works for Alfred Ingram. Ingram was here earlier this evening and threatened me. He indicated the accident was staged for my edification."

"Describe everything that has happened since you left my office," Prescott ordered. He huddled himself down in his chair, licked a stub of a pencil and held it over the notebook.

Carolyn detailed the incident in the park, describing the gray-haired man as best she could, and then recounted Ingram's visit and threat. "He said," she concluded, "that he would be back."

"Yes. But there are also perfectly logical explanations for the incident. The horse could have been out of control. You could have been in the way. Did Ingram say *exactly* that he had arranged the accident?"

Carolyn thought back. "Not in so many words," she had to admit. "But his implication was clear."

"I see." Prescott's tone indicated that he saw a great deal. Carolyn didn't like the turn the conversation was taking.

"Mr. Hood can confirm that I am being followed," she insisted.

Prescott turned questioningly to Hood, who tersely recounted their walk.

"And are you qualified to make such an experiment, sir?" Prescott asked.

"I was in the United States Secret Service for thirteen years," Hood answered briefly.

Prescott's eyebrows lifted. "I see. And in your professional judgment, did McAllister's actions indicate beyond doubt that he was shadowing Mrs. Bruce with sinister intent and not just taking an evening stroll himself?"

"He wasn't skilled enough to rule out all element of doubt. There were several points at which, had Mrs. Bruce turned, she would have recognized him. I cannot speak for his motives, but my impression was that he wished to ascertain her destination and purpose for being out and that he preferred that she not see him."

"But he didn't follow you the entire time?"

"It was obvious we were only strolling. He returned to the hotel to await her return in comfort."

"He may have had a more personal reason for his interest."

"You are being insulting, sir," Carolyn replied coldly.

"Not at all. My point, Mrs. Bruce, is simply this. There are sufficient questions to be resolved in this case so that we must guard against extraneous issues that may result only from strain and overwrought nerves."

"Superintendent Prescott—"

"Now, Mrs. Bruce, don't upset yourself. Ingram has been unpleasant, and in seeking to intimidate you, he is being unethical in regard to his professional principles. He is the most threatening of the things you have reported to me. He and that thing in the other room. However, you have a more serious concern, and that's the inquest tomorrow. Have you retained a solicitor?"

"Not yet."

"Then I feel it my duty to urge you most strongly to do so. Your reputation may suffer grave jeopardy and you should have expert counsel."

"But you said that witness was harmless."

"I didn't say exactly that. But no matter. The two additional witnesses we interviewed this afternoon alleged that they saw you push your husband into the flow of traffic."

"But that's absurd! I couldn't—I wouldn't—"

Prescott held up a cautionary hand. "The coroner will examine them closely. But you should have your own advice."

"I don't know anyone to contact."

"A friend of mine might be able to go with you," Hood put in. "Would you like me to call him?"

"Yes, please. If you would."

"If you will excuse me a moment . . ."

Prescott looked at Carolyn closely. She was shaken and upset, the control cracking a little. The case was a welter of unknowns. And he was tired and needed sleep. But as he rose and let his crew into the living room, he knew that the lovely and troubled Mrs. Bruce was the key to the whole matter.

Carolyn sat listlessly, numb. The only thing that she could clearly comprehend just now was that she was afraid. Afraid of Ingram, afraid of McAllister, of the witnesses, even of David, who, although dead, nevertheless still threatened. Even Hood, whom she had grown to think of as a friend in their two casual conversations, was not truly a friend. He was investigating her also. He was a professional agent first, as he had just proved. There was no one who would unquestioningly and instantly spring to her defense. Never had she felt so alone.

She looked up hopefully as Hood returned. "My friend can help you. His name is Alexander Adams. He will call you tomorrow when he gets to the office and arrange a meeting so that you can brief him on the case. He will go with you to the inquest and can argue in your behalf. The only hitch is that he is committed to a dinner meeting at six o'clock tomorrow evening. But surely, if the hearing is going to run late, it will be held over until the next day. You will find him quite able."

"How can I thank you . . . ?"

"Don't try. I wish I could go with you myself, but I have to go to Birmingham for a series of meetings. I could neither argue nor testify for you, so you are best off with Alex."

Prescott's men were moving quietly about in the bedroom, and the occasional pop of flashbulbs told of their activities. Prescott returned. "Mrs. Bruce, the fingerprint squad may take quite a while and it's very late. Do you want me to reserve another room for you tonight?"

"Yes, please."

"Tell Alex everything you know," Hood continued. "And also what you only suspect. He will be at some disadvantage in having no time to prepare, but he will be able to handle it."

"Mr. Hood, I have the feeling that Superintendent Prescott . . . that you . . . don't really believe me."

"We are neither one of us in a position to be biased, much as we might like to be."

"Whatever you think, whatever he thinks, I am afraid. For the first time in my life I am in something that I don't think I can handle myself."

"What's that, Mrs. Bruce?" Prescott asked behind her.

"She said she was afraid," Hood answered for her. "Could you give her some protection?"

"Of course, Mr. Hood. My men will be here most of the night, should you need them, and I'll leave word for one of them to remain here until Mr. Adams meets you."

"Thank you. That will be comforting."

"I'm sorry you have had such a shock. But you need not worry any more tonight. The hotel is sending someone up to unlock the suite across the hall. Well, I am off. I will see you tomorrow. Good night, Mrs. Bruce, Mr. Hood."

"Good night, sir."

Carolyn quickly packed a small bag which Hood carried across the hall for her. "I must go, too," he said. "Try to forget all this and sleep."

"I don't know that I can. I will have to take a couple of sleeping pills."

"I don't approve of that."

"I don't either. But tonight they will be useful."

"Well, then." He turned at the door to look at her. She was still able to smile, but it was a poor effort. "I will call you when I return."

"Thank you. Good night."

But as he softly closed the door behind him, Carolyn remembered something. "Mr. Hood?" she called after him. "Why did you come back?"

He turned in the hall with an enigmatic little smile. "Some other time we can discuss ESP and second thoughts. Not now."

"I see. Thank you for being so timely . . . again."

"Good night."

No, thought Hood. She didn't see. She didn't see at all. But, then, he hardly understood himself the urgency that had forced him to drive back through the dark streets to pound at her door. And if he could have described it accurately, he wouldn't have believed it of himself.

Carolyn dozed fitfully. She would fall off to sleep heavily for a few minutes and then would start awake, feeling a deep sense of loss, surprisingly painful, that McAllister was no longer a friend, that he had exposed himself as one of Michaux's and Ingram's henchmen. The odd-job designation no longer fitted. No doubt his actions of tonight were part of his new full-time duties.

She turned over again and curled up, her pillow bunched under her cheek, trying to forget how comforted she had felt Sunday night when he seemed so attuned to her need. Never in her life had she felt about a stranger as she had about James McAllister. Not wanting to leave him. That foolish desire to reach out and touch the fabric of his sleeve, to tuck her hand into his arm and feel a solid bond. Only briefly, during the few days of her engagement and just after her marriage, had she felt that way about David. Her relationship with David came to be such that it sometimes was a relief when he went off and left her. Loneliness by herself was somehow more bearable than the loneliness she knew when he was in town but too busy to be bothered with her. At those times he could look at her more impersonally than he would at his secretary, so coldly that it would chill the words in her throat, and she would go away and leave him alone, smarting from the relief in his eyes as he turned back to his work.

She had been with McAllister only twice, but she had formed the conviction that he could never look at her impersonally. His direct gaze encouraged her. His eyes lingered on her face as she talked. There was a little intimate expression around his mouth when he laughed with her. She wanted to talk, to share things with him, and he was eager to hear. He had subjected her to potent and powerful treatment, as smooth a line as any girl had ever heard. And she had fallen for it. How eagerly she had smiled her greeting last night. How hurt she had been when he abruptly left her standing in the lobby.

He had destroyed something in her by the cruelty of that thing in the other room. And because she had admitted to herself that she was interested in him, because she had almost revealed too much of her feelings to him to the detriment of her self-respect, because McAllister seemed so bound up in the events that were now threatening her, she found herself blaming him and hating him. She hated him for making her feel like a woman when she should be mourning her husband. Hated him for the eagerness of her own response to him. Hated him for bullying her and fascinating her while he did it.

The gray light of early morning has a way of diminishing the turmoil of midnight thoughts. When at last Carolyn rose, weary and unrested, to dress, she realized that McAllister was only a part of what she could not escape. She had her own resources, a solicitor committed to her defense, Prescott committed to justice, even Hood committed to seeing that an American citizen was treated fairly. And there were her own not inconsiderable wits. McAllister might be handsome and magnificently adept at making a woman feel cherished, but he was not omnipotent. At nine o'clock in the morning,

15
.

Carolyn was alone. She sat quietly, smoking, her eyes resting absently on a damp place in the wall. She could smell wet plaster. London's grime seeped in the windows. It permeated the ugly little room. The ashtray beside her was full. It was long past two o'clock. Carefully she shifted her position sideways, trying to avoid tearing her stockings on the splinters in her chair. She was very uncomfortable.

"Our coroners don't have courtrooms of their own," Adams explained as he returned from his restless pacing in the hall. "They have to take any space available. I would offer to find you a better chair, but there just aren't any."

"It's all right." Carolyn smiled. She liked Adams. Spare, white-haired and soft-spoken, he was quietly competent, his questions concise, his answers clear and candid. He had not sought to allay her fears by any platitudes. She knew her situation was serious. The grounds for optimism were now only in the person of the coroner himself. Dr. Edward Cooper was both a barrister and a medical doctor. In Adams' estimation he was the best of London's coroners. That was something, Carolyn thought. But it would not be enough. She lit another cigarette. Now her hands were shaking.

"The angle of impact was the determining factor in causing Mr. Bruce's death," Adams had explained to her that morning.

"How do you mean?"

"He wasn't run over by the vehicle. The internal organs were not crushed. He had started to fall, and because he was falling, the taxi's bumper was able to catch him and toss him into the air. He fell on his head and broke his neck. 'Fracture of the cervical spine' is the technical term. It killed him. But had he not been falling, his injuries would have been altogether different. Perhaps the result would not have been fatal. That is what the pathologist who conducted the postmortem believes, at any rate. That is what he will say at the inquest."

"What are you telling me?"

"The question that remains unanswered is what caused Mr. Bruce to fall."

Carolyn said nothing. Adams watched her closely. He had not yet made up his mind about his client. "What do the witnesses say?" she asked finally.

"You have gone to the most important problem. There will be several technical witnesses, such as the pathologist, the physician from the hospital, the constables who assisted at the accident, and so forth. With the possible exception of the pathologist, they are in no position to testify on the cause of Mr. Bruce's fall. One witness, Mrs. Christopher Lester, corroborates your account exactly. She even overheard the argument you were having with your husband."

Carolyn sighed.

"Mrs. Philpot is an eccentric." Adams paused. "She claims you pushed Mr. Bruce."

Carolyn nodded. "Prescott told me."

"We can discredit her. Her account is so garbled that I do not believe she was close enough to see exactly what did happen. She likes excitement. She is trying to make something out of this."

"Can she?"

"By herself she could not. But her testimony is given credence by two other witnesses, Adelaide Frye and Harvey Lisle. They are making the same allegation, and they are neither incoherent nor eccentric."

"But I didn't. I swear it!"

"You don't have to swear to me. We are not without resources. There's another witness, a man named Angus McIntyre. He was driving a panel truck that was directly behind the taxi. While he did not see you at all and did not see your husband until it was too late, he can speak on the erratic behavior of the taxi. If we can prove that the driver was guilty of dangerous driving, the cause of Mr. Bruce's fall becomes less important."

"Can we prove that?"

"I don't know. The driver still has not been located. His absence leaves large gaps in our information. The taxi was found abandoned in an old shed across the river at the Surrey Docks. It was wiped completely clean of fingerprints."

"Isn't that unusual?"

"Definitely. Scotland Yard finally found a fragment of your husband's suit in the radiator. That proved it is the vehicle that struck him. But that is all they can prove right now. It raises many questions indeed."

"Will it raise enough?"

"We will try to emphasize the unknown elements so that the jury will hesitate to decide homicide. I don't know whether we will be successful or not. The coroner will be fair, but a great deal depends on the witnesses. As it happens, the conclusions of the technical witnesses and the gaps in the story tend to support the theory that some foul play was involved in the accident."

"But there was. That man that my husband saw—"

"But he has disappeared. No one else claims to have seen him but you. He might as well not have existed."

Carolyn saw it all closing in. The room suddenly seemed darker to her. Uneasily she shifted her position, trying to get comfortable.

"There's the coroner now," Adams said. "I will see what is causing such a long delay."

Carolyn hardly heard him. Since noon she had been wrestling with Adams' assessment of her position.

"Coroners' juries in England have considerable authority, more, I think, than is the general rule in America," he had explained to her. "If they decide homicide, they can name the person whom they think responsible. They can name you. If no more than two of them disagree, the coroner will have no choice but to declare it a valid verdict, issue a warrant for your arrest, and commit you to trial at the next assizes. It may come to that today. Judging from the evidence available, I think it is highly possible."

The feeling of confidence she had experienced in the morning had faded. Now she felt completely without friends. Adams she could depend on, but a lawyer could do only so much. And it wouldn't be enough.

Adams was back. "We can go in now. Cooper wants to get started."

Carolyn put out her cigarette and followed him.

The hearing room was full. There was a little stir as they entered.

"There she is! She did it! I saw her do it! She killed him! Killed him dead! She's an evil woman!"

There was now much commotion. "You tell them, dearie," another voice said.

The coroner's stern voice subdued the hubbub. "Clerk, remove that woman from the room until she calms herself."

"I saw it! Taking me away won't change that! Others here saw her, too. She'll die for it!"

The clerk had a firm hand on Mrs. Philpot's arm. For a moment the woman glared at Carolyn. She was indeed an eccentric. Her wiry hair was scrambled and crammed under a navy-blue felt hat. An old lady's shoes, lumpy stockings, and a shapeless coat completed her outer attire. A Christmas ornament was pinned to her lapel. She clutched an enormous black plastic handbag to her bosom. She seemed sober, but a spot of color high on each cheek implied the ale she had drunk at lunch to cure her nervous excitement. The glitter in her eyes was not wholly sane. Carolyn suddenly felt more confident. She turned away and walked down the aisle to the chair Adams held for her.

"I'm sorry that happened," he said.

Carolyn didn't hear him. She was looking across the aisle, facing down a stare of pure malevolence smoldering in the eyes of a big man. He was solid, sturdy, tough-looking, with corded wrists and great hairy hands that stuck out of coat sleeves too short for him. His stringy hair was combed carefully over a sallow scalp. He looked away.

"Who is that man?" Carolyn whispered to Adams.

"I believe that is Harvey Lisle. Adelaide Frye is sitting just behind him."

Cautiously Carolyn looked again. She saw a large, raw-boned woman. Her lipstick was one of the new blood-red shades and so were her nails, which were thick and curved like talons. Her sculptured hair glistened with hair spray. It contrasted oddly with the conservative suit, new alligator shoes and handbag.

"Mrs. Lester and Mr. McIntyre are directly behind us and about three rows back. You'll have to turn clear around to see them," Adams said.

"I won't be that obvious."

Just then the jurors filed in. Most of them were middle-aged. All looked like working people. Anxiously they turned their attention to the unfamiliar atmosphere and terminology of an inquest. They looked at Carolyn curiously, but she could not tell from their expressions what they thought. Stolidly they took their seats. Again Carolyn looked quickly around. There was no one she recognized. Dr. Cooper rapped on the table and the little hum of voices ceased immediately.

"Ladies and gentlemen. This court will please come to order. In accordance with law, this jury is summoned to ascertain the cause of a violent and unnatural death. Law stipulates that such inquests are to be made in cases of suspected murder, accidental death, and death by accident arising from the use of a motor vehicle in a street or public place. Today inquiry shall be made into the death of one Mr. David Cartwright Bruce, an American, in an accident on Regent Street on Friday afternoon last. Is the jury prepared to take the oath? Please rise and hold up your right hands."

The words of the ancient oath were barely distinguishable in their collective mumble. "I swear by Almighty God that I will diligently inquire and a true presentment make of all such matters and things as are here given me in charge on behalf of our Sovereign Lady the Queen, touching the death of David Cartwright Bruce, now lying dead, and will, without fear or favor, affection or ill will, a true verdict give according to the evidence." Stressed heavily, the word "verdict" jumped ominously out of the oath. The jury lowered their hands, turned to stare at Carolyn once more, and then shuffled down into their chairs at the side of the room. The inquest had begun.

"For the first witness," Dr. Cooper said, "I will call Mrs. Carolyn Bruce. Will you please come and take the oath?"

Carolyn rose, was sworn to tell the truth, and took her place in the witness box.

"Mrs. Bruce, did you identify the deceased?"

"Yes. He is my husband, David Cartwright Bruce."

"How long were you married?"

"It would have been five years this coming May."

"Thank you, Mrs. Bruce. That will be all."

Gratefully Carolyn returned to her seat.

Two more witnesses, both constables, testified to the identity of

David Bruce and the validity of the passport he carried. They were dismissed quickly. The coroner waited for absolute silence.

"Ordinarily, ladies and gentlemen, this inquest would summon and question all witnesses here present," he said. "However, I am hereby postponing these interrogations. I was informed a few moments ago that additional information has just come into the possession of the police which bears directly and importantly on this case. It would be inappropriate to continue when a short delay would result in a more valid deliberation. Mrs. Bruce, you and Mr. Adams are requested to accompany the constable who is waiting for you in the hall. Everyone present is requested to be here, in this room, fourteen days from today at precisely two o'clock in the afternoon. This inquest is recessed."

"What is the new information?" Carolyn asked Adams.

"I don't know. He wouldn't tell me. But Mr. Bruce has been positively identified for the record. We can now obtain the necessary documents for burial. Shall we go?"

It was a short ride to Scotland Yard. Prescott was waiting and led the way to a chillingly bright and modern laboratory. It was indistinguishable from any other lab except that its green filing drawers were outsized and were sunk into the wall. A rotund official whose rosy cheeks and beery eyes were in ludicrous contrast to his macabre duties greeted them cheerfully. He slid out the middle drawer, lifted away the sheet and stepped back. Prescott ushered Carolyn forward. At his insistence, she looked into the drawer.

"Do you know him?"

"Yes. It's John Winfrey." Debonair and suave in life, Winfrey looked peculiarly shrunken in death. His eyes wouldn't stay closed.

"And this one?"

Marjorie Winfrey was in the drawer to the left. She had evidently had a more difficult time dying. There were deep bruises around her neck. The carefully coiffed red hair had been a wig. Carolyn gulped down the sudden nausea and turned away. But the attendant had opened yet another drawer.

"How many are there?"

"This is the last."

Slowly, reluctantly, Carolyn looked. A long silence passed. They watched her closely as she studied the cadaver. "He looks familiar," she said at last, "but I don't know him."

"Are you sure?" Prescott asked.

"Yes. Should I know him?"

"Not necessarily. We believe it is Michael Fanning, the driver of the taxi that struck your husband. His wife is coming in to make the identification, but it will be another hour before she arrives."

"I see. May I go now?"

"Yes," Prescott said. "Are you all right?"

Carolyn nodded. "Yes . . . just."

"Not a pretty sight, it's true. But better than some we see. Thank you, Mrs. Bruce."

Adams held the door for her. Carolyn could hear the last drawer sliding shut as they left the laboratory. "Can I drop you at your hotel?" he asked.

"Thank you, no. You will be late for your dinner meeting. You go on. I want to be alone for a while."

"I understand, Mrs. Bruce. Thank you. I'll call you tomorrow."

"Good night, Mr. Adams. Thank you."

Adams found a taxi immediately, and with a little wave, left her there on Victoria Street.

Slowly Carolyn buttoned her coat and pulled on her gloves. She breathed deeply. As the mist and the aroma from the nearby river hit her face, she knew how a prisoner must feel in his first moments of freedom. It was wonderful just to be able to walk alone.

16

.

Carolyn was acutely aware of everything around her. Westminster Abbey loomed darkly behind her. The lighted face of Big Ben showed six o'clock. In a moment it struck. Traffic poured off Westminster Bridge and rumbled past her, headlights glowing. She walked pensively, her hands in her pockets, mist gathering in the fur of her coat. She didn't mind. The mist and the growing fog were preferable to a dank government prison. It began to rain. A gust of cold air from the river behind her presaged colder weather. At the corner she stopped and looked for a taxi.

That was when she saw him behind her, the familiar figure in the military raincoat and slouch hat. The man in the park. The decoy. Ingram's man, dogging her again.

Frightened, she started to run.

There were no taxis and no policemen. She was alone. Scotland Yard was now too far away to reach quickly. The Defense Ministry on her right was closing for the night. And the parks were just ahead.

The man was closer. She could hear his leather soles on the pavement. Her breath came in gasps and her side caught as she ran. It was raining harder. Fog veiled the arc lights in mist. A car was coming, its motor distinctive. Please, she prayed, let it be a taxi.

The car neared, passed her and stopped. The door swung open and she veered toward it. Then she recognized James McAllister.

"Carolyn, get in."

She shook her head, backed away, and ran. McAllister leaped out and raced toward her. Another car was coming, a sedan. A Jaguar

Mark VIII, with a tall aerial on the back. Police car, she thought, and sprinted toward it.

McAllister grabbed her arm. "No, Carolyn. You are in danger. Come with me."

"Let me go," she gasped as he wrestled her to the car. She lashed out sideways at him, then slipped out of his grasp. He caught her, spun her around, and clipped her hard under the chin. As she crumpled he bundled her into the Mercedes.

The Jaguar had stopped behind them and the driver got out. Vaguely Carolyn saw a blue uniform. She fumbled the door open, trying to call for the protection of a policeman.

McAllister reached around her and swung the door shut again. "You stay put," he ordered angrily. He slammed the car into gear. The man on foot was directly opposite now. For the first time Carolyn had a full-face view. She would never forget that beaky nose or the dragging lantern jaw. McAllister jammed his foot on the accelerator. The car lurched forward. She looked behind her. Her pursuer and the uniformed chauffeur were getting into the Jaguar. It followed. After several blocks it turned off.

Carolyn darted a glance at McAllister. He was driving tensely, sitting forward, grasping the wheel with both hands, the street lights creating and then erasing shadows on his face. He guided the Mercedes through the traffic, seeking openings and taking chances to make them. He ran a yellow light and then a red one before he sat back. As they reached the highway out of London, the traffic thinned. McAllister shifted into fourth gear. The engine relaxed as they picked up speed.

Carolyn rubbed her chin reflectively. "Who are those men?"

"Ingram's."

"Where are you taking me?"

"Home."

She asked nothing more. The speedometer passed sixty. She knew the desperation of Ingram and Michaux now. There could be only one reason why they had let McAllister have his way so easily. He was Ingram's man. She took a deep breath, let it out silently, and began to think how to get away.

The car swung off the main highway onto a ramp that ended quickly in a deserted country road. A single arc light burned faintly. McAllister braked the car at the stop sign, reached over and lifted her chin, turning her face toward him, examining it in the dim light.

"You'll be all right," he said, releasing her and shifting gears. "There will be a red mark, but it will be gone tomorrow. I'm sorry."

"Sorry! You're sorry! And whose man are you?"

"Yours, dear heart. Yours."

He turned carefully onto the country road. It was raining hard now and sleet rattled against the windows.

"And Winfrey's too?"

"That's right. And Winfrey's too."

"Winfrey is dead. So is the taxi driver."

He looked at her sharply and then turned back to the road.

Carolyn huddled into the corner of her seat, as far away from him as she could get. He was going too fast, and the wheels slid a little on the macadam and gravel. Once the car skidded, and he swung the wheel, bringing it back under control and slowing down. She shivered. He reached and turned the heater up to a metallic roar without taking his eyes from the road.

They drove for a long time. Hedges turned the narrow roads into tunnels. The occasional signposts meant nothing to Carolyn. The directions they pointed to were as deserted and unreal as the route they were following. There were no trees and no other cars. Just hedges and sleet tinseling into the headlights.

McAllister turned again and they passed through a narrow village with stone houses that opened directly onto the road. Their windows were tightly curtained. The blackness followed the glow of lights so swiftly it increased Carolyn's sense of isolation.

Beyond a second village McAllister turned abruptly into a dirt lane. The car immediately jolted heavily into a deep rut, scraping its undercarriage. He throttled down to second gear. Trees grew together overhead. The eyes of a small animal gleamed and then winked out. The lane, now merely a track, forked twice before they passed through rusty iron gates that sagged brokenly into the mud and dead grass. A gas light on the porch flickered feebly and Carolyn sensed a low stone building, its walls covered with brown ivy. McAllister stopped the car, listened to the faint clicking of the motor for a moment and then cut it off.

The silence, and the blackness, closed in.

McAllister opened the door and pulled her out. Holding her arm firmly, he took her directly into the house and stood her before a fireplace. Logs were laid in readiness. The kindling responded instantly to his match. He pulled a tapestried settee to the hearth as

133

the flames curled hungrily over the logs. "Sit here. In a minute it will be warm. I bribed the maid to pack your overnight case. I'll get it now."

The moment the front door shut behind him, Carolyn rose. There was a French door to one side of the fireplace. She glanced out. It led onto an overgrown terrace. It unlocked easily. Carolyn stepped out. Moss and brick were underfoot. She moved quickly down the three shallow steps, across the yard to a group of bushes. There she concealed herself and looked around. A garden wall was to her right. The house was dark. McAllister had not followed. She darted off, ducked under other bushes, sending a welter of water and ice down on her shoulders. Then she groped forward until her hand touched the wall. Cautiously she followed it, seeking a place to pass through.

She almost fell over the stone steps, single big slabs set in the wall at sloping intervals. Fumbling for a handhold, she mounted the steps and reached for the top. McAllister grasped her ankle. "Where are you going?" he asked quietly.

Shock loosened her grip. She fell, with a little cry.

He caught her and dragged her away from the bushes to the open yard. She fought him, kicking, twisting, struggling to get free. He pinioned her arms easily, catching the flailing wrists and thrusting them behind her, holding her tight against him. She could not move.

"Carolyn. Carolyn," he said huskily.

"Let me go. Leave me alone!"

He suddenly went very, very still. To Carolyn his stillness was more terrible than his violence.

Deliberately, he bent his head and kissed her hard on the lips.

Carolyn remained motionless. Then furiously, murderously, she bit his lip until she tasted blood. He jerked upright. She tore away from him and raced toward the gate.

He looked after her, feeling his mouth with the back of his hand. Slowly he followed her.

When he reached the gate, Carolyn was not in sight. He broke into a jog. There were many hiding places on his land. He was afraid she would find one.

But Carolyn was too angry, too desperate to be thinking very clearly. Her only thought was to run from McAllister, and the quickest way to the village and help was straight ahead. Ruts and the cold gripping her wet boots impeded her progress, but she ran until her breath caught. Then she walked, and thought of hiding.

A primitive stone bridge she had not noticed before provided the first place. It was too dark to see a good way down, and she fell noisily, ending with her arm and hand in icy water. Cautiously she scrambled up, and hearing nothing, crept under the bridge. Her ears strained for any sound of McAllister, but heard only the wind and icy branches creaking. It was miserably cold. There was no place to stand except on two broad rocks in the stream. When they tilted her suddenly into water to her ankles, she realized she would have to take a chance. Awkwardly she clambered up the embankment. There was nothing there except blackness. She turned toward the village. Her hands and feet were dead, her ears hurt, and an ache in her thigh promised a big bruise. The heavy growth overhead blocked any light from the sky, but not the rain and sleet. Snow would be a relief. Doggedly she put her head down and followed the grass strip in the center of the lane. She didn't see McAllister until he stepped in front of her at the first fork.

"No one will believe you in the village," he said. "Come back to the house."

It was inevitable. She was too cold to fight him any more. He put his arm around her, and holding her wrists in his two hands, propelled her back the way they both had come.

The house, when they reached it, glowed with light, and the hall was gratifyingly warm. McAllister shucked his coat and took the damp fur from her shoulders. She watched him, her back to the front door, her hands on the knob behind her, as he took the coats into another room. Quickly she turned and fumbled with the handle, but he was back, reaching around her to slam the door shut again. He rammed the bolt home with an angry rasp, then wrapped a heavy wool blanket around her shoulders. He turned her and looked intently into her face. She was defeated, ruined and raw emotionally, frightened, exhausted, helpless. She was completely and totally his to break.

"Are you that afraid of me?" he asked softly.

She didn't answer, and he led her to the fire, where she collapsed on the raised hearth. He knelt beside her, taking her arm roughly to turn her to him. "Ingram is the one to be afraid of. Not I."

She shrugged away from his grasp. "There is no difference. You both work for Michaux," she said bitterly.

"Ingram will kill you if it suits his purpose. I would not."

She looked at him and turned her eyes back to the fire.

"You've met Ingram. You know what he's like. I thought you trusted me. You can't persist in thinking I had anything to do with that incident in the park!"

"Don't play games with me," she said harshly.

"I am not lying. Ingram engineered it. Not I. And Ingram is causing you trouble in court. Not I. Believe me. I am the only friend you have."

She drew the wool closer around her, trying to warm her hands in its folds. "And the mannequin?" she asked softly. "Who engineered that?"

"What mannequin?" He seemed genuinely startled.

"And the flowers. The black pall had your card."

"What black pall? I sent you yellow roses."

Her ears were hurting now as the fire became warm. She covered them with her hands, and when it didn't help, lowered her hands to her cheeks wearily.

"Here. Drink this." He rose, poured a large goblet of brandy from the decanter on the table and brought it to her, kneeling beside her again. She swallowed and gasped on the warmth of it. Then the tears came and wouldn't stop. She turned away, trying to control herself. The glass tilted and he took it away from her. "Carolyn. Tell me, please. This is something I know nothing about."

She tried to answer, but the sobs burst from her. She sank forward until her forehead rested on the stone hearth. Her hands hid her face from him. She was a contained woman. McAllister saw how painful it was for her to cry.

He lifted her away from the ashes, her body heavy in its grief, and folded her into his arms. She tried to push him away, but he held her against his shoulder until the last of her resistance was worn away by the tearing sobs.

"Tell me. Take your time, but tell me."

She no longer seemed to know him. Grief, fear, loneliness poured out. The occasional coherent word made no sense. He held her closely, rocking her a little, stroking the wet strands of hair from her face. "I didn't hurt you, Carolyn. It's all right. I did not hurt you."

"The mannequin," she managed finally.

"What mannequin? What are you telling me?"

"It was . . . sick . . . despicable."

"I don't understand you."

136

But the memory released another outpouring of emotion, and he had to wait longer before she began to control herself. When he finally thought she could listen to him, he tried again, holding her gently, speaking softly to her. "I don't know what happened, Carolyn. You must tell me."

Slowly she looked up. "Can I trust you, James? Can I? Or are you just like the others, pretending friendship to get something from me?"

"I know about the horse and I know about the inquest. I don't know about a mannequin and a black pall."

"There was a pall of black carnations. It was lying on a dummy. The thing was wearing my clothes and was chained in my bed. It was made to look like me. Your card was on the flowers. It said, 'I can't let you go.' I was afraid."

"My God, I should think so. Why did you think I could do a thing like that to you—to anyone? When you were so abrupt on the telephone, I sent you yellow roses, to try to tell you that I didn't want our friendship to end."

"Just before I discovered the dummy, I was at the window. I saw you run across the street and dash off in your car. I assumed you did it. Prescott didn't say anything to change my assumption. Don't you work for Ingram and Winfrey full time?"

"Yes, I do. But not that. My God, it's incredible. What did you do with the thing?"

"I called Prescott."

"And?"

"He said it was not your style. But I wasn't convinced."

"It's the sort of sadistic prank Ingram likes. I would guess he arranged it to frighten you. Now, listen. I want you safe. I want to help you if you'll let me. That's why I brought you here." He smoothed another strand of hair from her face, his fingers lingering beside her cheek, wiping the tears away with gentle hands.

"And am I any safer here?"

He smiled. "You can't find this place unless you've been here in daylight. And they haven't been. Were you indicted today?"

"They called it off at the last minute. But I would have been."

"You're being framed. Let me help you out of it."

"And in return you want the money David is supposed to have taken from Michaux?"

"I don't want the money."

"But Michaux does. And if you obtained it from me, you'd stand to gain with him."

He nodded.

"That's what you want, isn't it?"

"Let's say it's safer that way."

"What do you need to know?"

"How much he took, how he took it, where it is."

"You mean you don't know any of that?" She was incredulous. Hood had been right after all.

"No. They didn't know he had taken anything for a long time. Winfrey was suspicious first. Last September he accused David of embezzling from the two mutual funds, but particularly from the European Investors Fund, in which Michaux has the heaviest investment. David was furious and defended his innocence so convincingly that Michaux believed him. Then Winfrey retracted his accusation, apologized to David, and gave Michaux a report that seemed to resolve everything. But last month Ingram became alarmed and sent LeClere to America to audit the funds' assets and records. Sure enough, large sums had disappeared, but he was unable to determine the exact amount and who had made away with it. They suspected that David had stashed it in a Swiss account. When Ingram learned from you that such an account exists, they were convinced of David's guilt. Their contact in Switzerland said you have access to the account. Michaux needs this money to recoup some losses and start over. That is why they want you so badly. I think they would leave you alone if you returned it. Did David take it? How much is in the account?"

She regarded him gravely, wondering if she could trust him. He waited. Finally she sighed. "I didn't know there was an account. Prescott found the checkbook and gave it to me. There aren't any balances shown."

"Do you have the account number?"

"No."

"Are you sure? It would have six digits."

She thought of the locket. Her security, David had said. But to McAllister she shook her head no.

"We will have to go to Switzerland to find out about it. The bank has to have your signature and identification on file. Since he didn't give you the number, it may not be a numbered account; if it is, he must have made special arrangements to assure your access."

"You would go with me?"

"Of course. You know you can't go alone. Michaux and Ingram think you are in on it with David. You have seen how they are."

"Are other investors affected by the theft or is it just Michaux's money that's gone?"

"Of course there are others, many of them small shareholders in your own country."

"Would Michaux let me hold out their share? Would he accept payment through legal channels?"

"No. He can't afford publicity. The money didn't come to him under very legal circumstances."

"Then I don't want to risk myself to return stolen money to a thief. Let the Swiss keep it."

"He will kill you if necessary to get it."

"The dead can't write checks."

"Carolyn! The dead can take a long time dying. You would write it."

"And where would you be while this was happening? Or am I not any safer here after all?"

"I'm just one! I can swear you'll stay alive only if you help me."

"I doubt that Scotland Yard would let me leave the country. I am their primary suspect."

"Then we must break the frame. We'll make those two witnesses back down."

"How?"

"Rattle their cages. They were willing to testify against you for money. They should recant for money too."

She believed him. But still she was distrustful. "What were you doing in the hotel last night if you didn't have anything to do with the mannequin?" she asked.

"I was in the lobby when I called you. When you told me what had happened, I knew you were in danger. So I watched you. In fact, I followed you. When Jackson Hood joined you, I knew you were safe as long as you were with him. When Hood brought you in, I followed you to your suite. Everything was quiet, so I thought you were safe for the night. As I was going downstairs I saw LeClere and Ingram with Michaux. It's most unusual for Michaux to leave France, so I followed him to see why he had come to London. That is when you saw me, I suppose."

"Why did he come?"

"To get you and the money."

"If you help me, what about you and Michaux? He won't be pleased to have you working against him."

"I'll take my chances he will be arrested fairly soon. Anything we find out, you report to Prescott so the law can close him down."

"And if it doesn't?"

"I will risk it."

"What do you want from me?"

He studied her, his expression suddenly disturbing. She backed away from the intensity of his gaze. "I'll tell you what I will settle for," he said finally. "When you talk to Prescott, make a favorable recommendation for me. If you can, find out when, or if, they plan to arrest Michaux. Then warn me so I can get out."

"Can't you get out now?"

"Michaux doesn't just let people resign."

"And if the money isn't there?"

"Then I report that to Michaux."

She considered him gravely. Finally she nodded assent. It was a bargain, of sorts.

A slow grin warmed his face. "Good. You won't regret it. Now. You are soaked. Go take a hot bath and get into dry clothes. You are no good to me if you get sick. I'll get us something to eat. The guest room is through here." She rose, trailing the blanket, and followed him across the hall. "You won't run away again, will you?" he asked.

"You'd only catch me."

He laughed. "Yes, I would. And I'll go on catching you until you stay with me willingly. We'll eat in the living room."

Carolyn drowsed in the old-fashioned tub, hot water to her shoulders. She was relaxed, relieved that the last reckoning with McAllister had been postponed. It would be difficult to outwit him, but if there was money in that Swiss account, she didn't intend just to hand it over passively to Michaux. And her influence with McAllister was stronger than she had anticipated. Satisfied, she finally climbed out, found her wool robe in her suitcase, and dressed. Her hair was still wet. She pinned it back and left it hanging.

McAllister was waiting by the fire, a platter of cold cuts and bread, cups of hot homemade soup, and brandy on the low table before him. "Help yourself," he invited. She spread mustard on brown bread and made a ham sandwich. He filled her glass and they ate in silence.

When she had eaten, he offered her his cigarette case and held his lighter. They smoked quietly, their silence a restful one. "I want you to tell me everything you know about the testimony the witnesses plan to give," James said after a while. "I'll need to know about it for tomorrow."

"We talk to the witnesses tomorrow?"

"Yes. And when we finish with that, we'll fly to Switzerland. By Friday morning we'll know about the money."

"Do you think I'll be able to leave the country?"

"If we are successful tomorrow, it won't matter. If not, then you'll be back by the time they discover you are gone. Now, tell me."

She talked for an hour, describing the details for him. He asked numerous questions, drawing, while she talked, on the back of an envelope. Occasionally he made a note, and then surrounded it with borders of scrolls and leaves. When he was satisfied, he folded the envelope and put it in his pocket. Carolyn was hoarse from talking and cleared her throat.

"Thirsty?" He poured their glasses full. They sipped in silence for a moment.

"You are very thorough," she said.

"I have to be if I am going to represent you."

"You must be a good lawyer."

"I am."

She smiled. "How did David get involved with Michaux?" she asked.

"Several years ago LeClere met David at a bankers' conference in Paris. LeClere is Michaux's main recruiter, so he introduced David to Michaux. Michaux liked him and offered him a job. David accepted. When David returned to New York, he obtained the blessing of his bank to establish two mutual funds. Michaux funneled in the cash to get them started. The first shareholders were Michaux's own men, and they comprised the boards of directors. Michaux gave the general orders and selected a few investments he was particularly interested in, but otherwise David had free rein. The boards were supposed to check on him, but his record was so good that they rubber-stamped everything he did. He could get new funds from Michaux whenever he wanted. New investors were buying in. The records of both funds were excellent. Shares were in demand. And everybody was happy. Well, early last year the price of the shares began to slide. For a while the market situation covered for David."

"Until Winfrey got suspicious?"

"Yes. That was the first time. Since it was resolved so easily, David felt his position with Michaux was strong. When he found LeClere meddling in his books last month, he complained so bitterly that LeClere was called home. But LeClere had learned enough to know he needed a team of auditors. He recommended that he be given that team. Instead, David was called to London."

"Was that the meeting Friday?"

"Yes. I was there. David handled himself brilliantly. He agreed to the audit, even appeared eager for it. He seemed to satisfy them. At least, *he* thought he had. But they realized he had actually told them nothing. David was a fine talker."

"And the money?"

"He didn't admit there was any missing."

"I see."

"They were angry. Ingram ordered pressure on David to see if they could frighten him into some sort of admission."

"And what were you doing?"

"Listening. They don't welcome my opinions yet. I am in more than I want, but I'm not that involved."

"Was David murdered?"

McAllister looked at her sharply, saw the misery in her eyes and turned to study the brandy in his glass, rotating it between his hands to catch the firelight. "The timing seems all wrong for it to have been murder. They needed him alive to get the money. But the other things that have happened, especially the taxi driver's death, suggest maybe it *was* murder. You said Winfrey was dead. What about Marjorie?"

"She too. I identified the bodies this afternoon."

"I'm sorry you had to endure that. What was your impression of the accident at the time?"

"David *was* frightened. He suddenly was in a terrible hurry to get back to New York. The man who followed me today was following David then. It upset him terribly. But David stumbled so unexpectedly. It wasn't like him to be so clumsy. How were they going to scare him?"

"That was it. Winfrey was to order a man named Thorpe to shadow David and to let him *know* he was being followed. Ingram definitely did not plan to murder David. Something went wrong and no one in that argument at the Winfreys' Sunday night seemed to know what. Ingram was bitter. John and Marjorie were pretty silent. That's somewhat unusual. In conjunction with their murders, it may imply a double cross of some sort."

"What were you doing in the garden that night?"

He looked so startled that she smiled. Then he laughed—a deep, merry laugh with real enjoyment in it. "Trying to see what Ingram and Haskins were doing."

"And?"

"I didn't get close enough to hear. Haskins was Winfrey's man, but he and Ingram seemed to come to some sort of agreement that night. Haskins has a record for armed assault. He was Winfrey's hatchet man. He could have murdered Winfrey for Ingram. He could have murdered David, for that matter."

"Why would they have to kill Marjorie too?"

"I don't know. She was his partner in everything he did. Perhaps they thought she was as guilty as he was."

"What a group! I can't believe David didn't know about them."

"He knew. Some of Michaux's history isn't known, but it isn't difficult to find out about the others. You should know why he joined them better than I would."

She nodded. "Why did you?"

"Ingram referred a little business to me. There was nothing unusual or even illegal about the first assignments so I accepted others. One thing led to another. And the pay is quite good."

She stared into the fire. McAllister watched her as she twisted the sash on her robe. After a moment he reached out and stopped her hand. "Relax. You aren't still afraid of me, are you?"

She smiled. "A little."

"I just hope you are not as afraid of me as you were of your husband."

She looked at him sharply. "What makes you think I was afraid of David?"

"I know you. I knew him. Quite a few people had cause to fear him."

"Who?"

"People who had properties that he wanted. He was good at forcing them to sell out on ruinous terms. How did he persuade you to marry him?"

"I wanted to marry him," she answered. "What did he do?"

"Are you sure you want to know?"

"Tell me."

"The first example I knew of was the owner of some good property in central London. He was willing to sell at a fair value, but that wasn't good enough for David or Ingram. This man had a little daughter about four years old. David devised a plan which Ingram executed. The girl was kidnapped and kept in a shack in some woods in the west of England. She caught pneumonia and went without treatment for several days while the police searched. She was returned only after the owner gave in. And it was just a matter of a few thousand pounds or so."

Carolyn felt sick. "What happened to the girl?"

"She pulled through, but it was a battle. The man tried desperately to collect himself financially, but he was already heavily in debt and failed. He shot himself. His widow went into bankruptcy. The last I heard, she was clerking in a store in London and trying to learn to type. There are other instances of blackmail and extortion. A man with a sense of cruelty that refined couldn't have hidden it completely."

"And what was your role in this?"

He had hurt her badly. "It was some time before I knew them. Marjorie told me. She was my primary informant. I am sorry. You wanted to know."

She rose. "I don't want to hear any more. May I go to bed now?"

He ignored her outburst. "You are loyal to the memory of your husband, and I believe a wife should be loyal. But if you are to have any kind of happiness in the future, you cannot gloss over David's failings just because you married him. You cannot turn him into any kind of misunderstood hero, because he wasn't. He was totally amoral, and you should be honest enough with yourself to recognize and accept it and go on."

"I can take care of myself. Just you make sure you deal honestly with me."

He rose and took her arm, his fingers tangling in the hair tumbling over her shoulder. "No. I don't lie to you. And I will make you a promise. I promise that you will come out of this all right."

He extricated his fingers from her hair, stepped closer to her and pushed the falling strands from her face. He was looking directly into her eyes and Carolyn knew he wanted to kiss her again. She closed her hand gently over his wrist where it lay on her shoulder and put it firmly from her.

"I hope so," she said.

She stepped away and crossed the hall to the bedroom. He heard the door close and the old latch fall into place, locking her in.

17

•

Faint rustling awakened Carolyn. She raised her head. A new fire was burning in the hearth. Sunlight poured into the room. A door in the paneling she hadn't noticed before was open beside the fireplace. "Who's there?" she called cautiously.

"Good morning. I am Ida Connally." A little acorn of a woman came into sight at the foot of the bed. "I have brushed your coat. It doesn't look too bad. Are you ready for tea? Or would you prefer coffee?"

"Coffee, please."

Carolyn was almost dressed when Mrs. Connally returned with a silver coffee service. She poured the coffee into a thin bone china cup. It was very good and Carolyn complimented her on it.

"It's just coffee brewed in an old metal pot," Mrs. Connally said, pleased in spite of her modesty. She was lingering, obviously interested in talking.

"Have you been with Mr. McAllister long?" Carolyn asked.

"I've been here since long before he was born. His grandmother, Mrs. Stanhope, employed me to care for Mr. Stanhope in his last illness. By the time he died, Mrs. Stanhope was ill. And after she passed on, Mrs. McAllister was expecting. So I stayed on. I was here the night Mr. McAllister was born. A dreadful stormy night it was, and Mrs. McAllister was having a fairly difficult time of it. But what a fine, lusty lad he was. He looked just like Mr. Stanhope, which would have pleased him no end had he known. Captain and Mrs. McAllister were so proud of him. They had been married a long time and I think they had given up hope of having children of their own. Mr. McAllister was the only Stanhope and the only McAllister of his generation. He could have been terribly spoiled. But his nature is too fine for that. The McAllisters were such a close family. That was why Mrs. McAllister and James went to London with the captain when the war came."

"Yes. He told me."

"He did?" Mrs. Connally looked at Carolyn with greater interest. "He's never spoken of it to me. Mr. James was lucky to have his Grandmother McAllister. A fine woman, she was, God rest her soul, but poor, very poor. She did well by him. And he by her too. He didn't come back home until after she died fifteen years ago."

"He lives here full time now?"

"Yes. He goes up to London for a few days now and then, but when he comes back, he always says how good it is to be home. Just like that—'How good it is to be home.' Then the first chance he gets, he takes Old Maud—that's his mare—and rides over the place. He'll be gone most all day. When he comes in at dark, he eats a big supper and falls asleep in his chair. Old Maud is too old and he ought to sell her, but if I know Mr. James, she'll end her days in clover."

Mrs. Connally paused to pour more coffee for Carolyn before continuing. "Many people in the village have cause to be grateful to Mr. McAllister, me included. He always seems to know when someone is in trouble. Several years ago when my husband and I were both down with the bronchitis, Mr. McAllister came every night for a whole fortnight and cooked supper for us."

"Extraordinary," Carolyn murmured. She couldn't visualize David Bruce cooking supper for anyone, not even for himself.

"It's like him. He kept paying my wages too. That saved us, because my husband wasn't working regularly and there wasn't anything else coming in."

"It seems fair," Carolyn murmured.

"That's what he said. Said I hadn't missed any and I deserved it. And when young Sammie Harned was run over and his legs broken so bad he couldn't go to school, Mr. McAllister tutored him. The boy passed all his exams and didn't have to stay behind his class. But Mr. McAllister doesn't like to be thanked. It embarrasses him. He helps quiet like, and it's usually something unexpected but very thoughtful, like cooking or tutoring. Would you like more coffee?"

"No, thank you. I've had enough."

"Then I'll go and put breakfast on the table." She took up the tray, but at the door she turned. "I'm glad you came. He called up early yesterday morning and said to be ready for a lady guest. Sent me scurrying to clean, stock up and get things ready for you. He seemed real excited that you were coming."

"I didn't know I was," Carolyn answered. "How did he know?"

"He did say you hadn't accepted his invitation yet, but he seemed real pleased that you might. I am glad you did. He is alone too much. You'll find the dining room just beyond the drawing room."

James was already sitting at the banquet table, the newspaper spread beside him, when Carolyn entered the dining room. He was absorbed, meticulously checking the financial pages, his head bent as he ran his finger down the quotations. He looked up as she slipped into the chair beside him.

"There you are," he exclaimed. He folded the paper and turned to her eagerly. "I hope you slept well? The bed wasn't too hard?"

"I was too tired to notice."

"Good." He passed her the platter of eggs and ham. They ate in companionable silence. The rest of the house seemed bare, but this room was beautifully, even lavishly, furnished. Chinese vases, a pair of seven-branched candelabra, and portraits blended tastefully with Chippendale furniture. Carolyn liked what she saw and told James so.

"I'm glad you like it. I was surprised at what I found in the attic. The rest I bought from my winnings at cards. The portrait over the mantelpiece is on approval."

It was a portrait of a lady in an eighteenth-century morning gown, her head turned slightly, a gentle smile on her lips.

"Are you going to keep it?" Carolyn asked.

"Yes. She reminds me very much of you. When you are finished, we had better go. Are you packed?"

"Yes. I left the suitcase on the bed."

As Carolyn finished her breakfast, her mind returned to the things Mrs. Connally had said. Her picture of James McAllister was infinitely more trustworthy than the man Carolyn had seen so far. Carolyn wanted to believe her. She didn't dare.

The dark lane of the night before was not so long nor so forbidding as it had seemed in the sleet and rain. The trees lining the road would be a cool arcade in summer. Beyond them, in open fields, game birds were feeding.

"Pheasants?" Carolyn asked in pleased surprise.

"This is a game preserve. We feed the birds all winter and there is limited hunting in season. Look over there by the trees."

Carolyn's gaze followed McAllister's pointing finger. The doe blended into the underbrush and she didn't see it until, hearing the sound of the car, it turned and leaped into the bushes. She smiled with pleasure. "Do you hunt?" she asked.

"No. They are too much like pets. The deer are an expensive nuisance. They have to be tended as carefully as a herd of fine cattle or horses, but I like having them here. Mrs. Connally's husband is the gamekeeper. Shall I show you my favorite spot?"

"I would like to see it."

They crossed a crested stone bridge on the edge of the village and turned down the hill. James stopped the car beside a stone wall and helped her out.

The air was sparkling clear and quiet. The millpond mirrored the scene without a marring ripple. On the opposite bank a swan fussily preened her feathers, her neck turning gracefully. When she was satisfied, she slipped into the water. The wake of her swimming disturbed the scene like the train of a shimmering skirt. James leaned against the parapet watching the swan, his face relaxed and at peace, deeply happy. During her entire married life, Carolyn had never seen David look so contented.

"Now do you see what England offers?" James asked after a moment.

"You love it here, don't you?"

"It's home," he said simply.

"More than the Highlands?"

"I grew up in the Highlands and I'm fond of the place. But this is where I'll live." A serious, moody look crossed his face. "I want you to do something for me."

"What is that?"

"Don't take everything at face value. Look behind words and actions for the truths that motivate them."

"I can do that."

"I made you a promise last night, a promise I'll keep. But if you don't search for the deeper significance of things, it may seem that I haven't."

"I don't understand."

He turned and looked at her for a long moment. Then he smiled a little ruefully. "No, I suppose not. I'm talking in riddles." He reached and turned her chin into the light. "I hit you harder than I thought. I'm sorry." Awareness hovered then between them. A smile, one almost of sadness, touched his lips. His hand dropped to his side. "Shall we go?" he asked.

18
.

Carolyn gazed quietly out as they drove through the village and took the route they had followed the night before. In the daylight there was a warmth and a Constable charm to the dun landscape. McAllister demanded nothing from her in conversation. The rumble of his voice, with its faint overtones of Scottish brogue, was restful, almost hypnotic. It lulled her into lethargy and a strange fatalism. David and the accident seemed very far away and unreal. McAllister had taken over.

"Who lives here?" Carolyn asked. Her mind returned to the present as they turned through wooden gates and an idyllic scene opened before them.

"We'll talk to Mrs. Lester first. She should give us a frank account of the accident. It is nice, isn't it?"

It was a pretty house with a thatched roof. Flower beds were banked and composted, waiting for spring seeding. Two spaniels leaped around them barking, their paws furry and muddy.

"Let me do the talking," James said as he pulled the bell.

Mrs. Lester answered the door. A pencil was stuck through her curls. She seemed preoccupied. "Yes? It's . . . it's Mrs. Bruce, isn't it?"

"And I am James McAllister. May we speak with you a moment about the accident?"

"Well, yes, I suppose so. I've told all I know. Won't you come in?"

Her library was a comfortable jumble of books and papers. It wore the look of a much loved room. Carolyn began to feel more optimistic as Mrs. Lester cleared a place on the sofa and shooed another spaniel from the rug at their feet. "How may I help you?" she asked when they were seated.

"Since the inquest was postponed, you may not realize how very serious Mrs. Bruce's position is," James began. "But if you heard Mrs. Philpot's denunciation, you may have guessed the nature of the charges that would have been made against her."

"Yes. I don't understand it. We—I was very close to her and I saw everything that happened. I can't imagine how that woman could say what she did."

"We? Who is we?"

Mrs. Lester hesitated a moment, fingering and knotting her pearls. She made up her mind. "That was my subconscious speaking. And the only right thing to do is to tell you. I was not alone. A friend was with me and saw the accident, too. She didn't wish to become involved."

"Who is your friend?"

"Sophia Monroe. Mrs. Archibald Monroe. She lives on Bruton Place. We have been lifelong friends and I spend almost every Friday with her in town. I am a writer. Listening to other people's conversations frequently gives me ideas for my stories. Sophia helps me. She has a good eye and a good ear. We were watching you and your husband very closely, Mrs. Bruce. I can understand why she didn't want to become involved. Her husband is prominent in the government and it could be somewhat embarrassing for her to be seen in court. But if the circumstances are as serious as you say, she would be willing to testify for you. She would be a respected witness. It should help."

"Were all the witnesses familiar to you?" James asked. "That is, did you actually see those who attended the inquest at the scene of the accident?"

She considered carefully. "Now that you mention it, the only one I remember seeing was the driver of a white panel truck. He jumped out and bent over Mr. Bruce. He was quite distraught and it took him some time to calm down enough to tell the police what he had seen. He sat near me at the inquest."

"And Mrs. Frye? She is a large blonde woman. Did you see her?"

"She was at the inquest, but I'm sorry, I didn't see her at the scene of the accident."

"And Mr. Lisle? He was in a car in the lane nearest the curb."

"There was a car there, an older model green Morris. There was a man at the wheel, but I couldn't swear to his identity under oath."

James was making notes. Carolyn saw him write "Lisle, green Morris" and two question marks.

"You have been most helpful, Mrs. Lester, and we appreciate it very much. We will call on Mrs. Monroe. Her husband is a deputy minister of finance, isn't he?"

"Yes, that's right."

James rose to go. Carolyn thanked Mrs. Lester profusely. She felt that the older woman had literally saved her life. Words were totally inadequate for her gratitude.

"What a stroke of luck!" Carolyn exclaimed as they drove down the lane and took the road to London. "I feel reprieved."

James smiled but made no comment. Carolyn glanced at him. He wasn't as optimistic as she was, and it was an instantly sobering discovery.

Mrs. Monroe was at home. The uniformed butler showed them into an ornate French living room. Mrs. Monroe came in immediately. A Pekingese was under her arm. Carolyn and James exchanged glances. She put the dog down. It pattered immediately to James and curled against his leg, leaving long orange hairs on his black trousers.

"I have been expecting you. Susannah Lester called me. I hate publicity and do try to avoid it. I had no idea, though, that it would be considered anything more than an unfortunate accident. I am glad to help you, Mrs. Bruce, but I do hope it will not involve my being in court. Mr. Monroe would not like that at all."

"Can you tell us what you saw, Mrs. Monroe?"

Her account corroborated Mrs. Lester's almost exactly. Mrs. Lester had been standing just behind Carolyn's shoulder on the left, Mrs. Monroe on the right. "And then I saw your husband stumble. He seemed to trip over another man who was walking beside him. He tried to catch himself but couldn't."

"Can you describe the man?"

"He was a big man, middle-aged, gray-haired, from what I could see under his cap. He was wearing a gabardine coat. I saw him only from the back and profile. He was quite powerful-looking—big shoulders, big feet, big head—an athlete, maybe. He moved well."

James was scribbling once more. "Could you recognize him if you saw him again?"

"I might, especially if I saw him from that angle and in motion He jumped out of the way. People scattered when they realized the taxi wasn't going to stop. This man went on across the street and didn't return, as some of the others did. Since I didn't stay, I don' know what happened after that."

"Can you describe the vehicles around the accident?"

"The taxi, of course. A white panel truck and a green Morris in the near lane. Also, I recall a young man on a motor scooter. He jacked his scooter up on the curb and helped hold the crowd back."

"Can you describe him?"

"Long hair, scraggly whiskers, but a rather nice face under it all Dungarees and a brown corduroy jacket. I believe he may have been questioned by the police."

"Did you observe a big blonde woman near you trying to hail a taxi?"

"Not that I remember."

"Would you mind calling Superintendent Prescott at Scotland Yard and telling him what you have just told me?"

"Right now?"

"Please. Describe the man that Mr. Bruce tripped over. It may be quite important."

Mrs. Monroe left the room. Her shoes clicked on the marble floor in the hall as she crossed to the telephone in the library. James followed her to the hall door, where he stood, his head cocked, listening to her end of the conversation. He had resumed his seat beside Carolyn when Mrs. Monroe returned to the room.

"The superintendent will send someone to take a formal statement. Is there anything else I can do for you?"

"Thank you, no. We are most grateful to you. This will be a significant help to Mrs. Bruce."

"Then you are most welcome. Let me have the dog. He doesn't usually take to strangers. You must have a way with animals."

From the neighborhood of elegant town houses and expensive shops, James drove across London. Carolyn had to get the city map from the glove compartment and call the turns in their search for Adelaide Frye.

"Where did you get her address?" Carolyn asked.

"From the telephone book. Now, Harvey Lisle isn't in a business that benefits from a phone. I got his address from a reporter friend of mine who was at the hearing."

"You do have connections," Carolyn murmured. He looked at her quickly, but she missed his glance. She was bent over the map, turning it, tracing their route. "Turn left here," she said at last, "and start looking for the house number."

The Mercedes made its way cautiously down the dingy street. Garbage cans overflowed into the gutters and deprived dogs picked in the litter. Just past an old bomb crater, James parked carefully, avoiding a splatter of broken glass. Broken steps led into Adelaide's tenement, where an odor of dirty toilets and cabbage enveloped them. A pasteboard arrow tacked on the wall pointed to *Adelaide Frye—Massage—Second Floor*.

"This may be ugly," James said as he saw the sign. "But I can't leave you down here."

"I've seen prostitutes before."

"But have you visited one who lives like this? Let me go first."

Adelaide's door had accumulated the scars of numerous locks. A furry voice finally answered McAllister's impatient knocks. Grudgingly the bolts slid back and revealed a flushed Mrs. Frye. Yesterday's lipstick was smeared over her face and chin. A filthy wrapper hung open. She greeted James with a lascivious interest that changed to snarling reluctance when she caught sight of Carolyn. She tried to slam the door, but McAllister stiff-armed it violently against the wall and stepped inside. Carolyn followed. She had to catch her breath again. The flat reeked of sex and liquor. An empty bottle and two cheese glasses lay overturned on the floor by the bed. But the new alligator shoes and handbag were placed carefully side by side on the dresser.

"Who are you? What are you doing breaking down my door?"

"I'm Mrs. Bruce's solicitor. You do remember Mrs. Bruce, don't you?"

"What do you want? I told all I know to the police."

"You told all you know, but did you tell the truth?" McAllister asked.

Carolyn stood by the door. She didn't want to sit in the room's only chair.

"I don't know what you're talking about." The woman slouched to the window, raised it, and took orange juice and milk from the outside sill. She filled a teapot from the basin in the corner and put it on a hot plate. The odor of stale tea began to fill the room.

"No one saw you at the scene of the accident."

"I can't help that."

"For someone whose testimony is so important, I think it very strange that you didn't tarry to talk to the police on Friday afternoon."

"I couldn't wait for all that. I did my duty. I called in as soon as I could."

"You didn't talk to the police that afternoon because you weren't there."

"I was there."

"Were you, now? You waited so long, why did you bother at all?"

"I couldn't let her get away with it."

"I see." McAllister calmly plucked the alligator bag from the bureau, opened it and took out a roll of bills. "Where did you get this?" he asked.

"I earned it."

"How?"

She made a vulgar gesture.

"You're not in that class. You couldn't earn this much in six months. Who bribed you?"

She let out a stream of invective. McAllister grabbed her wrist and delivered a stinging slap against one cheek. "Who bribed you?"

"Nobody! I earned it."

Another slap. "Come on."

Carolyn watched, numb. There was an expression of extreme distaste on McAllister's face, and intentness too.

"You stinking bastard. You son of—" The flat of McAllister's hand cut her off.

"Do you know the penalties for perjury? For illegal prostitution? For accepting a bribe?" McAllister was leaning very close to her, spitting the words out, his fingers leaving white marks on her wrist. He lowered his voice. The deep purr was more menacing than his anger. "And do you know what your pals will do when they are through with you? I'll tell you. Remember the taxi driver? He was found in the Thames, his feet in a block of concrete. You'll be found the same way. Now, come on. Make it easy for yourself."

He read acquiescence in her eyes and released her. She snatched her wrist back and regarded him speculatively, rubbing the marks. "I'll tell you. For a consideration."

"If I like what you say, I don't turn you in. That's all. Now, what really happened?"

"You're right. I wasn't there. Late Monday night a man called me and asked did I want to make some money. I said sure I did. So he said to come to his hotel. I thought he wanted the usual, so I went."

"What hotel was that?"

"The one by Paddington Station. He gave me his room number, but he didn't tell me his name."

"What was the room number?"

"Two thirty-six."

"Go on."

"When I got there, he told me the deal. I didn't want to do it. When he threatened me, I said I would. He gave me half the fee and said I would have the other half when all the testifying was over. He told me what to do and what to say. He made me go over and over it. He even told me what to wear. As though I needed to be told that. I know what the swells wear."

"Did you ever get his name?"

"Herbert Smith, from Bristol."

"Describe him."

"A little chap. Late forties, maybe fifty. Black eyes. Kind of a greaser. He looked like a salesman."

"Was he an Englishman? Or a foreigner?"

"He did talk funny. Not very funny. Just a little. Canada, maybe."

"Would you recognize him again?"

"Sure."

"Have you seen him since?"

"No."

"Are you to see him again?"

"He said he would call and we would set up a time."

"What about Lisle?"

"Who is he?"

"He was a big fellow, going bald, at the inquest."

"What about him?"

"Was he bribed, too?"

"I don't know. I didn't see him before the inquest anyway."

"Was anything said to imply that Smith might have bribed another witness?"

"No. Yes, wait a minute. He did say I wouldn't be alone there— that my story would not be alone, I mean."

"Tell me exactly what he said about that."

"I asked him how he thought I could get away with it. He said I wouldn't be alone up there. That's all."

"Very well. Now I want you to call Superintendent Prescott at Scotland Yard and tell him what you told me. Ask for police protection."

She looked hard at McAllister. "Yeah, maybe I better. What's the number?"

Carolyn told her and they listened while she called. "He's not there. What do I do?" Adelaide asked, her hand over the mouthpiece.

"Who is that?"

"His secretary."

"Then tell her."

The secretary apparently asked why she was changing her story. "I'm scared. He was mean," Adelaide said. That must have been a satisfactory answer, because she hung up. "They're sending a car for me," she said.

"Good. Now get dressed. They will be here faster than you expect."

"You turn your back," she said. "Or better yet, send her out and we will have a party. There's plenty of time."

"I do my own inviting," McAllister snapped. "We'll wait outside until they come for you."

Carolyn and James watched from the stairs as Adelaide identified herself to the two constables. She flashed them a challenging smile as she entered the police car.

"She must love her work," Carolyn said. She was deeply relieved that they could leave the malodorous tenement at last.

He looked at her. "You sound surprised! Do I have a women's lib fanatic on my hands?"

"Just a pussycat. But they have claws."

"They bite too," he said, touching the tender spot on his lip.

At her expression, his laughter boomed. He reached and hugged her to him, his eyes alive in his joy of her. She left his grasp and ran down the front steps ahead of him. He was still grinning when he joined her at the car.

"If your friend Lisle is as cooperative as Adelaide Frye, we can go to Switzerland on the early flight," he said.

"My friend! He's your friend! Or rather, a friend of your friends."

"That's better." They laughed together. Carolyn's morale lifted.

His persuasive technique was crude. Having felt the force of his fist, Carolyn wasn't entirely out of sympathy with Adelaide. But she was relieved that the morning, at least, had succeeded. They glanced at each other, then looked away.

"Shall I call the turns for you?" she asked in a businesslike tone, and bent over the map.

The sunlight caught in the waves of her hair. She was lovely, desirable, her laughter refreshing and winning. It was the taste of what she would be without David Bruce. James wanted her, now more than before. But there was almost no chance that she would reciprocate his feeling. The awareness, the sensitivity, the consciousness of each other was a fragile thing, threatened by her alertness for the first sign of his betrayal. And when it came? It was so hurtful a thought that his fist tightened on the wheel and a sigh of pain escaped him. She looked up questioningly. In that instant he wondered how he could have struck her. He smiled tightly. "Guide me back to central London. I know where to go from there."

19

Lisle's boardinghouse was across the street from the city bus terminal. James found a parking spot and whipped the Mercedes into it with a neat twist of his wrist.

The woman who answered the door had been scrubbing. Her hands were still wet and shriveled. A faint scent of ammonia hung in the hall behind her.

"Does Harvey Lisle live here?" James asked.

"Yes."

"Is he in?"

"He works the seven-to-three shift. He comes in about three thirty."

"It's almost that now. May we go up and wait?"

"It's not permitted."

"The lady is tired. Do you have a place for her to sit down?"

"We have no public room here."

A five-pound note flashed in James's hand. The woman looked at it and at him. She nodded. The bill disappeared into her apron pocket and she took them up to Lisle's flat on the third floor. The building was clean but drab.

"Now, don't you disturb anything. He's particular about his things."

"Of course not."

The woman was interested. She eyed Carolyn's coat. "Well. I will send him up. Who shall I say is waiting for him?"

"Two friends. It's a surprise."

"But I need to know—"

"Don't spoil it for him."

The woman hesitated, then nodded. She reluctantly left them alone, looking backward curiously as she closed the door behind her. James waited a moment, checked the hall outside the door, and then bolted it.

"What are you going to do?"

James silenced her with a gesture, indicating she was to stand at the door and listen. Carolyn did as she was told while he methodically and rapidly searched the apartment. When he was finished, she unbolted the door again and sank gracefully onto the old Morris sofa. She leaned back and lit a cigarette. "Did you find anything?"

"Nothing that looks like sudden wealth."

"Maybe he spent it."

"On what?"

For answer Carolyn leaned over and fished a magazine out of the rack and showed it to him. Vulgar nudes and copulating couples. James leafed through it, raised his brows and handed it back. "How do you know about this?"

"It's difficult to miss."

"You've seen him. Is Lisle the type to spend a great deal on women?"

"He's not effete. Otherwise, I couldn't say."

"Then it's possible."

"Maybe he sent it to his old mother."

"Would he have an old mother? Stashed away in the country, perhaps?"

"It *is* hard to visualize, sure enough." Wearily she stubbed out her cigarette and put the ashtray on the coffee table.

"Tired?" James asked, coming to sit down beside her.

"Five whole pounds' worth."

He laughed. "Have some lunch." He broke a chocolate bar and gave her half. They munched in silence.

"Lisle won't talk as easily as Adelaide," Carolyn said, wiping her fingers clean one by one. "He will hit back."

"He's a tough chap, then?"

"He looks strong."

"Then I will play my part as Winfrey's employee." He took out his watch, making a slow ceremony of it. "Almost time. Go look and see if he's coming. Don't let him see you."

Some minutes passed. Once she turned to see James lazily study-ing her, his eyes half closed. She turned quickly again. Lisle was crossing the street below. "Here he comes," she said quietly. Mc-Allister rose and looked over her shoulder.

"All right. Take that chair there." He stood beside her, behind the door of the apartment.

Lisle had obviously been warned by the landlady that he had guests. He came in briskly. "Who's here? Ellie? Ted? Is it you?" Mc-Allister stepped behind him and closed the door. The little click of the latch sounded quietly ominous. Lisle whirled. His face closed. "What do you want?"

"I want to talk to you about the Bruce case."

"What's it to you?"

"The woman, Adelaide Frye, has changed her story. The old lady is crazy. Another witness has confirmed Mrs. Bruce's story. Herbert Smith has been identified and is in custody. The whole operation has come apart. We have Mrs. Bruce now, so it doesn't matter. She's going to cooperate. However, we cannot allow you to commit per-jury in public. There's a job we want you to do in about six weeks' time, so you can't go to prison. We want you to go to the police and tell them you were coerced into giving the statement you did. Then tell the truth."

"Who are you?"

"I work for Winfrey and Ingram."

"I don't know them."

"They set up the operation and sent me here."

The man's eyes flickered uneasily. He shoved his fingers into his hip pockets, teetered on the balls of his feet, flexing and stretching his muscles. He was a powerful man. "What's in it for me?"

"Big money this time. The operations are lucrative. With Smith removed, you get his cut of the profits in exchange for his share of the duties. If we like you, that is."

"And if I don't go to the police?"

"That's your choice, of course. But if you don't follow orders, we could no longer depend on your loyalty. You couldn't work for us again. In fact, you would be a threat." McAllister shrugged with Gallic expressiveness. "We can't run the risk that you will spill your guts some night and talk. But it's your choice." He pulled Carolyn roughly to her feet, and holding her wrist, turned to leave.

"Wait a minute." Lisle stopped him. "What do you want me to do?"

"Call Superintendent Prescott at Scotland Yard. Tell him what happened, who coached you, what you were paid, what you saw of the accident yourself and what you were told to say. The whole business."

"What about Clark? Won't he be arrested?"

"He's a liability to us now. The Yard is already onto him. It won't matter about him."

"When do I get my cut?"

"Beginning next month, a monthly cash salary of one hundred pounds. Plus special payment for any jobs you do. A Christmas bonus of one percent of the profits."

"One percent! That's peanuts."

"One percent of a million pounds a year? That's ten thousand pounds. More, of course, if it is a good year."

Lisle licked his lips. He wiped his face with a suddenly shaking hand, rasping the stubble on his chin. Carolyn waited apprehensively. McAllister seemed supremely confident. Once again she wondered.

"Don't I get anything now?"

"Certainly not. The police should have no suspicion of your connection with us. If you carry large sums around, they will be watching you like the royal lions. That comes later."

"I want some honest money, nevertheless. I'll need to pay my rent."

"Well—if you wish." James took his wallet from his inside pocket and counted out some notes. "All right?"

"Yes. The old bitch doesn't ask any questions if she's paid ahead."

"That's good thinking. You will be a good man, Lisle."

"Yeah. Do I tell the police I have talked to you?"

"Better not. Say your reason for telling the truth is that you were afraid of Clark and his associates. Don't mention our talk today or our plans. Any other questions?"

"When do I call?"

"Now. Do you have a telephone?"

"There's one in the hall."

"Go ahead, then."

Lisle left the room. James stood at the door watching, Carolyn beside him. Suddenly he shoved her roughly into the corner. Lisle

166

returned. "You double-crossing—" He lunged for McAllister, fists swinging. McAllister was ready. He blocked Lisle's fist, delivered a solid blow to his stomach that doubled him over and another to the chin that sent him reeling against the wall. Lisle fell heavily, jarring a table and overturning a pot of plastic flowers. He heaved the flowers at James and then tackled him. Both tumbled clumsily and rolled. Lisle's fists pounded James's face before McAllister could raise his knee and kick him solidly in the groin. Lisle screamed, loosened his hold and McAllister rose. Blood was running down his face. Lisle had split his eyebrow open.

"You damn fool," McAllister said coldly to the groaning man at his feet. "What's the matter with you?"

Lisle rose slowly to his knees, still holding himself. "You are not with Clark at all. You are with Mrs. Bruce. Wait until I tell them."

"You bloody idiot! What does it take to convince you? What do you think the purpose of that whole operation was? It was to scare Mrs. Bruce into giving us the money. It didn't work. So I had to go get her. I am taking her to the chief now."

"Then get her to give us the money and we will split it."

James laughed with genuine amusement. "Clark is as meek as a newborn babe in comparison to the others. You heard about the taxi driver that hit Bruce? Dead in the river, his feet in concrete. I know. I saw him put there. He crossed us. Did not do his job right. Now, you smarten up and go get on the telephone. I'll be listening to report to the chief." McAllister grabbed Carolyn roughly from the corner where she had been standing. "Now, you come along, girly, and don't give me any more trouble or you will be sorry again." He dabbed at the blood. His handkerchief was red.

"Don't call me 'girly'!" Carolyn snapped.

"I will call you what I please." McAllister took her arm, twisting viciously until she cried out. She made it a good shriek. "Girl-y girl," he sneered into her face. "Now, come on. God, have you ever seen such a dame!" he demanded of Lisle. "She's run away from me twice. But she won't run again. Will you, girl-y?"

Lisle was rising painfully to his feet. McAllister's byplay with Carolyn seemed to have removed his doubt. Slowly he crossed the room. They followed him. McAllister kept a tight grip on Carolyn's arm while Lisle telephoned. When he had finished, they went back to his flat.

"Now, you handled that just right," McAllister said. "You will earn your one percent. I can see that. We must go now. Anything else you want?"

"Her! What a lay!" Lisle grunted, his sallow skin suddenly shiny. "Will any broads like her come my way?"

James caressed Carolyn's arm possessively. "More than you will have time for," he said. "But I don't share this one. Now, remember. Not a word of our talk here. And you didn't see Mrs. Bruce either. I don't want the police after us before I'm through with her."

Lisle grinned. "Sure. I got you."

"Now, come on." McAllister led Carolyn from the room. She preceded him down the stairs and out of the house. In silence they got into the Mercedes. McAllister drove around the block and parked again in a side street. Through the intersection they could see Lisle's front door. They waited. Carolyn's arm hurt. He had given it quite a wrench. In a few minutes they saw a police car stop at Lisle's building. The constables went upstairs and in a moment returned with Lisle. Then they drove off.

"That's that," McAllister said. "I can't fly to Geneva looking like this. Can I use your suite to clean up?"

Carolyn nodded.

"Good. Can you drive?"

"Yes." They traded places. McAllister had to help her move the seat forward. "Remember. You are driving on the left."

"Sure."

He caught the coolness in her voice. He reached over and covered her hand briefly. "Did I play my part too well?"

She made no reply.

He took his hand away. "Before we leave for Geneva, call Prescott and learn about your new status. See if he'll tell you what Lisle tells them. Get names and descriptions if you can. If you noticed, I didn't mention any."

"Who do you think coached Lisle?"

"I need a description to know that. The name Clark means nothing to me. It must be an alias, as 'Herbert Smith' was."

"Who was Herbert Smith?"

"Now, he sounds like LeClere. Clark could also be LeClere. Or maybe Haskins. I doubt very much it was Ingram. He doesn't expose himself. And neither does Winfrey—did Winfrey, I mean. That business about Clark and Smith being in custody seemed like a useful fabrication."

"I didn't know how the driver died. Do you see him murdered?"

For answer he took a newspaper clipping from his wallet. "From today's *Times.*"

Carolyn glanced at it as she engaged the gears and swung the car into the street. "May I tell Prescott about Thorpe? Wasn't that his name?"

"Certainly."

"And who told me?"

"Of course. Wasn't that our agreement?"

"Suppose Lisle tells the police what you said? About the one percent and all that?"

"Let him. I didn't tell him my name. They will find out there is nothing to it soon enough."

Carolyn drove in silence, concentrating on the traffic. It was an odd feeling, driving on the left, and she wasn't confident. At the stoplight she looked at him again. He met her gaze. He was a mess. His shirt was ruined. His handkerchief was soaked. His eye needed a stitch to avoid scarring. There was a nasty scrape across one cheekbone. He wasn't bleeding any more, however. "And another thing," she said as the light changed and she swung toward Hyde Park, "don't ever call me 'girl-y girl' again. It's so . . . scummy!"

McAllister's laughter rang out. It was infectious, relieved, joyous even. "God knows what sobriquets I will give you before this is over, but, believe me, I prefer more endearing terms for you." His voice was soft, full of laughter. Carolyn had to smile with him. But her doubt remained.

20

No one seemed to notice McAllister's disheveled condition as they moved quickly through the hotel lobby to the elevators. At the door of her suite he cautioned her to silence, took the key from her hand, and preceded her into the darkened room. She stood beside the door while he searched quickly.

"It's all right. No one is waiting for you."

"Good. I could not stand a repeat of that experience." She moved around the room, opening the curtains and turning on lights. "Can I get you anything?"

"I have everything, I think." He walked to the bedroom, put down his suitcase, and dropped his topcoat on the chair. "I could use a drink. Whisky and not too much soda."

She made drinks, left his standing on the coffee table and took hers to the chair by the window. She was tired and let down. An unpleasant sensation of dissatisfaction with the way the two witnesses had been handled overrode her relief at the outcome of the interviews. James used his fists as easily as other men wrote memos. It made her uneasy.

In a moment James came out. Carolyn had to smile. Only an Englishman would wear such a dressing gown these days. He took up his glass, raised it in a little toast to her, and swallowed deeply.

"Shouldn't that cut have a stitch?" she asked.

"It's not as serious as it looks."

"But won't it scar?"

"Probably. But I won't be disfigured." He turned away from her, back toward the bedroom, but a knock on the hall door stopped him. "Are you expecting anyone?" he asked softly.

She shook her head. He gestured for her to stand still and opened the door himself. Jackson Hood's expression turned chillingly polite. "I have been trying to reach Mrs. Bruce by telephone," he said.

"Won't you come in?" Carolyn invited.

McAllister stepped quietly aside. "What happened to you?" Hood asked as he stepped into the room.

McAllister touched his cheekbone carefully. "A rather burly gentleman misinterpreted my intentions. I was clumsy and he was faster than he looked."

"Too bad," Hood said.

"Yes, it was. Please excuse me."

Hood watched James go into the bedroom and close the door. Then he crossed the room to Carolyn and pulled a chair closer to hers. "I didn't realize you knew James McAllister well," he said, his voice carefully impersonal.

"Not so well as you think. He has been helpful."

"Then he is here with your consent?"

"Yes. Three of the witnesses to the accident have told the police I murdered my husband. Fortunately, new information was obtained, so the inquest was delayed. I almost expected to spend the night in prison."

"Wormwood Scrubs is a dreadful place."

"Wormwood Scrubs?"

"The women's prison. Do you think now you won't be indicted?"

"I hope not."

"I see."

And Carolyn knew he had guessed all that she had left unsaid and did not approve of it. Today he was not the man who had smiled and talked of ESP. He was the professional representative of his government, inquiring politely after a citizen's welfare. His demeanor was as stern as it had been at their first meeting.

"The audits of your husband's affairs will go back for six years," he was saying. "Until we have access to Mr. Bruce's own records, we can only estimate the taxes and penalties owing. Based on information derived from our own computer records for the years 1966 through 1968, the amount due will approximate two hundred thousand dollars."

"Two hundred thousand dollars! I have no idea if the estate can handle that amount. It couldn't possibly be correct!"

"These estimates undoubtedly will change on the basis of additional information. You will be given complete details when you reach New York. You should talk immediately to your lawyer and accountant—the sooner the better."

"Yes. I will."

"The audits of the European Investors Mutual Fund and of the Greater American Growth Fund are still more serious. Information has leaked out that something is amiss with the two funds. The price of shares fell fifty percent by the close of business yesterday on the New York market. Trading in shares of both funds was halted this morning. The funds may be put into receivership. The Securities and Exchange Commission will probably sue, charging that the transfer of fund assets into worthless securities damaged the shareholders—and further, that cash and securities belonging to the shareholders have been spirited away. You see, large sums of money were removed from responsible banks and transferred elsewhere—we believe to David Bruce's own bank in the Bahamas."

"What do you mean, his own bank?"

"David Bruce has owned controlling interest in a private bank in the Bahama Islands since 1969."

"I didn't know," she said faintly.

He said nothing, but regarded her steadily.

"So you think my husband is responsible?" she asked finally.

"As I said the other day, he is one of two primary suspects. The boards of directors will be charged with complicity in the self-dealing. Others may be named as the investigations continue."

"And how was the spiriting away, as you put it, accomplished?"

Hood took several pages from his briefcase and handed them to her. It was a cable, summarizing the investment transactions of the two mutual funds since their founding. She studied the pages. For the first year all transactions involved trades in blue-chip growth stocks and in companies labeled in parentheses "Michaux Enterprises." Through low market periods in 1969 and 1970 large amounts of cash were held. Then in 1971 repeated small investments were made in six companies whose names were unfamiliar to Carolyn. At the same time major sums were invested in South African gold stocks. On August 13 and 14, 1971, all gold shares were sold. The proceeds were divided between American blue-chip stocks and the six unknown companies. The next month all the U.S. securities and some Michaux enterprise stocks were sold, and again the proceeds were invested in European **gold** and in the six companies. In late January 1972 the European gold was sold at the top of the market, and the proceeds were again split between U.S. securities and the six companies.

"I have never heard of O'Rourke Farms, Gray Company, Transatlantic Buildings, Machinery Specialty, Alpha, and Iptek," Carolyn said when she looked up.

"They are shell corporations."

"Are you sure?"

"Quite. They have no assets, no activities, no employees, nothing. They are merely conduits for money going elsewhere, mainly to the Bahamas and to South America."

"And then what happened to it?"

"That part of the investigation is still in progress. It will take some time."

"It's a sizable amount, isn't it?"

"Yes, it is. However, Lux Michaux has sold out."

"When?"

"The order was placed Monday afternoon and executed Tuesday morning. That set off the panic."

It was hard for Carolyn to comprehend all the implications of what Hood was telling her. She stared at the sheets, trying to add up the amounts.

"Did you notice the dates the gold shares were sold?" Hood asked.

"August 13, 1971."

"President Nixon's speech suspending gold convertibility and devaluing the dollar was made on August 15, 1971."

"Meaning . . . ?"

"That the funds may have possessed prior knowledge of the President's intentions."

"How could they have? Wasn't that a carefully held secret?"

"It was indeed."

The pages fell from Carolyn's lap to the floor. She understood what he was saying. "The Treasury documents . . ." she faltered.

"Exactly."

There was nothing to say. Blindly she stared out the window. Hood watched her. "There's more," he said after a moment.

174

"Tell me all of it."

"Appearances suggest, Mrs. Bruce, that Lux Michaux was as ignorant as the other investors and cannot in any way be considered culpable in this."

She nodded. That, at least, she knew. "You mentioned another suspect," she said faintly. "Who is that?"

"Mr. Bruce's deputy. He may have forged your husband's name on the investment orders. If not, and your husband becomes the only suspect, your position would depend on what happened to the money."

"I understand." She was silent, almost in reverie. Finally she looked directly at him. "Mr. Hood, I don't know at this time whether my husband was guilty or not. If he was, then I will do what I can to resolve the matter honorably, even if I personally have to take bankruptcy to do it. Are you going to arrest me?"

The last she had said in a faint effort to be funny, but he answered her seriously. It told her everything. "I have not been so instructed. However, you should not seek to avoid returning to your hotel. It would only make your situation more difficult."

"I have no intention of skipping the country, if that is what you mean. I have nothing to conceal."

A thin smile touched his lips without warming his eyes. "I hope not. Well, I must go." He rose as James came into the room. McAllister had changed his suit. The only evidence of his fisticuffs with Lisle was the vertical slit across his left eyebrow and the redness of his cheekbone.

"You certainly look better," Carolyn commented.

"I couldn't have looked much worse. Are you leaving already, Jackson? That didn't take long." He looked closely at Carolyn and then at Hood. "You upset her. What nuggets of gloom did you add to her troubles?"

"Are you Mrs. Bruce's lawyer?"

"Not exactly."

"Then Mrs. Bruce will tell you what she wishes."

"Very well."

Carolyn watched the two men eyeing each other. Jackson Hood was correctly formal in his pin-striped suit. His face was dour, his gray eyes flinty. He was rigidly impartial in manner, stern in his pursuit of justice and tax evaders. Carolyn couldn't condemn him. He was doing his job, and the nation's taxpayers were getting their money's worth from his services. James McAllister, on the other hand, was elegantly dressed, exotic, intriguing, dangerous, an enigma. Yet they were both good men. Their strength was in their faces and in the straight set of their shoulders.

"Thank you, Mrs. Bruce," Hood said politely. "Good day, James."

Carolyn rose, handed his coat to him and followed him silently to the door. The meeting wasn't ending well. She had lost Hood's sympathy. Even though she had it only if she could be proven innocent of complicity, the sense of loss was unnerving. At the door she reached and touched his arm. "Jackson, please. Are you sure of your information?"

Hood looked down at her. "I am sure."

"Jackson, you know there's more to this whole mess than you are turning up in audits. I know how eager the bureaucrats can become. They can get carried away. They can witch-hunt. The circumstances of my husband's death only make the issue more piquant. Please, caution them against excessiveness. Caution them to double-check the facts. Don't burden me with any false charges."

Hood's face softened. "I can do that for you. It's unnecessary, I assure you. But I will do it."

"Thank you. Thank you very much." A brilliant smile, dazzling in her gratitude, suddenly transformed her into a beautiful woman. James, watching from the center of the room, suddenly felt that, somehow, Jackson Hood had won a round.

The faintest wistful expression came into Hood's eyes. "I probably won't see you again, Mrs. Bruce. I have finished my work on the case. From now on, it will be handled by the New York office. But while you are here, if I can help you in any way . . ." He turned abruptly and left. Carolyn shut the door quietly behind him.

"Well?" James demanded. "Did he lower the boom?"

"No. He merely gave notice to duck. When do we go to Geneva?"

21

•

It was almost midnight when their plane landed at Geneva's International Airport. James had carried their suitcases on board, and now Carolyn followed him through customs ahead of the milling crowd. He changed their cash into Swiss francs at the airport's bank, made one telephone call, and then they were on the curb in front of the terminal. Several taxis were waiting. They took the first one as the other passengers straggled out and began searching for transportation.

Carolyn sighed. Had she known it was going to be such a long trip, she would not have consented to it. It seemed forever since Hood had left and she had gone to the telephone to call Prescott. James had followed her and cut off the connection. He took the receiver from her and shook his head.

"I thought you said . . ."

For answer he unscrewed the mouthpiece and dropped something into his hand. A small device glittered. She looked at it and then, startled, up at him. "Later," he had said as he replaced the telephone.

Suddenly it had seemed unreal. The dazed, almost dreamlike sensation stayed with her as they left the hotel through the servants' rear entrance and caught a taxi on a back street. "Whose was it?" she had asked quietly.

"I don't know. It is of American manufacture. It could belong either to the person you were calling or to my top boss."

The care he had taken to mention no names had heightened the unreality. She lapsed into silence until they reached Heathrow. There she had called Prescott from a public phone. James stood at her back, watchfully eyeing the crowd around them. To Carolyn he had seemed a little too obviously on guard.

Prescott had listened without comment while she described the man who had followed her the afternoon before and gave his name as Thorpe.

"How did you find that out?" Prescott asked.

"I had supper with Mr. McAllister last night. He knew."

"How convenient."

There was silence. Prescott wasn't going to help her. "Are there any developments that would prevent my going to Geneva tonight?"

"Were you expecting any?"

"I don't know what to expect any more."

"Then you will be pleased to know that certain fortuitous events have seemed to improve your situation."

"That *is* good news."

"Perhaps. It is all too neat and timely. Do you think the ubiquitous McAllister would know anything about it?"

"You should ask him."

"I will when I find him. Well, I cannot hold you here if you promise to return for the remainder of the inquest."

"Certainly."

"Where will you be staying in Geneva?"

"I don't know yet. I will be back in London tomorrow. I have kept my suite here."

"Will you call me when you return?"

"If you wish. Goodbye, Superintendent."

She was troubled and quiet on the flight to Paris, during the long layover there, and on the flight to Geneva. McAllister wisely left her alone. Now that they were here, Carolyn wanted only to sleep.

"Where to?" the driver asked over his shoulder to McAllister.

"Go to the Pont de l'Isle. I will guide you from there. And shut that window, please."

There was a jumble of French that Carolyn did not understand. The window beside the driver remained open.

"Where are we going?" Carolyn asked.

"You will see."

"Then you know Geneva?"

"Pretty well. I worked here for two months."

When they reached the bridge over the Rhone, McAllister directed the driver into the old town. It was bitterly cold. Carolyn huddled miserably into her fur coat, her ears terribly chilled. She shivered. James leaned forward and remonstrated with the driver in French. The driver shrugged and tried to close the window. The handle whirled around without effect. "The window is jammed," James said disgustedly. "But it's not too far now."

They rode in silence through narrow streets that reminded Carolyn of the Left Bank in Paris. James was sitting forward, giving instructions to the driver, who shrugged again and mumbled. In this part of the old town, there were few cars. James glanced behind them.

They were passing a park. The street was almost deserted. The taxi slowed, backfiring softly as it decelerated. A car was coming toward them. It drew parallel.

James suddenly swore and wrenched open his door. He hurled Carolyn down and threw himself over her, his head buried in her shoulder, as an object hurtled into the cab and exploded. The driver lost control and a second later crashed the taxi into the side of a parked car. They were thrown sideways onto the pavement. Carolyn landed hard, James on top of her. The recoil was still in her ears as he leaped up and raced after the other car. It had already careened around the corner. He gave up and came back, replacing the gun he carried. He pulled Carolyn to her feet. "Stand over there, away from the cab," he panted.

Furiously he flung open the front door, dragged the driver out, and threw him against the side of the car. He frisked the man swiftly, but found no weapons. "All right," he demanded in French, "whom are you working for?"

"Monsieur . . . I . . . nobody . . ."

James shook him furiously, as though he were a doll. He was as limp as one. His legs sagged and dandled. "Who did this? Who set this up? Were you paid?"

"No . . . yes . . ."

"Answer me!" McAllister's voice rasped harshly.

The driver looked fearfully at him, trembling. Carolyn could see spittle shining on his chin. "Please. I'll tell you," he whimpered.

"Do that. Now!"

179

"A man said to pick you up at the airport and drive you along here slowly. He jammed the window. He paid me. He said it was a little thing. He didn't tell me about a bomb. I needed the money. My little daughter—"

"Who was he? What did he look like?"

"He didn't say. He wore a ski mask on his face. I don't know." He moaned softly. "I'm sorry. I had no idea . . . My daughter . . ."

James let the man slump against the cab and slide onto the concrete. He dusted his hands in disgust and contempt and stood upright. "You're lucky it was only a low-grade bomb. If she had been hurt, I'd have killed you with these two hands." He turned his back on him and came to Carolyn. "Are you all right?"

She nodded.

"He knows nothing. But it has to be Michaux. You were right. He is not pleased with my helping you." The cabbie was creeping back into the driver's seat. James grabbed their suitcases from the front seat as the man backed the taxi away from the parked car with a rattle and tinkle of broken headlights. He gunned it down the street as a black Fiat came to stop beside them. McAllister turned to face the two men who got out and approached.

"Troubles, my friend?" It was an American voice, a cheerful, flat, Middle Western accent.

James put Carolyn behind him and slid his hand inside his coat. Immediately the men stopped warily.

"Relax, buddy," the man said. "You look like you need help."

"Don't come any closer," James warned. To Carolyn's ears his brogue suddenly seemed more pronounced in contrast to the familiar tones of home. "How long have you been following us? Who do you work for?"

The two Americans exchanged glances.

James stepped forward; his movement seemed menacing, stalking. "Were you responsible for that bomb?"

The shorter man glanced watchfully at his companion, looking for direction. "Now, take it easy," he said, but neither backed away. James moved quickly. His fist flashed out and caught the bigger man hard under the chin. The other man moved, reaching out, but James grasped him as he came forward, spun him around and slammed him against the car. Both hands on his coat lapels, he kept him in a tight grip.

"All right. Talk!" The man looked at his companion sprawled in

180

the street and then at Carolyn, huddling into her fur as though it could protect her.

"We are representatives of the United States Treasury. We are following Mrs. Bruce. Who are you?"

"I'm asking the questions. Do you have identification?"

"In my breast pocket."

McAllister found the man's wallet and flipped it open, turning it to read the card in the arc light. He released him. "All right, Chambers. The Swiss frown on such activities by other governments within their borders, but that's your worry. Who is he?" He jerked his head at the one lying in the street.

"My partner. His name is Blackerby. Who are you, anyway?"

"A friend of Mrs. Bruce's. Why are you following her?"

"All I know is that I was informed of her arrival and instructed to report on her movements. We are not to interfere in any way."

"To whom do you report?"

"Treasury headquarters in Washington."

"And did they give you the orders?"

"Yes."

"Do you know why?"

"No. Mrs. Bruce is a principal in a tax case is all I know."

"Very well. Have you noticed anyone else following her?"

"No. Do you say it was a bomb?"

"Yes. Not serious, though." He helped Chambers lift Blackerby to his feet and put him in the front seat of the Fiat. "You won't mind giving us a lift to our hotel? Our cabbie seems to have had enough for one night."

"You worked him over pretty good. Sure. Come on."

Carolyn silently climbed into the rear seat, moving over to give James room. The four rode in silence. Chambers kept glancing in the rear-view mirror at Carolyn. She moved slightly, out of the range of his leer. When the car stopped in front of the dimly lit hotel, she jumped out without waiting for assistance.

"Thank you very much," James said.

"You going out again?" Chambers asked.

"No. You will have an easy job tonight."

Chambers made a lewd gesture and jerked his head toward Carolyn, waiting beside the front door. "So will you. Think of us out here in this damn wind and give the broad one for us. Some guys have all the good assignments."

McAllister's hands clenched on the door. Then he stood upright. "Good night," he said tightly. When he came up to her, his face was so thunderous Carolyn said nothing, but preceded him quietly into the lobby.

22

Carolyn stood at the window of their tiny hotel room and stared into the park across the street. James had been gone three hours. She wondered if he would return.

Restlessly she checked her watch again and went to the door to listen for sounds in the corridor outside. There were none. She walked back toward the window, pausing at the battered dresser to look at the gun. James had given it to her. He had taken it from his shoulder holster, checked its magazine, and handed it to her, butt end first. "Do you know how to use this?" he had asked.

"No. I never have."

He cocked it for her. "Now, all you do is point and squeeze."

"You keep it. I don't like guns."

"You may need it. Bolt the door after me. When I get back, I will knock twice. Now, don't, promise me, don't open this door without hearing the double knock, even if it is me. Someone may be behind me. Understand?"

"Yes. I promise. Where are you going?"

"To find a way out of here. It's too dangerous for us to stay."

"Why? We don't care if the U.S. Treasury knows where we go."

"Michaux's men are down there, too. If they have orders to take you from here, I cannot stop them by myself."

"How long will you be?"

"Not long. You try to nap." He gripped her shoulder hard and was gone. She locked the door and gingerly put the gun on the dresser. There wasn't anything else to do, so she pulled a heavy comforter over her and was immediately asleep.

On awakening and seeing how much time had passed, she thought she had missed his knock. Cautiously she unlocked the door. The corridor was empty. What if he didn't come back? She had little chance of getting to the bank and then back to London safely. The techniques of self-protection were unknown to her. The gun was repulsive. She could never use it. As she stared, it seemed to grow until it was all she could see. The soft rap jerked her thoughts into alertness. It came again, a quick double knock.

"Who is it?"

"James."

With relief greater than she once would have thought possible, she let him in.

Immediately he rebolted the door, turned out the lights, and without speaking further, strode to the window and drew the curtain aside.

"James, where have you been? What kept you?"

"I got caught in the kitchen. The charlady was mopping the floor. I couldn't get back upstairs until she left." The normality of his voice reassured her in spite of his tense posture.

"Where were you, then?"

"In a pantry cupboard. Here. I helped myself to some confections." He handed her two éclairs wrapped in wax paper. They were crushed but light and fragrant. Her anger exploded.

"James! My God! Thugs surround us and you filch cupcakes in the kitchen! What if you had been discovered? What if—oh, damn!"

"I was quite safe. It was a big pantry." He spoke absently, still looking intently out.

"How many are down there?"

"Come here. I will show you."

He reached and brought her to stand in front of him at the window. One hand rested on her shoulder. The other held the curtain aside. "Do you see the black Fiat just to the right of the crosswalk? That's Chambers' car. He's alone now. The other one went home. The third car behind him belongs to Ingram's men. There are four of them, two patrolling the front of the building and two the rear. They are armed, I think. Here comes one of them now."

The man below paused at the corner, looked about, and then strolled past the hotel. He walked without purpose, turned and retraced his steps as Carolyn watched. "Then we are trapped?" she asked.

"Yes. I don't know what their orders are, so we must go. It will be more risky later."

"Where *can* we go?"

"A friend of mine has a studio in Carouge. That's an artist's colony about ten minutes from here."

"They'll follow us."

"Not if we are careful."

"Won't they watch the bank?"

"They aren't there now. I went down and checked. That probably means they expect us to leave here at nine o'clock. They may wait until ten o'clock before they figure we are not here. By that time you will have transacted your business at the bank and we will be gone."

"If we are very, very lucky. How do we get past them?"

"I had hoped to find at least part of a clandestine route I knew when I was here. There are several in this part of Geneva, most of them cutting between Rue Bourg du Four and Rue Farel around the cathedral. But there wasn't time. I couldn't remember how to find it in the dark. We will just have to slip past them."

Carolyn had no delusions about that. Her body slumped. "When will this nightmare be over?" she murmured.

He let the curtain drop and took her shoulders quietly. "Soon. I promise you." Her hands went to her elbows as though she was cold. He was intensely aware of the fragile feel of her arms and back, the subtle scent of her perfume. Softly, almost surreptitiously, he laid his cheek down on her hair and drew her closely against him.

"James . . . please . . ." She stepped out of his embrace and snapped on the table lamp.

He followed her and touched her arm, stopping her there by the table. "Being with you all day, loving you, not being able to touch you—it's more than a man can endure."

She made an impatient gesture. "Don't . . . please . . ."

"I know. I know how you feel, what you are thinking. You loved David Bruce. Now he's dead, and I'm out of line." He hesitated a long moment. "But dammit," he continued in a rush, turning a haggard face to her, "dammit, I love you. And I'm going to tell you so now, while we have a quiet minute to ourselves, before it's too late for me."

"James . . ."

"Yes, it's true. I want you. I want to take you in my arms and kiss you and make love to you until we are both weak from the joy of it. But my dearest heart, I don't want you for my whore, like Chambers did out there. I want you for my wife. A day on the lam isn't enough. I want you all the time. And I'm not going to let you get away from me. When this is over, when you've had time to decide what you want to do and what you want to be tomorrow and next week and the week after, I'm coming for you. I pray that there will still be hope for me, for us. I—" He stopped and made a poignant outward gesture with his hands. "We'll see," he concluded, "on your terms."

The tension and impatience faded from her face. A gentle smile began in her eyes and then touched her lips. Incredibly, he saw, she was no longer angry with him. "It may take a very long time, James. I can promise you nothing. I can tell you only that I will never forget you. Now, hadn't we better go?" Without waiting for an answer, she touched his arm briefly and went to get her coat.

He looked after her, his craggy face suddenly worn and lonely and hungering. "That's not enough." There was bitterness and regret in his softly spoken words. She didn't hear, and he went again to the window and looked out. His face hardened. His hand on the curtain tightened. His expression as he studied the street below became frightening.

23

•

They left the luggage for the hotel to forward and slipped out of the room. There was no one in the hall or on the dingy service stairs. Carefully, silently, with McAllister leading, they made their way to the ground floor. It was very early, but the staff was already in the kitchen eating breakfast. Carolyn glanced questioningly at James. He listened a minute and then gestured for her to come forward. They passed the kitchen doors and stepped through the swinging doors to a dimly lighted vestibule. No one seemed to observe them. James let the door fall quietly shut. More double doors opened onto steps leading down into the alley.

"When we step outside," James whispered, "wait for me. Stand in the shadow while I reconnoiter."

Carolyn nodded. McAllister opened the outer door barely enough for them to get through. Once outside, she concealed herself in the darkness. James moved along the wall to the top step. He listened a moment and then moved swiftly. Carolyn could see the faint outline of his form as he ran silently across the street and out of her sight. She waited, glancing behind her at the servant's entrance, watching anxiously for his return. The faint hum of the city and of the wind were the only sounds. Then, noiselessly, he was back, gesturing for her to come. He took her hand and led her to the right, away from the main thoroughfare toward a darker, narrower street.

Suddenly a man briskly entered the alley ahead of them and strode purposefully toward the hotel. James pulled her into the deep entrance of a storehouse and blocked her closely into the darkest corner. They waited. When he had passed, Carolyn realized she had been holding her breath. McAllister took her hand again and they hurried to the street. They walked for several blocks, toward the towering spires of the cathedral. Once they cut through a courtyard. They finally found a taxi parked by the old city hall, its lights out, its driver dozing behind the wheel.

"Will you take a fare?" James asked in French.

The driver roused himself and swung open the rear door. "Certainly. Where to, monsieur?"

"Carouge. Then I will call the turns for you."

McAllister was still gripping Carolyn's hand, but his face was so set and anxious, she made no protest. She studied his jagged profile as he stared watchfully out the window. A few minutes ago she had doubted him. Twenty-four hours ago she had run in fear from him. Yet now she was trusting him with her life, and it no longer seemed a risky bargain. By voluntarily giving her the time she needed, he had strangely altered her feeling for him. He had removed the guilt she had felt for liking him, had made her willing, even eager, to continue their relationship. Yet why should he still doubt that she would welcome his friendship? Couldn't he depend on her gratitude? He must believe that he couldn't. And there it was again. He knew he could not be trusted. She took a deep breath and let it out slowly. He felt the change of her mood and turned to her from the window.

"How did we get away from the hotel so easily?" she murmured, hoping that her voice held the proper blend of casualness and curiosity.

"We didn't."

"I didn't hear anything."

"There wasn't anything to hear."

"What did you do?"

"Went up behind him, squeezed his carotid artery, and then bundled him into a dark doorway."

"Won't he be discovered?"

"Certainly. It was a bit of luck that the others were elsewhere at the time. I took his money and threw his wallet in the gutter, so I hope they will think it a simple robbery. It will take them a while to find him and then to discover that we've gone."

"They can tell that by picking up a telephone and calling the room."

"I disconnected the switchboard."

"Is the man dead?"

"No."

"Did he see you?"

"No."

"Then they don't know we've gone. It worked just as you said it would."

"I hope so."

But he sounded doubtful.

James found the key to the studio in the flower box and let them in. Immediately distrustful, Carolyn hesitated on the step. He read her mind. "Come on. I called Maurice while I was out. He left the key for me."

He led her in and shut the door. "Let me see how he left his room. Maybe you can sleep for a couple of hours."

Wearily she dropped her coat, glanced around the artistically cluttered studio, and sank down on the sofa. When he returned, she was asleep. He stood for a long time gazing down at her, then gently covered her with her coat. One hand stirred in the fur and was still. He left her there.

Someone was chasing her. She ran, crying, across a newly plowed field, stumbling over the furrows, rising with pain to run again. There was a house. If she could reach it, she would be safe. The pursuer grabbed for her. She jumped onto the porch, lost her balance, and fell into the rough grass.

Tiny things were in her vision. A yellow flower. Blades of grass, each one divided vertically. A minute weed with three sprigs. A big hand came into her view. She had to choose. The follower behind her or the hand beside her. Her palm lay open. The hand touched her palm. She closed her fingers over it and held on.

The warmth of the hand brought her instantly out of her nightmare. James was leaning over her and she was clinging to his fingers. Her face was wet with tears. She brushed them away.

"You must have had a nightmare."

He handed her a cup of coffee and she sat up and sipped gratefully.

"Where did you say your friend was?" she asked.

"I didn't. He's with his mistress. She's a show girl. Maurice is a bad artist but a good friend. I shared expenses with him here when I was in Geneva years ago."

"It's fortunate." There was silence a moment.

"What's bothering you?" he asked.

"Do you often use force in your work?"

"Only when my friends are threatened with murder and mayhem."

"Wasn't there any other way with Adelaide?"

"Mercenary as she is and inured to petty crimes of one sort and another, a show of determination seemed appropriate. Lisle was different. He saw through my ruse and would have stopped us. I would guess he has dozens of misdemeanors to his credit and probably is overdue to spend some time in prison. Now, listen." He spoke softly, intensely, leaning forward. His eyes held hers. The anger flickered just below the level gaze. He looked dangerous. "They sold you out for sixty pounds apiece. Don't spare one thought for them. To get you out of this scrape, I would have bashed their heads together until they cried for mercy. I don't approve of violence. I wish it had been unnecessary. But anyone who would condemn another person, an innocent stranger, to prison for life for money is as low a type as ever crawled in the gutters of London. They weren't suffering any remorse for you. Spare yourself remorse for them."

His voice changed, became less impassioned, more curious. "You know, it's always amazed me that people who sell their souls accept so little for them."

"No doubt it's a reflection of their view of their own worth."

"I suppose so."

"I'm grateful to you for what you've done for me. Just saying thank you seems inadequate, somehow. But thank you very much."

"We're both the worse for wear." He touched his eye carefully. "Is it coloring up?"

"Yes."

"I'll borrow your makeup. That should hide the worst of it."

The idea of James McAllister using makeup amused her. She laughed outright. There was a bond between them, a comforting warmth, a little challenge.

"Are you ready to go?" James asked.

190

24
•

A bank official was unlocking the door as Carolyn and James mounted the front steps to the bank. He ushered them immediately to deep leather chairs and then glided away, his steps noiseless on the soft carpet. There was no sound except the low hum of electrical equipment. The atmosphere was so churchlike that Carolyn found herself whispering.

"Were we followed?"

"I don't think so. There's a chap in a gray topcoat reading a paper at the kiosk across the street. He didn't look like a pedestrian. I'll watch him while you have your meeting. If I think we will need help in getting away, I'll interrupt you."

"The vice-president will see you now, Mrs. Bruce."

Carolyn followed the secretary into Emile Voss's elegantly furnished and paneled office. Voss shook her hand with a courtly little bow and pulled a leather chair closer to his desk for her. "How may I help you today?" he asked when he had resumed his seat.

"I believe my husband, David Cartwright Bruce, of New York City, had an account with your bank."

The expression on the thin, almost ascetic face did not change. Voss waited for her to continue.

"He was killed in an accident in London last Friday. Questions have arisen that make it necessary for me to ascertain the status of the account without delay. Do I have access to it?"

"I am indeed sorry to hear of your loss, Mrs. Bruce. It is tragic,

tragic to die so young. It is sad. But may I have your passport? There are some formalities."

Carolyn handed it to him. Then, at his request, she signed a small index card. "Do you have the account number?" he asked.

"I believe so. Twelve-twelve-seventy."

"Please write the numbers here."

Carolyn complied.

"If you will excuse me a moment."

He left her alone. Carolyn had time to notice a pair of Klee originals on the walls and a Giacometti statuette on the credenza before he returned, accompanied by the president of the bank, Mr. Chernay.

"Could you give me that account number again, madam?" Voss asked when the introductions had been completed.

"Twelve-twelve-seventy. Here. You may read it for yourself." She opened the locket and extended it on its chain for him to see. Both men looked.

"Yes. A moment more, if you will be so kind."

Through the half-opened door Carolyn could see the two men studying a folder, comparing her passport and signature cards with bank records, murmuring together. When they returned they looked so grave that Carolyn hoped she did not have access to the account after all. Or better still, that there was no account. But the hope lasted only a moment.

"Please forgive the delay. Only Mr. Chernay and I know the account numbers. In the case of this account, we must be very sure."

"What is unusual about this account?" Carolyn asked.

"We are a small bank, madam. This is a large account." Voss handed her the folder, opened to the proper page. "The balance is on the bottom line."

Carolyn looked at them for a long moment. Both men were apprehensive. Then, deliberately, she dropped her eyes to the bottom line of the yellow computerized ledger sheet. There it was. Enough to kill for.

"Is this francs or dollars?" she asked.

"Ah. Forgive me. Francs. In dollars that comes to . . ." Voss made a few rapid calculations on a small electronic computer on his desk. "It comes to $65,365,252.10 at today's rate of exchange."

"How much?"

He wrote it out on memo paper and handed it to her. She looked at the balance in her hand. She felt nothing. Then, carefully, she put the folder down. The two men watched her anxiously.

"How do you want it?" Chernay murmured.

"Want it?"

"In dollars, francs, marks, yen, pounds sterling, or gold?"

"No. I don't want to take it with me. Not now, anyway."

Their expressions relaxed. They exchanged glances. "Then, madam, how may we serve you?"

"Do you have a complete record of all transactions since the account was opened?"

Voss handed her additional ledger sheets. Slowly she turned through them. On the first day of each month, a deposit had been made. They began with $25,000 a month five years before and rose rapidly to $125,000. That must have been David's salary, Carolyn thought. His commissions on profits were deposited quarterly and ranged as high as $236,000. The really big deposits began after August 14, 1971, and corresponded roughly with the dates she remembered from Hood's information. There were only minor withdrawals. It was all true.

She looked up. "Gentlemen, at some point this money will have to be returned to the United States. For the moment it is safer here. Do you pay interest on your accounts?"

"Certain accounts, yes. Not this one."

"I will instruct you later about transfer to an interest-bearing account. Meanwhile I would like a complete record of the account, including the currencies the deposits were made in and the banks from which the funds originated. I would also like a photostat of each deposit record and check, front and back. In fact, Mr. Voss, if it is possible, I would appreciate a complete record of every transaction, communication, letter or telephone call my husband may have had with this bank and through this bank, with any other bank in the world."

"It will take a little time, but certainly it is possible."

"Good. Please make three sets of the information. Mail one copy to me at my New York address. Seal the second set in an envelope marked 'Private—hold' and mail it to my lawyer in New York. Here is his address. And please send the third copy to Detective Chief Superintendent Elsworth Prescott, Scotland Yard, London."

"Do you wish to take a notation of the balance with you?"

"That won't be necessary. The balance is engraved on my memory."

They looked at her sharply when they heard the fervor in her tone, but they said nothing.

"There's one last thing." She reached for the memo pad on the desk and wrote a single line on it. Then she turned it so they could read it. "Is that possible?"

"Yes. Certainly."

"Then make it a part of the record."

"Indeed, yes. Anything else?"

"No, I think not." Voss clipped Carolyn's written instruction to the folder, excused himself, and took it away. "My husband was a business associate of Lux Michaux of Paris. Are you acquainted with him or his affairs?" Carolyn asked Chernay.

"Only by name and reputation. He is not a customer of this bank."

Discretion is the fortress of the Swiss banking system, Carolyn thought, as Voss came quietly back into the room. "Mr. McAllister wishes a word with you, madam," Voss said.

"Please ask him to join us."

When McAllister had been introduced and seated, Carolyn continued. "My husband and his business partners had a serious disagreement. Since his death, I have been threatened and followed. I am being followed now."

"Indeed?"

"Does that window face the street? Is there a man in a gray topcoat by the kiosk?"

Chernay rose and carefully drew aside the curtains. "Yes, there is such a man."

"I wish to avoid him. Do you have an exit in the rear of the building that Mr. McAllister and I might use? We suffered an unpleasant experience last night. I do not wish a repetition."

"Where are you going from here? Do you have transportation?" Voss asked.

"We are going to the airport. Once we are away from the bank, we can make arrangements for our transportation," McAllister answered.

Voss looked at Chernay. "Madame Chateaureaux?" he asked. "Is she in the bank this morning?"

Chernay nodded. "If she isn't, it's the first day she's missed in years." He turned to Carolyn. "Is this a matter for the police?" he asked.

"It is a matter for the British police, not for yours. That is why I wished a copy of the information sent to them."

"Very well. Perhaps Madame will help you. It will make her feel five years younger. Mr. Voss, will you see if she has arrived?"

"Certainly, sir."

"Madame Chateaureaux is a woman of great charm and courage," Chernay said. "She is also something of an adventuress. I dare call her that only because she is the first to admit it of herself." The barest twinkle showed in his eyes. It was gone before Carolyn could decide that it was there.

"Ah, Madame Chateaureaux," Chernay said as Voss escorted a distinguished old lady into the office. "How well you look. May I introduce Mrs. Carolyn Bruce and Mr. James McAllister."

"A Scotsman," Madame said to James in heavily accented English. "I loved a Scotsman once."

"And?"

"There is no 'and.' He went to war and was killed."

Carolyn watched Madame bemusedly. Such uninhibited conversation from the regal figure in dove gray was incongruous. Yet she had once been a beauty. Much of it was still there in the fine black eyes and good cheekbones. Madame was a lovely old lady. And the knowing eyes were young.

"Are you in trouble with the police?" Madame asked McAllister bluntly.

"No."

"With whom, then?"

"A man named Lux Michaux," Carolyn answered.

"I know him. I don't like him. You are fortunate that I don't. Yes, I will help you. Emile, may I trouble you to bring Jacques to me?"

"Certainly, Madame."

Her chauffeur came promptly and was instructed to bring the car, with its curtains down, to the rear of the building. Madame would feign a slight illness. Mrs. Bruce and Mr. McAllister would assist her into the car. It was as simple as that. Jacques bowed himself away. "I have the thought, Chernay, that you had some such idea as this in your mind," Madame said when Jacques had gone.

"We remembered your car," Chernay replied. "And I knew you. I thought it possible." He smiled rather fondly at her.

"I've had precious little adventure in my life lately, as you know," Madame replied. "And I dislike to be dull. Well, shall we go?" She took her handkerchief from her voluminous handbag and pressed it to her lips as her body slumped forward. "How is this?"

"Very good," Chernay approved. "Mrs. Bruce? Mr. McAllister?" They took their places one on each side of Madame, holding her arms. Chernay and Voss went ahead.

Madame was a good actress. She gasped and stumbled and murmured all the way down the corridor, through the main lobby of the bank, and down a second, shorter corridor to the rear exit. Carolyn and James kept their heads low. Jacques sprang out to assist them into the car, then quickly took his place behind the wheel. The car moved away sedately from the curb and turned into the main thoroughfare.

"How was I?" the old lady asked in a satisfied tone.

"Magnificent," Carolyn replied fervently. "You should go on the stage."

"I was on the stage at one time—for several years, as a matter of fact. I was a dancer. But I acted a little, too. Did anyone observe our departure?"

McAllister looked carefully out around the curtain. "No. He's still there. And there is another one with him. They haven't seen us."

"Good. Then I will take you directly to the airport. You should not risk a taxi now."

"Madame, how can we ever thank you?" Carolyn began.

"Hush, child. Chernay was quite correct. Things have been very dull for me since my husband died. I am along in years, and while I am able to get about quite well, my friends are not, and so I live very quietly. But I have had much excitement in my life. I miss it, even while I enjoy the peace and rest. Chernay is a nice young man, one of the few who dares to tease me a little. We gossip together. He doesn't look the type, I know. I discovered it quite by accident and have enjoyed it immensely." Carolyn smiled. She couldn't imagine Chernay gossiping.

"My dear," Madame continued, "I have had five husbands and a long life. I know the worst advice is the advice you don't ask for. But I am going to give you some anyway, and because you are a

196

polite young lady, you are going to listen. I hope you are woman enough to take it."

"Tell me." Carolyn smiled.

"The only thing worthwhile in this world is love. You can derive comfort from the love of your friends and your family. You should arrange your affairs so you are never without either, if you can. But that doesn't substitute for the love of a man. Get yourself another husband." She sighed a little. "I would marry again, but Joseph spoiled me. The men I meet are poor shadows in comparison to my memory of him."

"And if I should have the same problem?" Carolyn asked.

"You won't," Madame replied bluntly. "Be happy, my dear. You are so young and so lovely. Your happiest years are ahead of you if you have courage enough to grasp them."

Carolyn liked Madame Chateaureaux. She was still smiling when the car pulled under the airport shed.

25

*

The Boeing 707 flew in sunlight. Carolyn stared out the window and thought of sixty-five million dollars and Madame Chateaureaux. McAllister dozed beside her, his hands clasped together. His knuckles were cracked and scraped. They looked swollen.

The light paled. The clouds lost their whipped-cotton look and became moist and runny. The plane seemed to hesitate. Then, reluctantly, it sank through the flying streamers of moisture and landed in London's own peculiar grayness. Rain dashed against the Plexiglas windows and mingled with oil and jet fuel in circular rainbows on the black tarmac. By the time they deplaned, passed through customs and headed into town, it was dark.

They drove in silence. Now that there was no longer any reason for them to be together, Carolyn did not want McAllister to leave. He glanced at her several times. When they reached the turnoff to her hotel and were stopped by the light, he turned to her. "Have supper with me." He sounded almost desperate.

She nodded.

He drove to a restaurant near the center of the city. It was open for dinner but was deserted at this early hour.

The headwaiter greeted McAllister by name and showed them to a table in an alcove. "The usual, sir?"

"Two of the usuals, Claude. And we'll order now. The trout, I believe, for both of us."

"Right away, Mr. McAllister. It is unusually good today."

Cream sherries arrived promptly. Carolyn sipped gratefully. The wine was superb. James toasted her with his glass.

"Madame Chateaureaux really hurt your feelings, didn't she?" he asked after a moment.

"Yes, she did," Carolyn admitted. "How old would you say she is?"

"Nearer eighty than seventy. Perhaps she is eighty."

"Five husbands and considering a sixth!"

"And several lovers. Her last husband died while I was in Geneva. As I recall, he was an explorer and archeologist and several years younger than she was. There was as much written about her in the news accounts at the time as there was about him. According to one article, she married her first husband for love, the second for wealth, the third for position, the fourth for a title, and the fifth for love again. Her lovers included dukes and archdukes and maybe a prince, although never a king. She should write her autobiography."

"You should have suggested it to her."

"I was enjoying it all too much."

She laughed as the waiter placed two platters of beautiful trout amandine before them. Green beans. String potatoes. A smooth white wine. They ate without conversation. By the time the coffee came, the lights had been dimmed and the tables had filled quietly with diners. The discreet hum of voices, the small clink of cutlery, the crisp squish of crushed ice against wine bottles reclining in coolers surrounded and isolated them.

McAllister watched her through the haze of his cigarette smoke. The character he had sensed when he first saw her at the Winfreys' had been displayed in their hours together. Her face had become beautiful to him. Lovingly he studied its lines and curves, the wide gray eyes, the light dusting of down on her cheeks. He hoped she cared for him more than she wanted to admit. But she didn't trust him. She hadn't told him of the account.

Carolyn looked up suddenly and caught the appraisal in his eyes and the darker, more brooding expression under it. She smiled slightly. He was grateful that she hadn't asked what he was thinking. That was a silly woman's question, and she wasn't a silly woman.

"You know," she said, "your eye looks painful."

He reached for her hand, which was toying with the spoon, and laid it against his cheek. "Never forget, Carolyn Bruce, that I love you."

She shook her head as he released her hand; he rose, excusing himself with a murmur. She watched him tread the narrow aisle to the rear of the dining room. He was absent several minutes. When he returned, she was gone.

Sitting with her back to the door, Carolyn did not see Ingram until he stood beside the table. His thick body blocked her only escape. A trench coat covered his arm.

"Please come with me," he said softly.

"No. I am with a friend."

Ingram moved the coat slightly to one side. It took a moment to identify the black metal circle pointed at her as the muzzle of a gun. "Not another word. Come now."

He took her upper arm, lifted her out of the chair, and directed her out. Carolyn started to speak to the cloakroom attendant, but Ingram's chubby fingers closed into her arm. He took her coat and then forced her out the door. A car stood at the curb, its engine humming softly. Ingram shoved her into the back seat, where LeClere waited. Haskins drove.

"Where are you taking me?" Carolyn tried to speak calmly, but her voice trembled.

"You know about the money in the account. Lux Michaux wants to hear of it from your own lips."

"How did you find me?"

"We have been following you since you left the airport. That restaurant does have good food, doesn't it?"

"Nice of you to let me eat it," she snapped.

She looked out the rear window, but the gun brought her back to face the front again. "He's not following you," LeClere said smoothly. "Relax. We have a few minutes' drive ahead of us. Perhaps you haven't seen this section of London?"

"Take that gun out of my ribs," Carolyn demanded.

Ingram didn't move.

"Really, my dear Albert," LeClere interceded, "it isn't necessary at this juncture."

Ingram withdrew the gun to his lap but kept it cocked in her direction.

They passed Kensington Palace and drove through streets that were dark and dimly lighted by gaslights. There were no pedestrians and no cars. After a while the car turned into stone gates and stopped. Ingram and LeClere helped her out. She couldn't run. They gripped her arms as they walked her to the door.

The building once had been an elegant town house. Now it was a fashionable apartment house. Carolyn glimpsed parquet floors and plaster ceiling rosettes as they climbed the stairs to a second-floor apartment. Their hands on her arms prevented escape. Ingram's fingers dug painfully into a sensitive nerve. She tried to pull away, but it only made it worse.

Ingram opened the door with a latchkey and pushed her in ahead of them. Carolyn had an impression of an all-white room before a jocular greeting claimed her attention.

"There you are, my dear Mrs. Bruce. Do come in. I hope my colleagues have been courteous. Come and sit here by me."

"Lux Michaux," Ingram murmured.

The speaker was repulsive. He hunched in his chair like a giant vulture. The expensive clothes defied fit and bunched awkwardly about his thick body. Pendulous ears framed a sagging pear-shaped face. A diamond winked on his little finger as he smoked. He reeked of cigars.

"Here. Right here, where I can look at her. And give me that," Michaux ordered.

Ingram sat Carolyn in the chair by Michaux, plucked her purse from her lap and dumped its contents on the desk. Michaux studied the pile curiously, picking up each item and examining it before laying it to one side. He was toying with her, Carolyn thought, building tension. She schooled herself to sit calmly. Finally Michaux picked up the two checkbooks. The first was for her New York account. He looked at the balance, grimaced and tossed it aside. The second was the Swiss bankbook. He tapped it on his fingers thoughtfully. A damp little smile played on his lips.

"You know what I want," he said. "If you will just make out a check payable to me for the amount your husband stole, we will be done with our business together, and after I have cashed it, you can go."

"I have told Mr. Ingram and I will tell you—"

"I know what you have told him. American courts take too long to resolve such things, especially when the government is involved. No, I want my money now."

"I cannot give it to you."

Michaux let his eyes crawl over her. His lips were wet. "A pity you are so stubborn. Perhaps you can be more persuasive, Guillaume."

LeClere sauntered forward. He had a roll of adhesive tape in his hand.

Carolyn knew immediately what he was going to do. She bolted for the door.

The suddenness of her movement caught them off guard. She had the door open before LeClere caught her.

"Let me go!" she screamed.

LeClere spun her around, clasped one hand over her mouth and wrenched her arm behind her back and up between her shoulder blades. Keeping her arm in that position, he wrestled her back and held her down while Ingram bound her to the chair. The tape had the clean, antiseptic smell Carolyn remembered from her childhood.

She waited apprehensively. Ingram lit a little cigar. He was smiling pleasantly.

"Well, Mrs. Bruce?" Michaux asked.

"The money belongs to everyone who invested and lost in your enterprises. You've already gotten out."

"Ah," Michaux said. His thick lips stretched into a satisfied smile. "Then the money is there. I thought as much."

Damn, Carolyn thought. She had given away something he hadn't known. They had been bluffing. She clamped her mouth shut, determined to say no more.

"All you have to do is sign the check and fill in the amount. Well?"

Carolyn said nothing. She thought of McAllister.

Michaux signaled LeClere again. He stepped lightly forward, pointing his toes a little. Carolyn noticed for the first time that he was effeminate. The realization was not reassuring.

At the desk LeClere picked up a letter opener. He turned it in the light, showing off the steel blade and the handle inlaid with bronze filigree. Carolyn saw that it was not a letter opener but a stiletto. Scalpel-sharp and deadly, it was a weapon for footpads. And for LeClere.

He turned the knife before her eyes, balancing its blade lightly on one hand, breathing audibly. He glided around behind her. Suddenly, like a dancer, he whirled, wrested her head back and laid the blade against her throat. Carolyn's body tensed and arched against the adhesive. Then she realized it was the broad side of the blade. It was cold against her throat. She closed her eyes and the moment passed. LeClere released her.

Then, gently, without warning, he drew the blade across her left hand, just below the knuckles. Incredulously, Carolyn saw the thin red lines appear and form into globules. She felt pain. She spread her fingers and let the blood drip on the white carpet.

"Now are you ready to sign the check?" Michaux asked softly.

"No."

"Your devotion to the laws of your country is admirable, but under the circumstances very silly. You have led a sheltered life. You have never known pain. You have no idea how much you can hurt. Or where the most tender places of your body are."

The soft whisper triggered Carolyn's imagination. She glanced at LeClere and Ingram. Their eyes glistened. They hoped she wouldn't give in too easily.

How long had she been here? There was a clock on Michaux's desk. Maybe twenty minutes. She couldn't remember. Could she stretch it twenty more minutes? Maybe thirty? That would be almost an hour in all. If McAllister hadn't come by then, she would sign anything they wanted.

Michaux was watching her closely. "Do you know," he asked, "that you can even love your torturer? It is an interesting relationship. Love and hate. Pain and ecstasy. It will be so easy for you." His words hissed sibilantly.

"You will get your money if you present a proper document showing the claims."

"The check."

"No."

"Very well." Michaux signaled to Ingram.

Ingram smiled. Then, carefully holding his cigar upright so as not to lose the ash, he stepped forward. With the tiniest, most delicate flick of his finger, he dropped the ash down the front of her blouse. It fell between her breasts and bored into her flesh. Through the tears in her eyes, she saw Ingram drag deeply on the cigar. The new ash glowed red.

Ingram unbuttoned her blouse. His pudgy fingers slid the straps down over her shoulder and exposed her breast. He found the place, low down and inside, where the skin was the whitest and most delicate. Then, deliberately, he snubbed the cigar out against its soft curve.

Her scream was as long and as startlingly painful to her senses as the merciless end of that cigar. Suddenly Michaux's cigar was in Ingram's hand. Carolyn gasped and writhed to escape the hands that played on her breasts, ripped aside her blouse and enjoyed burning the delicate body. She screamed and sobbed and prayed to faint. Through it all Michaux chuckled softly.

"Fun-and-games time?" The cool voice cut into her consciousness. Gasping, she tried to look up as McAllister strolled into the room. He pocketed the latchkey he had used to get in and shut the door behind him.

"James," she sighed. It hadn't taken as long as she had thought.

"Impatient as always, Lux? And entirely unnecessary. She is quite reasonable, provided you approach her reasonably." He walked quietly forward into the room.

"Not as reasonable as you think, Mac," Michaux barked. "She admitted she has the money. But she is stubborn about the check and secretive about the amount. What did you find out?"

"Of course she has the money." James glanced at Carolyn. She blinked for clearer vision. His eyes were cold as they rested on her. Cold and yellow and unsympathetic. Suddenly her senses stilled in premonition. Something was wrong. He was a stranger.

"She has all of it, I should guess," McAllister said. "But this is hardly necessary. You should have waited for me. You get more from her in other ways."

He sauntered to the desk and took up the stiletto. "Yours, Le-Clere? Beautiful. Nice balance. It's too bad you ruined its value by sharpening it electrically." He savored the weight and heft of it in his open hand while the three men watched him. He closed his fist over the handle and suddenly whirled on Carolyn.

"No! James!" she cried.

He laughed. With two swift strokes he sliced the tapes holding her wrists. He stood over her, the knife still in his hand. His eyes were on the ugly blisters on her naked breast. Softly he drew his fingers down over the injuries and then covered her, laying the blouse over the angry burns. Even the light touch of satin hurt and she cringed away from it. He stripped the tapes away and dropped them on the floor.

"I went with her to Geneva," James continued in an impersonal, explanatory tone over his shoulder to Michaux. "That was a nice

205

assignment for a change. A good traveling companion. Plenty of expense money. We could have done without your thugs by the park. And the goons around the hotel were a nuisance, too. But all in all, perhaps they were useful. Getting away from them gained her confidence."

He knelt and cut the tapes from her ankles. Carolyn tried to rise. "Sit down and stay there," McAllister commanded harshly. She obeyed. Her legs were too weak anyway.

He rose and tossed the knife on the desk. "It was the Geneva bank, as you had determined," he continued. "And the money is in the account. The account number is twelve-twelve-seventy and the amount is— Don't be so slow, Lux. Write out the check there. You can do that much for her."

Michaux nodded eagerly. "And the amount?" he asked in a hoarse whisper. "Stop tantalizing me with your success. How much?"

"Wait a minute. Bruce earned some of it legitimately. You paid him a retainer and a percentage of the profits, didn't you? How much did he earn in the five years he worked for you? You owe that to her. In fact, you should grant her a bonus of the auditing fees she's saving you. Don't you agree, Guillaume?"

LeClere's face whitened. He stepped forward.

Michaux waved him back impatiently. "No bonus, Mac. How much is in the account?"

"How much did you pay Bruce?"

"About four and a quarter million dollars."

"Well, then, subtract that amount from $65,365,252.10."

"Ah." Michaux let his breath out in a long satisfied sigh.

"How did you know that?" Carolyn couldn't contain her cry.

McAllister turned to her politely. "How? A listening device, of course." He slipped his hand in his pocket and removed a tiny earpiece with a narrow cord. He held it up between thumb and forefinger for her to see. He took the receiver from the other pocket. It looked like a pack of cigarettes in a black case. "The transmitter is in the hem of your coat, Carolyn. You obligingly went to sleep Thursday night. I didn't have to drug you, although I was fully prepared to do so. I slit the hem and dropped it in. Let's see."

LeClere handed him Carolyn's coat. He searched the hem with his fingers, found the tiny disk and slipped it out. "See? I sat on the other side of Voss's office and heard every word you said." He dropped the bugging device on the desk in front of Michaux. "Keep these. They are quite useful at short range. Is the check ready?"

Michaux handed it to him. McAllister mentally calculated the amount in his head.

"I can add and subtract," Michaux growled. "What's the matter with you?"

"Nothing. Nothing at all, providing your financial problems don't rob me of my fee or Mrs. Bruce of her pension. She is a widow, after all. Hand me that book. And your pen."

Silently they were passed to him. McAllister approached Carolyn. She looked at him, fury blazing from her eyes. "Your signature, Mrs. Bruce, please."

"No."

He leaned over her. His big body blocked her view of Michaux. Tension throbbed in the room. His eyes glittered with determination, his face was hard, and his mouth was set in a severe line. There was no hint, no remnant of the James McAllister who had said he loved her. It was all for this purpose. There was no help for her.

"Sign it," he rasped.

She signed it.

McAllister let out his breath. An expression flickered briefly and was gone. He took the check from her and stepped back. "Well, now. Here you are, payable to the order of Lux Michaux, $61,115,252.10. You are back in business. What are you undertaking this time? Prostitutes? Stock swindles? Torture?"

He was laughing harshly, his back to Carolyn, when something thudded outside the apartment. The door burst open. Carolyn turned curiously, saw a battery of blue uniforms and heard the barked order to stand and freeze. Michaux lunged forward. His chair crashed against the wall. There was commotion. Ingram had a gun. A shot cracked. Carolyn leaped for the door.

"Carolyn! Get down!"

More police piled in and sprinted after Michaux. Another shot. Two shots. A splinter of glass. There was a searing in her leg. Carolyn stumbled.

"Carolyn!" McAllister hurled himself at her and brought her heavily to the floor under him. The breath rushed from her body. She felt sick. James had betrayed her.

26
•

When Carolyn came to herself, she was lying on the sofa in Michaux's apartment. Woolly blackness obscured her vision. She waited, her eyes closed. In a moment she could turn her head and see clearly.

James was kneeling beside her, an anxious expression on his face. "How do you feel?" he asked.

"What happened?"

"The police came. It's all over now."

"The police," she murmured. "Yes. I remember." With the return of memory, her voice went flat. She closed her eyes. Tears soaked through the heavy lashes.

"Carolyn."

She turned her head away.

"Carolyn, look at me."

There was no response.

"Carolyn, please . . ." A frantic note was creeping into his voice. Slowly she turned to him. Her gray eyes were remote.

"I know how you must feel. The important thing is, it's over and you are all right. When I saw those two hurting you . . . Carolyn, don't look at me like that!"

"Whose side are you *on*, James?"

"Yours, dearest heart. Believe me. You must believe me. Everything I told you was the truth. If I could—"

"That's enough." A sharp voice cut across McAllister's pleading one. "Constable, arrest this man."

Carolyn turned to the speaker. Prescott was standing over her, glowering at McAllister. A policeman came and took James's arm.

McAllister waved him back and leaned intently nearer to Carolyn. "I love you. As God is my witness, I didn't lie to you about that."

She looked at the white graven face, the love and pleading in his eyes. She made no answer.

"Come along now," the constable said briskly.

James lifted Carolyn's inert hand. He ran his thumb gently over the cuts, then closed his other hand over them, with sadness, it seemed to Carolyn, sadness and renunciation. Then he rose.

"Just tell me one thing," he said. "Was the check good?"

A slow smile began in her eyes. "No," she said.

"That was your secret written order?"

"Not to honor any check I didn't present personally and alone."

He grinned. "That's why I love you. When I'm free, I'll come. You can decide then whether you want to see me."

"Constable," Prescott ordered impatiently.

The officer led McAllister away, out of Carolyn's sight and out of the apartment. She sighed deeply. It was a relief just to lie with her eyes closed, listening vaguely to the murmured voices as the police led away the men arrested. Someone had been killed. She wondered who it was.

"Mrs. Bruce?"

She must have drifted off. It seemed that some time had passed. She didn't know whether she had fainted again or slept. It was Prescott, his hand on her shoulder. "Mrs. Bruce, the ambulance is here to take you to the hospital. You have been hurt. Is there anyone you want me to notify?"

"No. Yes. Yes, there is. Please call Jackson Hood of the American Embassy."

The ambulance took her to a cavernous city hospital. Her injuries were efficiently but impersonally treated and she was put brusquely to bed in a dreary room overlooking an elevator shaft. Alone and exhausted, she almost regretted having asked for Hood. She didn't want to admit David's perfidy. Reason had told her to expect it, yet a hope had remained that there was no Swiss account and no money. No wonder David had never confided in her. He probably had regretted marrying her as well. Tears were burning her cheeks when there was a soft rap on the door and Hood stepped quietly in. He brought a bunch of violets and laid them gently in her hand.

"Violets in February?" was all she could say.

"One of England's little miracles. How do you feel?"

"Relieved that it is over."

"I should think so. I talked to your doctor. He won't keep you here long. My sister and I want you to come to stay with us. Will you?"

She hesitated.

"I want you to," he added.

"Then, yes. Thank you very much."

"Good."

"Jackson. David's deputy isn't guilty of forgery."

"I know. I received a cable today clearing him."

"And I have control of the money."

"I know that too. I also know what you're going to do with it."

"How could you know that? I haven't told anyone."

"ESP. Remember?"

After he had left she turned her face into the coolness of the flowers and cried softly. She fell asleep with them still clutched in her hand.

Jackson Hood proved himself a wise and sensitive friend as well as a warmly gracious host. In the serenity of his comfortable town house, Carolyn slept away the fatigue of body. His easy sympathy and his sister's ebullient personality soothed her weariness of heart. By the time a smiling and genial Prescott called on them, she was eager to discuss the case. He gave the most important news first.

"You can return home whenever you wish, Mrs. Bruce. There is now no reason to believe you are responsible for your husband's death."

"The witnesses?"

"They have confessed to giving false statements. Guillaume Le-Clere intimidated and bribed Mrs. Frye and Harvey Lisle into incriminating you. They will be prosecuted, of course. Another highly reliable witness has come forward and corroborated your account of the murder. No jury would indict you now."

"Then it was murder?"

"Most definitely. We have full statements from the principals involved."

"From Lux Michaux?"

"Not from him. He was killed in the shooting."

"Who is responsible for the murder, then?"

"That's the extraordinary thing. We know who planned it. But we don't know who carried it out."

"You don't know . . ."

"Let me go to the beginning. You already know most of the background of the case. But what you may not know is that Winfrey was trying to blackmail your husband."

"No. I didn't know."

"Exactly. As soon as Bruce began siphoning away mutual fund assets, Winfrey called his hand. But Bruce had the trump card. Somehow he had found the evidence to convict Winfrey of his partner's murder some years ago. Winfrey had to back off. But he had a problem. He had inadvertently made a comment to Michaux implicating Bruce. Fortunately for Winfrey, Bruce was willing to help him smooth that over. It lasted until Ingram began to suspect trouble a couple of months ago. He questioned Winfrey, who had to agree to an investigation. That was when LeClere went to New York and made his recommendation of a team of auditors. Appalled at the cost, Michaux and Ingram decided to do it the cheapest way. They called Bruce to London, without, however, telling him the purpose of the meeting. Bruce found out anyway and suspected that Winfrey had exposed him. He said just enough to Winfrey to scare him badly.

"The meeting last Friday convinced LeClere and Ingram that Bruce wasn't going to collapse and confess and give the money back. Acting for Michaux, Ingram ordered Winfrey to put a tail on Bruce and to arrange some traffic mishap sufficient to scare him into admitting guilt and returning Michaux's money. Winfrey hired Thorpe for the job—the man you reported, Mrs. Bruce. But Winfrey secretly hired a second man and ordered him to murder Bruce, using Thorpe's accident as the cover.

"Well, the plan worked except for one little detail. The driver of the taxi, Michael Fanning, failed to stop. Winfrey was uneasy. He ordered Haskins to keep an eye on Fanning. When Haskins located Fanning, he discovered that Ingram's men had also found him. But more important, he learned that Fanning had seen both Thorpe *and* the murderer. He reported this to Winfrey, who panicked and ordered Haskins to eliminate Fanning. Haskins complied and disposed of the body in the Thames."

"That was putting a great deal of trust in Haskins," Carolyn murmured as Prescott paused to light his pipe.

"And so far it had been justified. Haskins and Winfrey had been together so long it didn't occur to Winfrey that Haskins could defect until Haskins didn't report for work. He lost precious time trying to find him. When Haskins' perfidy finally dawned on him, he had time to get his wife at the American Embassy but not to get away. Ironically, Haskins, now in Ingram's employ, stopped them. Their game was over, but in a frantic effort to save themselves, they told Ingram everything they thought he wanted to hear. Specifically, they said you had access to the money and knew all about it. Then Ingram began putting the pressure on you."

"But who murdered my husband?"

"We don't know. Winfrey told Ingram before he died that the man's name was Norman Long. Haskins received a vague description from the cabbie. But the name is an unknown alias and the description could fit any middle-aged man of medium height. Winfrey arranged it personally with Long, and probably even *he* didn't know Long's real name. Thorpe swears he did nothing to cause the accident. Someone else did it all for him. He doesn't know who. He saw no face. But he said it was an expert job."

"He could be lying," Hood suggested.

"Possibly. But I am inclined to believe him. They all seem genuinely puzzled by the identity of Norman Long. They were not sure that there was another person until Winfrey confessed it. They even briefly suspected you, Mrs. Bruce, which gave them the idea of framing you when Thorpe remembered overhearing Mrs. Philpot."

"I hate to think of Norman Long being free!"

"So do I. Undoubtedly he is a professional killer who is far away by now. We've queried Interpol. All the others, however, will come to trial."

"You haven't mentioned James McAllister."

"He will be released this afternoon. We have nothing to charge him with."

"Nothing?"

"Nothing. He ordered a dozen yellow roses sent to your room about seven o'clock Wednesday evening. The hotel florist arranged them and put them in the usual place to be delivered. They weren't there when the bellboy went to get them. No one knows who moved them, but we found them in the garbage the next morning. The pall was made by the same florist for a convention of American morticians that was meeting at the hotel. Macabre, I must say." Prescott paused reflectively.

"And the dummy?"

"There were no fingerprints on it, but Ingram admitted it was his idea. LeClere dressed it. And Haskins delivered it."

"The horse?"

"Ingram's idea again. Haskins rode."

"But wasn't McAllister one of Michaux's men?"

"Yes. But he himself has done nothing illegal. He was unarmed at the time of the shooting. He has not assaulted anyone. He is not a partner in any of the illegal business ventures. He has revealed his role and the others have corroborated it. Before he met you he had offered, for a fee, to persuade you to give up the money. They considered permitting him to do it, but decided against it when they saw his regard for you. When he went to Switzerland with you anyway, they thought he had allied himself with you and would take the money for himself. Thus the problems you had in Geneva. But when he brought you back to London, they believed they had misjudged him. But taking no chances, they grabbed you. He followed. The rest you know. And while James McAllister seemed to be omnipresent, *I* know of no accusation to make against him. Do you?"

"No. No, I don't. But how did you know to come that night?"

"We received an anonymous tip."

"Anonymous! Was it from McAllister?"

"I have no idea who it was from. I wish I had. I would like to thank him."

Hood cleared his throat and shifted in his chair. There was an odd glint in his eyes as he watched Prescott. Carolyn looked from Hood to Prescott's bland face and back to Hood. She wondered what Prescott had said that had meant more to Hood than it had to her. Then she knew. Hood had been a Secret Service man. He had worked under cover. He would recognize an intelligence operation when he saw it.

"Do you think James McAllister is a police agent?" she asked Hood when Prescott had left.

"The thought occurred to me. It is logical except for one thing. Scotland Yard generally doesn't use undercover agents. McAllister might have been playing both sides against the middle, either for your sake or for his own. He may have been in communication with Scotland Yard. He even may have been the anonymous tipster. But I don't believe he is a police agent." He looked at her closely when she made no reply. His lips tightened. McAllister was not mentioned again.

Carolyn stood with Jackson on the observation platform of Heathrow Airport and watched a hearse pull up to the Boeing 747 below. Uniformed men carefully lowered the casket to a dolly. Two British officials and Richard Riley, representing the American Embassy, inspected and approved the casket seals and signed the proper documents. Then it was lifted to a conveyor belt. The six-sided English coffin poignantly emphasized the shape of the body inside. Seeing it disappear into the bowels of the giant plane, Carolyn thought she could have no greater sense of finality, even when she would watch its descent into the ground in a New York cemetery. From now on she was alone.

Her flight was called. Silently they moved toward the gate. She turned to him. "Thank you for everything. You and your sister have been splendid and I'm grateful." She held out her hand and Hood took it. His handshake was as genuine as he himself.

"I'm glad you called me. I have to be in New York next month. May I call on you then?"

"Please do. I would like very much to see you." His grip tightened. Then, impulsively, he raised their still clasped hands and in an awkward little gesture, kissed hers. It was totally unexpected, and they were both surprised and embarrassed, yet warmed. They laughed a little together. Suddenly there was nothing, and yet everything, to say.

"Carolyn—"

"No. I must go. I'll see you in New York." She turned away and was quickly passed through customs. On the other side she waved. Hood's austere face wore a grin. She smiled back, wondering how she had ever thought this man cold. She had measured up to the rigid code of honor by which he lived. Her reward was his warmth and esteem, the courtly kiss on the hand, a gentleman's salute to a lady, a pledge given and received.

Slowly the passengers passed security and filed out to the plane. As she waited to mount the steps, Carolyn's eyes turned toward the luggage compartment and lingered there. An ignominious way for David to return home. Tears flooded her eyes suddenly. She ducked her head and stepped out of line, fumbling for a handkerchief to brush them away. Then, without quite knowing why, she turned a little and looked up.

McAllister was standing on the platform. Coatless, his hair blowing in the wind, he looked exactly as he had in Winfrey's drive when she had first seen him. Their eyes met. Eagerly he stepped forward, trying to speak across the distance. But his words were interrupted by Jackson Hood's appearance on the platform. Hood saw him, stopped, and turned sharply to find Carolyn. She looked from one to the other, then smiled that peculiarly brilliant smile that they had seen only once before and now prayed to possess. Then she turned, ran up the metal steps and boarded the plane. She did not look back.